Dance Like Nobody's Watching

Missy and Dan – Summer Lake Book Three

SJ McCoy

A Sweet N Steamy Romance

Published by Xenion, Inc

D0927575

Dance Like Nobody's Watching Copyright © SJ McCoy 2014

Published by Xenion, Inc.
First Paperback edition 2017
www.sjmccoy.com

This book is a work of fiction. Names, characters, places, and events are figments of the author's imagination, fictitious, or are used fictitiously. Any resemblance to actual events, locales or persons living or dead is coincidental.

Cover Design by Dana Lamothe of Designs by Dana
Editor: Kristi Cramer of Kristi Cramer Books
Proofreader: Aileen Blomberg

ISBN 978-1-946220-09-7

Dedication

For Sam. Sometimes life really is too short. Few xxx

Chapter One

Missy heaved the vacuum cleaner into the back of her minivan and sat down next to it for a minute. She was worn out. Another cabin cleaned, another day done. She stared out at the late afternoon sun sparkling on the lake and smiled. She might be exhausted, but she was paying the bills. If she kept picking up cleaning contracts the way she had been doing, she might soon be able to hire someone to help. It was the tail end of the busy tourist season now though. Maybe it would be best to wait 'til next year, even if it did mean she had to keep working every minute she could. At least every minute that she wasn't with Scot.

He was away overnight with the Robotics Club. They had made it to state finals. He'd been so excited to go. Missy had wanted to chaperone, but had decided to be brave and stay home when she'd heard him chattering with his friend about how cool it would be to be off on their own. He was growing up. She didn't want to be that mom who was always hovering. Still, it was hard.

She closed the back of the minivan and got in. The cabin she'd just finished cleaning was way up in the foothills on the Eastern shore of Summer Lake. It would take her a good half hour to get back down into town. For once she would have an evening home alone. It had been so long she wasn't even sure what to do with it. She'd been so tired lately; she had an idea that it might involve an early night.

She jumped when her cell phone rang and the sound came through the car speakers. She'd never had one of those hands free set-ups, never really wanted one, but last weekend Scot and Dan had rigged something up so that her phone synced with the stereo system. She swiped to answer.

"Hello?"

Holly's voice filled the van. "Hey, Miss. How you doing, sweetie?"

"Hey, Holly. I'm good, thanks. How about you?"

"Great. Listen, will you meet us for dinner at the Boathouse? The guys are all pumped up after a big meeting about Four Mile. Em's in LA this weekend and I could use some female company to dilute the testosterone."

Missy laughed. "So, the three musketeers are full of themselves, are they?"

"You would not believe the way they carry on. They're driving me crazy! Say you'll come down. I don't want to be the lone female and besides, I haven't seen you in weeks."

Missy sighed. She'd been working so much she hadn't had much chance to catch up with her friends lately. "Sorry, hon, but Scot's away tonight and I've got dinner for one and an early night with my name written all over them."

"You don't have to stay late. Just come for a while. Do us both a favor. Please?"

Missy thought about it. She had to eat and she sure didn't feel like cooking just for herself. "Okay then, but I'm not staying long. What time?"

"Yay! We're heading down there in a few, so as soon as you're ready."

"Okay, I'll get there when I can. It'll be good to see you."

"You too. See you there."

Ah, well. It would be good to see the gang. It was a pity Dan wouldn't be there. She had to stop thinking like that though. He had a girlfriend. She was lucky that he spent as much time as he did with Scot. The two of them spent most of their weekends writing computer programs and building robots. She smiled to herself. She was grateful that Dan had taken such an interest in her son. Scot had come out of his shell these last few months. What she had to do was stop hoping that Dan would take an interest in her, too. She'd never seen the appeal in the sexy nerd type 'til she'd met Jack's younger brother. She sure understood it now. Unfortunately for her, his business partner's sister had always seen the appeal and had laid claim to him years ago. She wrinkled her nose. What could she expect him to see in her anyway? A single mom who cleaned other people's houses to scrape out a living. It was pointless to keep daydreaming about him.

She pulled out onto the South Shore road and joined the traffic heading into town. Tourist season might be winding down, but the weekends were still quite busy. There would no doubt be quite a crowd at the Boathouse tonight. She pulled into her driveway and smiled at the sight of Dan's huge RV parked behind the house. It was massive. It probably had more livable square feet than her house did. Hell, it was probably worth more than her house. These days all Dan used it for was to store computer equipment that he and Scot were working on.

After a quick shower, she sat in front of the mirror putting her makeup on. Normally she wouldn't bother with much for a night like this, but those dark circles under her eyes needed some help. She chuckled to herself, wondering if it was physically possible to apply mascara without sticking your tongue out. Impressed with the lift her makeup gave her, she decided to wear the new top her brother had sent as an early birthday present. Once she was done, she was pleased with the result. No one would ever guess how tired she felt from the way she looked. She closed up the house and set out to walk the five minutes to the resort.

"Hey, Miss!" As she entered the restaurant, Ben called to her from behind the bar. "Come here, would you?" He let himself through and gave her a hug. "I haven't heard from you for days, bud. I was starting to get worried, and I've missed you in here."

Missy smiled. "I've missed you too, hon, but if you keep sending me places to clean—and don't you dare stop—this is how it's going to be."

"Yeah, we need to talk about that. I don't understand how you're doing it. I thought you would have hired people on by now. Have you figured out how to clone yourself or something?"

She laughed at that. "I wish! If I could do that though, you know you'd be seeing more of me in here."

Ben put an arm around her shoulders. "Well, you're here now. That's what counts. I'm glad Holly talked you into it. Come on, she's out on the deck with Pete, and you're never going to believe who's with them."

He started walking her through the bar. She was grateful that he kept his arm around her. At her height, it could be difficult to push a path through a crowd. Since everyone in the place knew Ben as the owner of the resort, they made way for him to pass as they smiled and waved in greeting. When they reached the deck, she really couldn't believe her eyes. Holly and Pete sat talking with one of her favorite people in the world.

"Michael!"

At the sound of his name, he jumped up from the table and picked her up off her feet to spin her around. She laughed as she wrapped her arms around his neck.

"Little Missy! You've still not had that growth spurt then?" As always, his Australian accent reminded her of how far this friend had drifted from Summer Lake.

She slapped his arm. "Good things come in small packages. Now put me down!"

"No chance, darl'." He spun her around again, making her dizzy. "You're the best little package I've got my hands on in a long time. No way am I putting you down just yet."

"Michael Morgan, put me down!" She laughed and beat her fists against his chest as he wrapped both arms around her waist.

"Can't make me!"

"Can too!" She wriggled 'til he loosened his grip. She looked up into laughing green eyes as he let her slide to the floor.

"Missy Malone, you are still the bossiest little critter I ever met."

She laughed. "You can bet your ass on that one, buddy."

Ben looked at Holly. "Can you imagine what it was like going to school with this bunch?"

Holly laughed.

"Yeah," said Pete, "Especially these two. Missy Malone and Michael Morgan. Double trouble in the middle of roll call.

"Hey, it was all her," laughed Michael. "She was the ringleader. I just tagged along behind like a lovesick puppy."

Missy pushed him. "You! You were the one that caused all the trouble." She turned to Holly. "Watch out for this one. Causes trouble wherever he goes, he does." She looked back at Michael, "Anyway, what the hell are you doing here? Did they kick you out of Australia?"

She noticed his eyes darken for a moment; an almost imperceptible shadow crossed his face before he laughed. "Nah, I just got bored of it. Was feeling homesick. Missing you, critter. And thinking about how much fun we had here as kids, I thought it'd be good for Ethan to spend some time here too."

"Oh, my God! Ethan's with you?"

"He is, he's with my folks tonight, but I'd love to get him and Scotty together."

"Oh, we have to. Scot won't be back 'til late tomorrow night though. How long are you here for?"

She watched Michael exchange a look with Pete before he replied. "That's a real good question, Miss. Hopefully it's for good."

"What? You're moving back here?" Michael had been a great friend, one of the gang, from kindergarten through high school. He'd gone to college in Australia and lived there ever since, though he came back at least once a year and brought his son, Ethan with him.

"I'm thinking about it." That shadow crossed his face again. She'd have to get him alone and ask what was going on. She knew him too well to question him in front of people. "We'll definitely be here 'til the holidays, so you'd better get used to it." He picked her up again and swung her around.

"Put me down!" she laughed.

Michael plopped her down into a chair and drew up another for himself, as close as he could get it. "I'll put you down for now, critter, but we've got some catching up to do." He winked at her then looked up at Ben. "So, is this everyone? You said Em's in LA?"

"She is, but her husband Jack is on his way. He went to pick up his brother Dan at the airport."

Missy felt the familiar tingle of excitement at the mention of Dan's name. "I thought Dan wasn't coming this weekend?"

"So did he," said Pete, "but with Em and Scot out of town, the Benson boys decided to get some brother time in. Jack sent Smoke to fly up to get Dan in the company jet this afternoon. In fact," Pete peered across at the parking lot, "I think Jack just pulled up."

Missy leaned over the railing and craned her neck to see if she could see the truck.

Michael wrapped an arm around her waist and pulled her back into her seat. "Careful critter, we don't want you falling into the lake now." He laughed.

Missy laughed with him. "Okay, just keep your big hands to yourself, mister!" She scooted her chair further away from him, but he just moved his own so he was right next to her again, a big grin on his face. He rested an arm along the back of her chair.

"I'm just looking out for you, darlin'. I've missed being your bodyguard." He raised his eyebrows and cast an appreciative glance over her. I could get used to guarding that body."

"Michael Morgan, you are one big flirt! It never worked on me. What makes you think it's going to work now?"

He dropped his arm to her shoulders and pulled her towards him. "Now, my little critter, I've got all the time in the world to work on it. You know you won't be able to resist a sustained charm offensive."

"Pete!" she laughed. "He's picking on me already. Make him stop!"

Pete laughed. "Sorry, Miss. I never could make myself heard once you two start up. I'm staying out of it."

"See. Not even perfect Pete is going to stand in my way. There's no escaping it. We were meant to be and I'm back to claim what's mine. He pulled her from her chair and into his lap. As she laughed and tried to get away, he planted noisy kisses on her cheek and the top of her head. Even though it was only Michael, it felt good to have a man's arms around her again. She just wished it were...Dan! As she wriggled to escape, she saw Dan and Jack approaching the table. Jack smiled, amused by their antics. Dan's face was completely still, his eyes fixed on her. He cocked his head to one side. She loved it when he did that. It was so damned sexy.

Holly was the first to greet them. "Hey guys. Seems like there are more members to the original Summer Lake gang."

"Yeah," said Ben. "Meet Michael, Missy's partner in crime. If Pete, Missy, Em and I were the gruesome foursome, then Missy and Michael were the terrible twins."

Missy slid back into her own chair, while Michael stood to shake hands. "Nice to meet you. I'm sorry I didn't make it to the wedding."

"No problem," said Jack. "We didn't exactly give people much notice. I'm glad you're here now though. I know Em will be thrilled to see you."

Dan shook Michael's hand and muttered a greeting. He looked put out. She had to stop imagining that it was about her. He had a girlfriend, for God's sake! Still though, his big brown eyes were fixed on her and she knew that look well enough to know there was a lot going on behind the serious face.

"Now that we're all here, is anyone ready to eat?" asked Ben, tapping his menu. "I'm starving."

The others nodded their agreement and began to study their menus. Missy knew what she wanted and looked around at the others in amusement. They ate here often enough, they should know the menu by heart, but they all had their heads down. Except Dan. He was looking straight at her. She wished she could figure out what he was thinking. She smiled at him and was rewarded with his slow smile in return.

"Did you hear about the first round of the robotics competition yet?" he asked.

"No, Scot hasn't checked in. I'm hoping he'll call, but he may forget." Dan's eyes twinkled, sending a shiver of tingling excitement through her. She could stare into those eyes all day long. Preferably all night long when they twinkled like that. "Don't tell me he called you?"

Long dark lashes lowered over his eyes for a moment and his hand came up to his face, rubbing the stubbly scruff she longed to feel against her skin. His slow smile spread. "Only because he needed help to figure out some adjustments."

"Yeah, right." Missy laughed. "And I'll bet the two of you talked for twenty minutes and he told you all about what's going on?"

Dan smiled. "Well, yeah. We did and he did."

Missy was happy that Scot was coming out of himself, voluntarily calling someone. He had always been more comfortable with computers than people. She didn't even mind that it wasn't her he wanted to talk to. She loved that they were so close, but knew it wasn't healthy for her to be his whole world. She couldn't believe how lucky they both were that he had Dan. "Come to the bar with me, and tell me what he said?" she asked. "While this bunch decides what they're eating. They can add my chicken sandwich to the order."

"And my burger," said Dan as he sprang to his feet to follow her.

Dan had been so excited to tell Missy about his phone call with Scot. He was thrilled that the kid had called, and had asked him to tell his mom how well the team was doing. He'd been glad that Scot was going off to the competition, but a little sad that it meant he'd have no reason to be in Summer Lake this weekend. When he'd talked to Jack yesterday, he had suggested Dan should come anyway. Some brother time would be good. Some alone time with Missy would be even better, if he could find a reason. She'd just given him one. He knew he shouldn't be taking every opportunity he could get to be around her, but he couldn't help it. Seeing her with that Michael guy had dampened his excitement. It had stopped him dead, but it shouldn't have. It wasn't logical. He came up here to see Scot, not Missy. It wasn't reasonable of him to hate seeing her with another guy. She wasn't his and he was supposed to be with Olivia anyway. Unfortunately the logic and reason he usually relied on refused to kick in, in fact, it abandoned him when it came to the feisty little lady in front of him.

His excitement had returned when she'd asked him to come inside with her. As he followed her through the crowded bar, his arm shot out just in time to stop a guy who was backing up and about to step on her. The place was heaving. She turned around to thank him and someone else pushed into her. She stumbled forwards. In a moment she was pressed against him, looking up into his eyes.

His arms instinctively closed around her, holding her to him. He could feel every beat of his increased heart rate and knew exactly where all that blood was rushing to as he held her even closer than was necessary. Her full breasts felt warm and soft against his chest. Her arms came around his waist and she laughed up at him.

"My hero! You saved me. Thank you."

With any other woman, he would think she was mocking him, but he knew Missy wouldn't do that. She understood him. Besides, from the way her pupils were dilated and from her increased heart rate that he could feel matching his own, he'd guess she felt this attraction the same way he did. But shit! What to do with it? For a moment he looked down into her gray eyes, savoring the feel of her in his arms.

"Whenever you need a hero, call me. I'll save you any time." Where the hell had that cheesy line come from? With a smile he forced himself to let her go. "How about you follow me?" He stepped in front of her and held his hand out behind him. She took hold of it and stayed close as he forged them a path through the crowd to the bar. Miraculously, there was one empty stool. He pulled it out for her to sit and stood close to shelter her from the jostling crowd.

"It may take us a while to get served," she said.

He smiled. "That's okay. I'll catch you up on Scot while we wait." From the look Ben had given him when they'd left the table, he'd guessed they'd probably have gotten a drink sooner by staying outside and letting Ben take care of it. Dan was more interested in getting a few moments alone with her than getting a drink, though. And getting her away from that Michael guy.

"So what did he have to say?" she asked. "How are they doing?"

"They're doing really well. They placed first in their section in the first round. He wanted me to help him get some modifications ready for round two in the morning. He said to tell you not to worry if he doesn't call 'til late. They're going to be working on the robot for another couple of hours yet. You know how that goes."

She laughed. He loved the way she laughed so much. "I'll be surprised if he calls at all. I do know how it goes. I've had his whole life to get used to it. And these last few months, while he's been working with you, I can see it's not just a Scot thing. You're just as bad."

It was weird. When Olivia said stuff like that to him, it felt like a criticism. When Missy said it, it made him smile. It felt like she understood him and, even better, that she liked him anyway. "It's called dedication, Miss. And you know, he gets so involved in what he's doing, he forgets all about time." Dan had always been that way with his work, but now it was how he felt when he was with Missy. Time disappeared when he was with her. He felt guilty about making the comparison, but time dragged with Olivia. She talked so much. About things that didn't interest him. "You don't mind that he called me?"

She put her hand on his shoulder and smiled. "Mind? Dan, you have no idea how glad I am that he called you. Thank you so much. I mean, of course I want to talk to him, and I did want to ask him about my laptop, but it can wait 'til he gets back."

"What's up with your laptop?"

"It's frozen up again. He put some partition thing on it, and I keep doing something wrong. It only takes him two minutes to fix it, but I can't figure it out for the life of me."

"I could take a look at it."

"That'd be great, if you get chance."

"We could take a look after we've eaten if you like?" What was he saying? He'd come to see Jack. He could fix her laptop tomorrow. She was looking up at him. He had no clue what she was thinking. Was he being too pushy? Should he take it back?

"That would be wonderful, thank you."

He grinned. Wonderful indeed. "Okay, well let's get these drinks and go eat, shall we?"

~ ~ ~

Dan shifted in his seat in Jack's truck. No one had been up for a late night of it. They'd said goodbye to the others and Jack had offered to drop Missy off on the way home. Dan had been trying to figure out what to say to Jack. He hadn't figured it out yet, and now they were pulling up at Missy's place.

"There you go, Miss. Was good to see you. Don't be a stranger. You'll have to bring Scotty up for dinner one night when Em's back."

"I'd love that. Thanks, Jack. Give Em a hug for me."

Jack grinned, "Oh, okay then. I think I can manage that."

Missy opened the door to get out. Dan had to say something now or he'd be riding away with Jack and kicking himself as he went. He looked at his brother. "I said I'd give Missy a hand with her computer. I'm going to stay here. I mean in the RV." He hadn't known what reaction to expect, but it wasn't the one he got.

A huge grin spread across Jack's face. "Great. Give me a shout in the morning. I'm beat, and now I get an early night without having to keep you entertained."

That was a lot easier than he'd feared. He looked at Missy, who had climbed down from the truck, then back at Jack. His brother raised his eyebrows and gave him a knowing smile. "Call me in the morning. We need to talk about this. In the meantime, have fun, little bro."

Dan grinned back at him. "Thanks, Jack. See you tomorrow." He climbed down and waved as Jack drove away with a beep of his horn.

Chapter Two

Missy fumbled with her key as Dan stood close behind her on the doorstep. All the little hairs on the back of her neck were standing on end. It was as if even they felt the tingly excitement that had been coursing through her ever since he'd put his arms around her in the bar.

"Do you need a hand?" His breath tickled her ear as he spoke.

"Got it," she said as she managed to unlock the door and push it open. She hurried inside, needing to put a little distance between them. She shouldn't be enjoying the feel of his closeness this much. She knew he was seeing someone else. Yet Missy wanted to feel his arms around her again, look up into those big brown eyes, and kiss him senseless...for starters!

"I'll get my laptop. There's beer or wine in there, if you want anything." She ran up the stairs, laughing at herself for wishing she could drag him up there with her.

"Would you like a glass of wine with me?" he shouted after her.

"Yes, please." She grabbed her laptop from the bedroom and started back down the stairs. When she came into the kitchen he was holding two glasses of wine, smiling at her. She caught her breath. He was perfect. Tall, but not too tall for a shrimp like her. Muscled, but more wiry than bulky. His green T-shirt stretched over him, doing a very poor job of concealing the lean, well-defined chest and shoulders it was supposed to be covering. She met his eyes. They were twinkling again. Oh, boy!

"Thanks." She turned away and set the laptop on the table. Sitting in front of it, she jabbed at the keyboard, trying to make the thing wake up. "See, I can't make it behave!"

He put her glass on the table and looked at the screen over her shoulder. "Be gentle with it. I think I'd freeze up too, if you poked at me like that!"

She laughed. "I'd never poke at you. There's no need. You always behave exactly the way you're supposed to."

He reached over her shoulder and tapped a couple of keys. She tingled all over as he leaned closer.

"What if I misbehaved?"

Was she hearing things? Letting her imagination run wild? She turned her head and found herself face to face with him. He cocked his head to one side, his eyes dead serious as she looked into them. Damn! Why did she always want the ones she couldn't have? She jumped up from her chair, not realizing he had his glass in his other hand. He managed to cover himself in red wine as he moved quickly out of the way.

"Sorry," she gasped.

"No, I'm sorry," he said, not meeting her eyes. "I shouldn't have said that."

She grabbed some paper towels and started dabbing at his shirt. "It's okay, honey. I wish you would misbehave, but we both know you're not going to. You have a girlfriend and I have a son. Now let's get you out of this before it stains."

He kept his eyes lowered as he pulled his T-shirt up and over his head. Oh, this was cruel and unusual punishment, his body was as beautiful as his smile! He was lean and hard with a dusting of dark hair she wanted to sink her fingers into. And ink! She'd never have pegged him as a tattoo guy. He stepped closer and she dragged her gaze away from the string of Chinese characters that ran down his side and disappeared into the waistband of his jeans. He was so close now. Without conscious thought her hands found their way up to his shoulders. His arms fastened around her waist and, for the second time in one evening, she found herself pressed against his chest. He smelled wonderful. Some musky cologne that made her want to breathe him in.

"You wish I would misbehave?" His voice was low. She watched his lips move, wondering what it would be like to kiss them.

She reined herself in. "Dan, honey." She couldn't help but sink her fingers in his hair. "In a different world, a different life, I think we could have great fun misbehaving together. But you have your girlfriend to think about and I have Scot. I would never do anything to hurt either of them.

His gaze softened as he looked down at her. "I understand about Olivia, but how could we hurt Scot?"

Oh, such a typical man after all! Didn't care how he might hurt a woman and didn't understand how he could hurt her son. She let go of him and stepped away, angry now. "You...." The sound of the doorbell cut off the choice words she'd been about to lay on him. Who the hell could that be at this time of night? She turned away from Dan and went to see, leaving him bemused and shirtless in the kitchen.

She opened the front door. "Michael!"

"Hey critter!" He held up a bottle of wine. "I told you we needed to catch up. No time like the present." He stepped inside and grinned at her. For once, Missy was speechless. What game was he playing? Showing up at this late hour and coming in without waiting to be asked.

"I'll be on my way then."

She turned to see Dan, still shirtless, face unreadable, standing in the kitchen doorway. Oh, for God's sake! What had she ever done to deserve this mess?

"Sorry." Michael had the good grace to look embarrassed. "I didn't realize. Didn't mean to come barging in and interrupt." He looked from Missy to Dan.

"No worries. There's nothing to interrupt." Dan came out with his T-shirt in his hands. He nodded at Michael, then fixed her with hurt brown eyes. "Goodnight, Missy." Then he was gone.

"Damn! Sorry, critter," said Michael. "I had no idea there was anything going on between you two."

Missy rolled her eyes. "There isn't. Whatever that just looked like, there really isn't." Right now she wished that she'd stayed home tonight. She let out a deep breath and looked at her old friend.

He grinned. "But you wish there was, right?"

She wrinkled her nose at him. "There's no point. He has a girlfriend and I have Scot to think about."

"Ouch. He didn't strike me as the cheating type, but you know, those quiet ones can be the worst. Want a glass of wine and you can tell me all about it?"

Missy couldn't believe the way this whole night had turned out. "Why the hell not?" It wasn't like she was going to be able to sleep any time soon for thinking about what had just happened with Dan. "But there's really nothing to tell. You said you wanted to catch up. You can tell me why you're really here. Come on." She went into the kitchen. "Let's have that drink." She looked at her laptop. Her home-screen waited patiently for her for the first time since Scot had left.

~ ~ ~

Dan let himself into the RV and flopped down on the sofa. How had all that just happened? There was nothing logical or reasonable about his behavior back there. The only restraint he'd shown had been not following her upstairs when she'd gone to get her laptop—and that had been a struggle he'd almost lost! What had he been thinking? He hadn't been thinking at all, had he? Wh*at if I were to misbehave?* Had he really said that out loud? What was happening to him? What was Missy doing to him? He closed his eyes and covered his face with his hand.

Ever since he'd first come up here to meet Scot, he'd been attracted to Missy. She was so beautiful, inside and out. Her long dark hair, her steel gray eyes that lightened when she laughed and darkened when she got angry. And man had she been angry with him when that Michael guy arrived. He couldn't for the life of him figure out why though. Maybe he should have stayed put and waited for Michael to leave? With so many confusing emotions involved, he'd followed his instincts and walked away. It was too late to go back now. All he could do was try to figure out why she'd been so angry.

He knew he had to break things off with Olivia. He wasn't looking forward to that. He bit the inside of his lip at the thought. Yeah, that wasn't going to be pretty. He should have stuck to his guns last year. She wasn't even interested in him, really. These days she only wanted to talk to him about the business—at least the money side of it. She didn't understand or care about his work. He couldn't remember the last time she'd even smiled at him. She was too busy telling him and Steven what to do. They'd had some fun in the early days, but that was three years ago. Even then, she'd never lit him up the way Missy had from the first time he'd met her.

Missy said she wouldn't hurt Olivia, he understood that. He didn't want to hurt Olivia either, not that he thought he'd hurt anything but her ego. What he didn't understand was why Missy had said she wouldn't hurt Scot. How could their seeing each other hurt the kid? He'd already asked Dan a few times if he was going to date his mom. He chewed on his lip, trying to puzzle it out. People could be so confusing, with the weird emotional significance they attached to things. He'd be the first to admit that he could be quite clueless, but he usually understood and appreciated where Missy was coming from. He shifted on the sofa and folded his hands behind his head as he stared up at the ceiling.

Missy had said she'd love it if he misbehaved. He smiled at that. She was attracted to him too. He knew it, could see it, had felt it the two times he'd held her to him tonight. His smile faded; but that Michael guy was there now. She'd been sitting on his knee earlier, and now he was sitting in her kitchen, where Dan wanted to be. He jumped up from the sofa and went to peer through the blinds. The kitchen light was still on. He didn't know if that was good or bad. This was too confusing.

He went to the bedroom, the one he and Scot had set up as a workshop. Sitting down, he fired up the computer. Time to get back to a world that functioned purely on logic and reason, a world he understood and felt comfortable in. He opened up a file of code Scot had been writing and smiled. It was brilliant. He opened a new file and his fingers flew over the keyboard as he typed code of his own and wrote the program that would allow Scot's idea to work.

~ ~ ~

The banging in his head sounded like drums, or was it thunder? He opened one eye and saw the letter 'P'. He sat up and stretched. He'd fallen asleep at the keyboard again. The banging hadn't stopped. He pushed the sleep out of his eyes, wondering how long it would take.

"You awake, bro?"

Ah! It wasn't inside his head. "Almost," he shouted back. "Come on in. It's open."

He emerged into the hallway as Jack let himself into the RV. He was carrying two coffee cups and a large grocery bag. He looked Dan over and raised an eyebrow. "You know some day you're going to end up with a permanent imprint of the letters, 'A', 'S' and 'D', on your left cheek."

Dan rubbed his eyes and nodded. "Yeah. I guess. I was working."

"I gathered." Jack smiled. "Want to tell me how the rest of your evening went?"

Dan took the coffee his brother held out with a grunt of thanks and went to sit at the table. "I don't know."

"You don't know how it went?" Jack sat down opposite him. "Or you don't know if you want to tell me?"

"Both." Dan took a slug of his coffee and waited for the caffeine to hit his system. Jack was looking at him expectantly. "I screwed up. I'm not even sure how or why. Then that Michael guy showed up looking to share a bottle of wine with her. So I left."

"Whoa," said Jack. "How do you think you screwed up?"

"Well...I kind of ended up without my shirt and with my arms around her." He could see a smile playing on his brother's lips.

"And?" Jack prompted.

"And then she got mad at me about Olivia and Scot. And then that Michael arrived. And I just got out of there. And...."

Jack held up a hand. "Slow down. What has Olivia got to do with anything?"

"Missy said she'd never do anything to hurt Olivia or Scot. I understand we can't start seeing each other while Olivia is still my girlfriend, but I don't see how we could hurt Scot, do you? Am I missing something? I really like the kid, he really likes me!"

"Okay, first of all, Olivia is still your girlfriend?"

Dan put his hand to his face and chewed his thumb. "Yes, but...."

Jack scowled at him. "Then what the fuck did you think you were doing last night, Dan? I can't stand the girl myself, but you have to end it with her before you can think about starting anything with Missy."

"I know! I just can't think straight at all when I get around Missy. She shorts out all my circuits."

Jack smiled. "I can see that, and it looks like you have the same effect on her."

"Hmm." Dan drank some more of his coffee. "I was hoping so, until I saw her with that Michael guy last night, and then he showed up at her house later." He chewed on his thumb some more.

"I think he's just one of the gang," said Jack. "They're all so close, you know. For a while there, I was jealous of Ben with Emma, but they're just really good friends. I'm sure it's the same with Miss and Michael. And anyway, you've still got Olivia around. What's the deal with that? I though you broke it off with her last year."

"I tried."

Jack shook his head. "Tried?"

"Yeah, she didn't want to break up. She said we didn't have to see as much of each other. I think it's more about Prometheus than about me. She likes being in charge of the business."

Jack shook his head again. Dan knew that look on his face. It meant he disapproved, and somehow expected Dan to know why. He didn't. "What?"

"You need to get that woman out of your company and out of your life. She doesn't understand software and she doesn't understand you. She just wants the money, and the control over her brother."

Dan hung his head. "Yeah, Steven's been pretty stressed about her lately. She's been talking about some deal that will make us all a lot of money. As if we needed more. I manage to avoid her most of the time, and I get up here weekends."

"And you still call her your girlfriend?"

Dan pulled a face. "That's what she calls herself. I just agree because it's easier than arguing. But as soon as I see her, I'm going to tell her. Even if I don't get a chance at anything with Missy, she's made me realize that I'm capable of feeling major attraction for a woman. I didn't think I worked that way."

Jack grinned. "Then we need to see that you do get a chance with Missy. I don't think it's about how you work, or what you're capable of. It's about finding the one person that makes you feel that way. Why don't you take a shower, and I'll make us some breakfast."

Dan smiled. "You brought food?"

"Sure did, little bro. Western omelets, home fries, and pancakes will all be ready by the time you're showered. After we've eaten, I want you to come back up to the house with me. I'm working on the plans for the Four Mile development, and I want to run a few things by you, if I can."

"Sure." Dan smiled to himself as he went to get a shower. He loved getting to spend time with Jack and felt proud that these days he had valuable contributions to make to his brother's property developments.

The smell of food drew him back to the kitchen before he bothered to get dressed. He secured his towel around his waist and sat at the table. Jack put a plate in front of him. "There you go, more fuel for all that muscle you're building. I gotta say, you're looking pretty ripped."

Dan grinned. "Yeah, that gym thing is great, thanks. I never saw the appeal in it. Never figured out why you spent all that time pumping iron, but it's addictive, isn't it?"

Jack laughed. "It sure is. I'm glad you got into it. I've been trying to figure out what I can set up at Em's. I might get the same one I sent you, since you're getting such great results."

Dan held up his arm and flexed his biceps. "I'm liking it," he said with a grin. "I want to get Scot interested too. It's a great way to make sure you do something other than sitting on your ass staring at a screen all day."

"You're getting really close to him, aren't you?"

Dan put his fork down. "I am. I love the kid. But, Jack, what do you think she meant about hurting him? I don't understand."

Jack brought his own plate and two fresh coffees to the table before he sat down. "The way I see it, Missy is grateful for everything you're doing for Scot. She's probably afraid of messing that up. I'm guessing she thinks that if you two start dating and then break up, it would affect your relationship with him."

"How?" Dan didn't see it.

"Well, with most guys, when they stop seeing a woman, they don't have anything more to do with her. They certainly don't keep hanging out with her kid."

"But that's separate." Dan frowned. "What I do with Scot is for Scot, and for me. Not for Missy."

"I know that, and I think Miss does too, but maybe she sees it as too much of a risk."

Dan ate his omelet in silence. Once it was gone, he looked up. "So, what am I supposed to do?"

"About Scot? I don't know. But there's not much point dwelling on it until you tell Olivia that you're over. Whatever might or might not happen with Missy, you need to finish it with Olivia, get her out of your life."

Dan nodded. "I'll call her. Tell her I want to see her tomorrow night when I get back."

"Good. Why don't you go do that and get dressed while I clean this up? Then we can get up to North Cove."

"Okay."

Dan locked up the RV and followed Jack out to his truck. He fastened his seat belt and looked back at Missy's house, wondering what she'd be doing today. The front door opened and Michael stepped out. Dan froze in his seat, Missy was laughing in the doorway. Michael turned and hugged her and she reached up and kissed his cheek. Jack pulled away. Missy looked over at the truck. For a moment her gaze met Dan's; she looked even paler than usual, then Jack turned the corner and she was gone.

Dan stared straight ahead. His head was full of white noise. Michael had spent the night with her? He didn't know what to do with that thought. Couldn't process it.

"What's up?" asked Jack.

"Did you see that?"

"See what?"

Dan could feel the tension around his temples. "Nothing."

Chapter Three

Missy leaned against the doorframe. "Blimey, are you okay, critter?" Michael looked concerned. "You just went white."

She took a deep breath then let it out slowly. "I'm fine."

"You don't look it. Let's get you back inside." He took her arm and led her back into the kitchen. She collapsed into a chair. "Did you see them?"

"Who?"

"That truck that just pulled out was Dan and Jack."

"Oh, shit! And they saw me leaving your house first thing in the morning?"

"Dan sure did."

"Oh, shit! That's not going to do you any favors, is it?"

Missy blew out an exasperated sigh. "It doesn't make any difference. So, I have a little crush on him. So what? It's not like anything's going to happen. "Michael looked at her. "Then how come you're still white and shaking, critter?"

"Because I wish it could. But now, on top of the fact that he has a girlfriend and the fact that I would never risk jeopardizing his friendship with Scotty, now he thinks I'm screwing my old buddy, too!"

Michael waggled his eyebrows. "If he thinks it anyway, want to prove him right?"

She looked up at him. "You are the world's biggest flirt, you know."

He grinned. "I know. It usually works pretty well for me too. You always were a tough nut to crack."

"Michael, honey. You are adorable. I'm sure I'm the only woman around here who doesn't adore you, at least not like that."

"So you do adore me in some way then?"

"Of course I do, and you know it. You're still one of my dearest friends, and I'm so glad you're back. I hope you're back for good, but you and me? We're never going to get together, it would never work."

Michael laughed. "Who said anything about getting together? I was just talking about screwing your old buddy."

Missy laughed with him. "You are such a whore!"

"Am not. Just wanted to make you laugh. See, you've got some color back in your cheeks."

"Thanks, but I need to get going. I've squeezed a couple of extra jobs in today while Scot's gone."

"Shouldn't you be getting some rest? Ben said you've been working your ass off all season."

"I have, but I have to." She checked her watch. "And I really need to move. How about I call you when I know what time Scotty will be back and we'll see about getting him and Ethan together?"

"Sounds good."

She closed the door behind them and locked it. She looked around, wondering who else might see them and make assumptions about Michael leaving her house on a Saturday morning.

"Don't worry about it, critter," said Michael. "There's no-one around. It might do your man some good to think I did more than spend the night here. The way he left last night, I'd say he's got it bad. This might make him wake up and give the girlfriend the flick." He walked her to the minivan. "Call me later then?"

"Will do, and good luck today. I hope you get some good news."

"Thanks, me too."

Missy got in the van and started it up. She watched Michael walk back towards town and shook her head. So much for her night home alone!

She'd managed to keep a lid on her attraction to Dan for the last few months. At first she'd been so excited at such a sweet and handsome guy becoming a part of her life. Then as she'd watched how close he and Scot were becoming, she'd become apprehensive about getting involved with him herself. She was scared that an ending between the two of them would mean an ending between Scot and Dan too. When they'd been paired together in Emma and Jack's wedding, they got along so well she'd started to think that he was a risk worth taking. Then he'd dropped the bombshell about his girlfriend, Olivia. She had no idea what kind of relationship they had; he'd been up here every weekend for months. She did know though that Olivia was involved in his business, his software development company in San Jose.

Once the van had stopped making its morning noises, she pulled out and set off for the East Shore. She had two huge rental houses to clean out there today. It would be good money. Hopefully she'd get back in time to put her feet up for a while before Scot returned. This time, if she got the chance, she really would just stay home and hide. Last night's events had proven that was her wisest move. Thinking of Dan, bare-chested in her kitchen, remembering the feel of his arms around her, made her want what she couldn't have. And then Michael showing up like that. He had a whole mess on his plate. She was glad to have been there for him to talk to, but damn! The timing couldn't have been worse—last night, or this morning.

~ ~ ~

Dan's phone buzzed in his pocket. He smiled when he pulled it out and checked the display. "Hey, champ! How's it going?"

"Awesome! We got through the second round and we're in the semis tonight."

"Tonight? I thought you were coming back tonight."

"We were, but they had to delay some of the rounds, so now its semis tonight and finals tomorrow. Hold on...."

Dan smiled to himself as he heard Scot talking to someone. It sounded like he was telling them how to reprogram a circuit. It was good to hear him sound so animated and confident when he spoke.

"Dan, you still there?"

"Sure am."

"I gotta go. Will you tell Mom for me?"

"I think *you* should call her, bud." Dan thought it best for Scot to call Missy himself, for many reasons.

"I will. But later. I forgot last night. If you call her first, she might not chew my ass...me out so bad."

Dan chuckled. For a kid who was supposed to struggle socially, he had a pretty good handle on how people worked—and how to manage them to his own advantage.

"Say you will? I really gotta go."

"Okay, but only if you promise you'll call her later. She misses you."

"I know. I will. Thanks, Dan. Bye."

Dan's smile faded as he hung up. With Scot gone another night, would Missy spend it with Michael again? When he'd finally admitted what was bothering him this morning, Jack had tried to convince him that Michael was just her friend. But why had he needed to stay at her house?

Jack came out onto the front deck where he was sitting. "That was Em on the phone. They got done with their meetings early, I'm sending Smoke to fly her up, so she'll be back later."

"That's good." He liked Emma. "It'll be good to see her."

"Yeah, you sound thrilled. What's wrong?"

"Scot just called. They made semis and he's staying another night."

"That's great, isn't it?"

"It is, *but* he asked *me* to let his mom know."

Jack smiled. "I told you about the time Em spent the night at Ben's?"

Dan nodded.

"I know how easy it is to think the worst, but that doesn't make it true."

Dan hoped so.

"Why don't you call her now? Get it over with and ask her to come out tonight. Em wants to go listen to the band when she gets back."

Dan dialed Missy's number from memory. He had it stored in his phone, but he liked to tap out the numbers each time, so he wouldn't forget it.

"Hello?"

"Hi. It's me."

"Hi."

His mind froze as the silence lengthened.

"Can you hear me, Dan?"

"Yes. Sorry."

"Do you want me?"

He bit his lip so he wouldn't tell her just how much he wanted her. "Yes. Sorry. Scot called."

"Great! How's he doing?"

The eagerness in her voice made him smile, despite his nervousness. At least they shared one simple and straightforward thing; they both loved the kid. "He's great, they made semis and he's supervising repairs on the 'bot."

"I'm so proud of him."

"Me too. Thing is though, semis aren't 'til tonight now, so they're staying. If they make finals I doubt they'll be back 'til tomorrow night."

"Oh, it's running over then?"

"Yeah. He asked me to let you know. He said he'll call you later."

She laughed. "Just like last night?"

"Hopefully tonight will work out better than last night."

She didn't say anything.

"Emma's getting back tonight and we're all going to the Boathouse. Please will you come, Miss?"

"Dan, honey. I'm exhausted. I need a rest."

"Please come?"

"Just for an hour. And, Dan?"

"Yes?"

"That wasn't what it looked like this morning."

"Good. I'm glad."

"Okay. Well. I'll see you tonight then. And thanks for letting me know about Scotty."

"You're welcome. I'll see you later."

~ ~ ~

Missy put her phone back in her pocket. What had happened to her resolve to stay home and get some rest? Dan's voice. That's what had happened. *Please come?* How could she say no? She folded her cloths and started lugging the vacuum towards the door. One house down, one to go. Maybe she'd have time for a quick nap when she got home.

~ ~ ~

"Can you drop me off at the RV?"

They were on their way to collect Emma from the airport. Jack grinned, "You mean, at Missy's?"

Dan nodded, a slow smile spreading across his face. "I do."

"Sure thing. We'll see you guys in the bar."

"Thanks."

A few minutes later, Jack pulled up in front of the little cottage in town. "Later, bro."

"Yeah, later."

Dan walked up the path and knocked on the front door. Perhaps he should have called first? Missy opened the door and smiled.

"Well, hello! I thought I was meeting you all there."

"Yes. Sorry. I wanted to come see you first."

"Don't be sorry. I'm not. Come on in."

She stepped back to let him pass. He'd wanted to talk to her about Scot, and Michael, and Olivia, all the complicated stuff, but his mind was freezing up again. She was so pretty. Her hair was tied up in a ponytail, with wispy bits hanging around her neck. She wore a white tank top, which, from his height, gave him a great view of her impressive cleavage. The top was tucked into a pair of yoga pants that showed off a lusciously round backside and very shapely legs. Little feet with shiny pink toenails peeked out the bottom.

He brought his hand to his face. His fingers met stubble. Damn! He'd forgotten again. "Sorry, I should have shaved."

She smiled up at him. "I like it."

"You do?" Olivia always harassed him when she saw him with anything more than five o'clock shadow. It didn't look professional, apparently. He realized he was blocking Missy's way in the hall, but he didn't move. "Miss, I need to talk to you."

"How about we take this in the kitchen and get a glass of wine? I promise to try not to throw it on you this time."

He smiled and went through to the kitchen. "I threw it over myself."

"Yes, but it was my fault."

"No, Miss, it was my fault, but I would like to finish what we started."

She spun around to face him, corkscrew in her hand.

"I mean finish the conversation, not the part where I...." He gave her a shy smile. "Though I would like to finish that too, someday soon."

To his relief, she smiled back at him. "I was about to lay into you and you want to finish the conversation?"

He shrugged and took the corkscrew from her hand. He opened the bottle and poured two glasses of wine while he spoke. "I'm happy to skip that part and fast forward to the part where I explain myself?"

"Okay. Let's try that. I think I'm too tired to lay into you right now, anyway."

She did look tired. As she had for weeks.

"You said you'd like it if I misbehaved."

She sat down heavily in one of the chairs. "I also said that we both know you won't."

"Right, because of Olivia and Scot. You need to know that I rarely see Olivia outside of work these days. You already know I never see her on the weekends. I've asked her to meet me tomorrow night when I go back so we can talk, and end it. We should have done it months ago."

"I don't want you to finish it with her because of me, Dan."

"I'm not." Now she looked confused. "Well, I am and I'm not. I'm doing it *now* because of you. But even if you say no, I needed to end it anyway."

"Say no to what?"

"To going out on a date with me, and if you like it, to keep doing it?"

She rested her chin on her hand and looked at him across the table. "But I have to think of Scot." She was wrinkling her nose at him. He thought that was a good sign. Maybe? Good or bad, it was so damned cute!

"I have to think of Scot too, you know. I didn't understand what you meant last night. I didn't understand, because it never occurred to me that anything that happened between you and me could affect him and me. I wouldn't let it. Miss, you have to know how important he's become to me? Even if you ended up hating me, and throwing things at me, and never wanting to see me again, I need you to understand that I'd sneak around behind your back to keep my friendship with him going."

She looked shocked. Oops! "You'd sneak around behind my back?"

He smiled. "I said that to make a point. Even if you hated me, I don't think I'd have to sneak around. We both know I'm good for him."

Her face relaxed. "You are. You'd have to make me a solemn promise, though, that no matter what happened, you wouldn't let anything change what you and Scot have."

"And you'd have to make me the same promise. That you wouldn't keep him away from me, or me from him."

She looked even more shocked. "I would never do that! Whatever is best for him is all that matters to me."

"Can you understand that's how I feel too? That's why I couldn't understand what you meant last night."

"Really?"

"Yes, really. I'm sure we'd work it out. Divorced people manage it all the time, even when they hate each other."

She laughed. "I suppose so."

"The way I see it, we need to make each other that promise. We both need to talk to Scot, and I need to talk to Olivia." He felt better now. It was starting to look logical. There were steps to be followed. A sequence of events. It made sense. He looked across the table at her. Her eyes were light gray, happy. She was smiling. She moistened her plump lips with her tongue and everything started to spin again. He needed to hold her face between his hands, kiss those lips.

"I'll make you that promise now, Dan. Whatever happens, I will not let it affect Scot, or your friendship with him."

"And I promise you the same, Miss." He stood up. "Want to shake on it?"

She stood and shook his hand. She had a firm grip and looked him straight in the eye. He kept hold of her hand and pulled her closer. "Want to seal it with a hug?"

She hesitated. "We shouldn't. Not until you're single."

She was right, but he needed to feel her in his arms again. He cocked his head to one side and gave her a pleading look. "Just a little hug?"

She shook her head, but she didn't move away.

"You hugged me last night. How about we recreate the moment? He pulled his T-shirt up and off. Her pupils dilated as she looked at his naked chest. He reached an arm around her waist and drew her to him. Her hands came up to his shoulders, setting his skin on fire as she looked into his eyes.

"We shouldn't."

"We're not. Not really. This doesn't count as a new hug. It's just finishing off last night's hug that got interrupted." Shivers ran down his back when she buried her fingers in his hair. Her full breasts pushed at his chest. He closed his arms around her waist and held her tighter. "Not hugging."

"Mm," she murmured. "Not hugging."

He looked down at her upturned face, trusting eyes searching his own, moist pink lips begging him to kiss them. He lowered his head. She closed her eyes. He stopped with his lips a fraction of an inch from meeting hers. He breathed in the scent of her. She smelled like the beach. It was killing him not to close that final tiny distance and kiss her. He could feel that she wanted him to; she was pliant in his arms.

~ ~ ~

Missy opened her eyes. She was clinging to him, pressing herself against him. Longing for the moment his lips would come down on hers in the kiss she'd been daydreaming about for months. But he'd stopped. His deep brown eyes met hers. She was tempted to close the gap herself. Kiss him and to hell with it. But it wasn't right. Whatever his story with Olivia might be, Missy had never, to her knowledge, kissed another woman's man. She wouldn't start now. Even though the man in question was Dan.

"See," he said without pulling back at all. "Not hugging. Not kissing."

His lips were so close to hers, she could feel them move. "Not kissing," she agreed. "But I want to." She licked her lips and parted them slightly, bringing them as close as she could without touching. His mouth mirrored hers. She could feel his warm breath. He brought his hands up to cup her face. She clung to his shoulders as he moved his mouth down over her throat. Though his lips never touched her skin his breath fanned her desire. He moved back up, gently blowing the side of her neck, sending hot shivers racing down her spine. They were holding each other so close she could feel his hard-on pressing into her belly. She wanted him so badly she could no longer remember why they shouldn't. He framed her face between his hands again. As his lips came closer, she closed her eyes and held on to him, just to keep herself upright. It wasn't his lips, but his nose, that met hers. She opened her eyes and came back to her senses as he rubbed noses with her. "We shouldn't do this should we?" she asked, hoping he might find it too hard to agree.

"Not yet, beautiful. But we will, won't we?"

She wrapped her arms around his neck. "Yes, honey. We will."

Chapter Four

The bar was crowded when they got there. Dan smiled at her. "Want to stick behind me this time?"

Missy nodded. He stepped in front of her and she took hold of the hand he held behind his back. She smiled as she felt the calluses on his fingertips. All those hours on a keyboard had left him with the same scars as Scot. She stuck close as he pushed them a path through the Saturday night crowd. Dan stopped to let a girl with a tray full of drinks pass in front of him. Missy was jostled from behind until she was pressed up against his back. He tightened his grip on her hand and looked back over his shoulder.

"Are you alright?"

She squeezed his hand. "I'm good." She was quite happy to be pressed up against him like this, especially his muscular backside. She was tempted to slide her arms around his waist, but she didn't. Next weekend. She'd be able to do that then. When he was free. One week waiting was a small price to pay. He moved forward again. She followed, wishing they'd been held up a little longer. They found Pete and Holly out on the deck.

"Hey, guys," Pete greeted them.

"Hey," smiled Missy.

Holly caught her eye and grinned, shooting a look at Dan and back then raising an eyebrow. "I'm glad you came. Is Scot not back?"

"No, not 'til tomorrow night, by the looks of it." She smiled at Dan. "But I understand he's having a great time."

Dan smiled back, but said nothing. He didn't tend to say much when they were all together.

"Jack and Em should be back soon," said Pete. "They stopped in, but Em wanted to run out to her Gramps'. Ben's going to try to join us too, and maybe Michael."

Missy felt bad. She'd completely forgotten to call Michael.

Pete looked at Dan. "Did Jack get a chance to talk to you about Four Mile?"

Missy rolled her eyes. "Seriously, Hemming? Do you ever think about anything but work?"

Holly laughed. "He does. I can vouch for it, but only one thing."

Missy put her hands over her ears. "I'd rather hear about Four Mile! Sorry, Pete. Go ahead."

Pete looked at Dan, "Women, huh?"

Missy watched the slow smile spread across Dan's face as he looked down at her. "Yeah, women." His eyes twinkled. She really had to wait another week before she could kiss him?

He looked back at Pete. "Yeah, Four Mile. It's an interesting proposition. A fiber optic community. I'm not sure it would make sense, financially. But you'd know that better than me. Technically, it's feasible and it'd be an interesting project."

"Yeah, I'm not sure it'd work financially, but I want to understand it better, to know whether it's even worth crunching the numbers."

Holly looked at Missy. "He's about to start asking questions, I can tell. Come dance with me, sweetie?"

Missy looked at Dan. He had that look on his face. She could tell he was engrossed, thinking about the technical details of whatever it was they were talking about. She smiled. "Sure. We won't be missed here."

Pete caught Holly's hand as she stood. "Want me to come, sweetheart?"

She leaned down to him, her long hair swinging in a curtain, behind which she kissed him. "You're fine, Bigshot. We'll be back."

As Missy stood, Dan put his foot over hers. "Save me a dance for later?" How she wished she could lean down and kiss him, like Holly had just kissed Pete. She nodded happily and he removed his foot.

"Holy hell, chica!" said Holly once they'd pushed their way to a space on the dance-floor just in front of the stage. "Last night you had Michael all over you, and tonight it's Dan that's the lovesick puppy!"

As the song came to an end, Missy caught the lead singer's eye. He smiled down at them and gave a little wave. She liked Chase; all the band members were good guys. Holly watched the exchange.

"Have you got some new pheromone perfume or something? And can I borrow some?"

Missy laughed. "You don't need it. Pete's like putty in your hands."

Holly grinned, "Yeah, but he doesn't stay like putty for long!"

"Sorry, Holly, but that is too much information!"

"Well, that's better than *no* information! What's the story with Dan? What's happened? It's obvious something has."

Missy grinned. "We're going to go on a date!"

"You are?" Holly's eyes were wide. "Oh, Miss, that's awesome!" Then she frowned. "Didn't you say he had a girlfriend though?"

"Yes, but he's going to end it with her when he goes back. After that we can go on our date. I'm so happy, Holly. You know how much I like him."

"I do. I'll be keeping my fingers crossed for you, sweetie."

As they danced, a couple of guys came to dance beside them, trying to move in. Tourists, by the looks of them. Missy looked up at Chase as the song ended. He winked and spoke into the mic.

"Guys?" Holly nudged the guy next to her. He looked up at Chase. "A word to the wise? You couldn't handle the trouble that comes with these two. I'd dance away, if I were you."

The guy grinned up at him, apparently thinking Chase meant the fun kind of trouble. Chase shook his head seriously. He jerked his chin over to where Dan and Pete were standing at the edge of the dance-floor

Holly rolled her eyes. "He does that all the time. Thinks he's so intimidating."

Missy smiled as the two guys moved hurriedly away from them. "To most people he is. *Very* intimidating."

Holly grinned. "I know, but right now I'd be more scared of Dan. Look at him! He's like one of those silent ninjas who's going to take people down with some crazy karate shit, before you've even seen him move."

Missy laughed. He did have a don't-mess-with-me air about him when he was rattled. Apparently, right now, he was rattled. She knew she shouldn't, but she liked it. She smiled at him and watched his face relax as that beautiful smile spread.

His eyes only left hers when Jack and Emma appeared through the crowd and Jack clasped a hand on his shoulder. As Dan turned to greet his brother, Emma spotted Missy and Holly and waved. She pecked Jack on the lips and started elbowing her way across the crowded dance-floor to join them.

"Hey, girls! Isn't this great? I get back early *and* we get Miss out for once. We need to make the most of this, close the place down." She waved up at Chase. He smiled at her, then scanned the edge of the dance-floor, no doubt checking for Jack.

Missy laughed. "He still likes you, Em, but Jack put the fear of God into him."

Emma looked more pleased than she should as she denied it. "He doesn't. He's become a friend to both of us. Anyway, do either of you know what's up with Dan? He was with Pete and the two of them looked ready to kick some serious butt."

"They thought the tourists were moving in on their women," said Holly.

Emma stopped dancing and stood still. "*Their* women? Dan's girlfriend isn't here is she?"

"No," said Holly. "He's done with her because he wants to be with our Miss."

Emma squealed and clapped her hands together. "Oh Miss! Really? That's so cool! You're going to be my sister-in-law!"

"Slow down, Mouse! We're talking about going on a date after they're finished, not getting married!" Marriage wasn't on Missy's wish list.

Emma laughed. "That's what I said. And Holly. And look at us now!"

"Yes, and I'm very happy for you. Getting married, settling down and no doubt having kids soon. But I'm a bit different,

Em. I don't do things the way most people do. When you reverse the order and you have the kid first, like I did, you settle down by yourself and you get on with it. Marriage gets knocked off the list."

Emma smiled her sweet smile, the one that always meant she thought she knew better and was so smug in the knowledge she wasn't even going to argue about it.

"Forget it, hon," said Missy.

"Yeah," Holly grinned. "You should know by now, Em. You can't convince people of things they're not ready to hear. It didn't work with me, did it?"

"No, but you got there eventually."

"And so will Missy. Come on. Let's go get a drink."

Missy followed them off the dance-floor. She loved Emma and Holly, but they had no idea what life was like for her. She'd raised Scot by herself, always had to work hard for everything, and lived a very different life than they had. She couldn't expect them to understand.

Ben and Michael had joined the guys at one of the big picnic tables out on the deck. Missy headed straight for the end of the bench and squeezed on next to Dan. She could do without Michael stirring things up with his flirting tonight.

"Hey, ladies," said Ben. "I brought us a bucket of beer, thought that was easiest, but I can go get whatever you like."

"I'd love a beer," said Holly, plucking one from the ice.

Dan looked at Missy. She nodded. He grabbed one and twisted the top off before handing it to her.

"Thanks, hero," she murmured. He winked at her before he turned back to the others.

"Are you starting to rejoin the living, Miss?" asked Ben. "Getting you out two nights in a row is a big deal these days."

"I know," she said. "But I think I might be using up my quota. I'm not staying late tonight. I'm too tired and with all the cleaning I've got lined up, you might not see me again for months."

"Okay, so there are two things we need to talk about," said Ben. "First, I'm thinking I'm not going to give you any more contracts 'til you hire a team to help you."

Missy was horrified. She needed the money. This trip of Scot's had been a big expense, and now she would have another night's hotel cost on top. She couldn't afford to be paying other people to do work she could do herself.

"Don't look at me like that, Miss. I mean it. You're doing the work of at least four people. I'm not surprised you're always exhausted."

All heads around the table turned towards her. Dan edged closer to her on the bench. She was grateful for his silent support. She felt incredibly uncomfortable. Everyone there was worth millions in their own right. Everyone except her, and maybe Holly. The rest of them would never need to work another day in their in lives, if they chose. While she needed to clean multiple toilets every day, just to make ends meet. It didn't normally bother her. They were her friends. But in this moment she was acutely embarrassed.

"Whatever. We can talk about that on Monday. What's the other thing you need to talk to me about?" God, she hoped it was nothing else that would embarrass her!

Ben seemed to realize he'd made her uncomfortable. "Yeah. The other thing is about you saying you won't be out again for months. You have to come out for your birthday. Seeing as you've been working your ass off, I thought you should have a party. You haven't had one for years. Missy's costume party used to be something we all looked forward to. Now everyone's back up here most of the time, I thought it'd be good to kick-start the tradition. What do you say?"

She smiled. She used to love her birthday parties, and she knew the others did too. They'd been expensive and a lot of work to organize though. She hadn't had the time or the energy to pull one together for the last few years. She'd done one for Scot's birthday a few months ago and had decided that would be her annual goal now. "It's a nice idea, Ben. Thanks for thinking of it, but there's no way I could fit it in." She wasn't going to say 'afford it'. "It's only a couple of weeks away."

Ben grinned. "All you'd have to do is organize your costume and show up. I'll take care of the rest."

"I'll help," said Holly.

"And me," added Emma. "Say you will, Miss? We all used to love your parties and you deserve one."

Dan leaned against her. She didn't dare turn to him with everyone still looking at her, but it felt like encouragement. She looked at Ben. "You really wouldn't mind organizing it?" She did love the idea—especially if she didn't have to pull it together, or foot the bill.

"I wouldn't have offered if I did," said Ben with a smile. "Go on, say yes. You know you want to. Let it be my birthday present?"

She wrinkled her nose. He was such a good friend. Always had been. What was there to think about really? It'd be fun, and boy could she use some fun. "Okay, yes. Thank you. Let's do it."

Everyone smiled. Everyone except Pete. He fixed her with his supposedly powerful stare. It didn't bother Missy though,

never had. He was such a big softie really. "What, Hemming?"
she asked. "What does perfect Pete want now?"

He laughed. "I have one request."

Holly groaned. "Always so demanding. Sorry, Miss."

"Don't worry, Holly. He's been this way since we were kids.
You're not going to change him now."

"My request is, if you're going to pick a theme, we don't have
to wear anything too demeaning."

Missy burst out laughing remembering a very grumpy Pete, a
few years ago, in a ridiculous pixie costume she'd made him
wear for losing a bet. Emma and Ben joined her laughter.

Pete glowered round at them. "If it's anything too degrading, I
may have to be in San Francisco that day, whatever day it is."

Holly grinned at Missy. "You have to fill us in?"

"No, Miss," said Pete. "You don't. You really don't! Just tell us
what the theme is for this one, so I can decide if I can handle
the humiliation."

Missy was still laughing. "I'll need some time to think about it,
Pete. Let's eat, can we? I don't think well on an empty
stomach."

"Good idea," said Jack. "I'm starving."

~ ~ ~

Dan picked at his fries. He was enjoying himself this evening.
He liked these people. They'd become his friends over the last
few months. He liked that he could dip in and out of the
group up here. He only stayed as long as he felt comfortable,
then he went back to his computers and his work. No one
minded. Usually he spent more time with Scot than with the
rest of them, but not this weekend. This weekend he didn't
feel uncomfortable at all.

He was still sitting a bit too close to Missy, but she hadn't moved away, in fact she kept giving him a grateful little smile. She was enjoying herself, being with her friends, laughing and telling jokes. She brightened the whole group. He enjoyed seeing her happy. She still looked tired though. She'd finished eating and he noticed that her beer was empty. He pulled another from the bucket and offered it to her. She smiled at him. "Thanks, hero."

He popped the top with a grin. He liked it when she said that.

The band was playing a set of country music. "What do you think?" asked Ben. "The guys thought some country would go down well with the weekend crowd in here."

"Works for me," said Jack. "But then we're just country boys, huh, Dan?"

Dan grinned and spoke in the Texan drawl he'd mostly lost over the last ten years. "Yes sir, thankin' you kindly sir. Just a pair of good-ole, down-home, southern boys."

"Oh, my God!" cried Holly. "That is so damned sexy. Do it again!"

Dan laughed as Pete nearly choked on his beer. "Excuse me? Fiancée of mine!"

Holly laughed at him. "Sorry, Bigshot, but that is damned sexy!"

"S'true partner," Jack drawled. "All the purdy lil' ladies sure do love us country boys."

Emma smiled at him. "They most certainly do, Tex."

Missy laughed. "Okay between this conversation and this song, I just decided the theme for the party."

Everyone went quiet to listen to the band. Dan recognized the song immediately. He smiled at Missy. "Cowboys and Angels?"

"Yep! It's great, don't you think?"

He did.

"I reckon that'll work for us little bro, don't you?" asked Jack.

Dan grinned. "Sure do. Tall, dark and Texan."

"Oh, I can go for that," said Missy.

"I can live with it," said Pete.

"What do you think, ladies?" asked Missy.

"I love it," said Emma.

"Me too," said Holly. "And if we can all get into the city one day, I know the perfect place to get angel costumes."

"Slutty angels?" asked Pete hopefully.

Holly smiled at him. "We'll see."

"At least we won't have to search too hard for costumes," said Pete. "I'll bet you two Texan boys already have something that will work?"

"Maybe," replied Jack.

"Looks like it's just you, me, and Ben shopping for cowboy gear," said Michael.

"You'll have time," said Missy. "And you know what makes it even better?" She looked really happy now. "It means Chance might come to the party since it won't be a costume for him, just work clothes."

"Chance is coming?" asked Ben.

"Yep!" Missy grinned. "I talked to him last week and since my birthday falls on a Saturday he said he'd come for it."

"That's fantastic!" said Michael.

"Chance is really coming?" asked Emma. Her hands were clasped to her chest and she had a dreamy look on her face.

Missy laughed. "Yes, Em, he's really coming."

"Oh, Miss, that's the best news I've heard in ages! I get to see Chance!"

"Um, hello, wifey?" Jack put an arm around Emma's shoulders and gave her a gentle shake. It didn't shift the rapturous look on her face, though. "Hello? Your husband is sitting right here, remember?"

"Oh!" Jack laughed as Emma's hand came up to cover her mouth. "Oops! Sorry. But it's Chance!"

Jack looked at Missy. "Who is this Chance character? And do I need to worry?"

"He's my big brother," said Missy proudly. "He is wonderful. You can't blame Em. He has that effect on everyone."

"Yeah," said Ben. "You need to lock up your women when Chance is around. He's awesome."

Jack raised his eyebrows at Pete, who laughed. "Sorry, partner. You really can't hold it against Em. I think even I have a crush on him. He's just one of those guys, you know? Good looking, good guy. He was like the home town hero, captain of the football team, played guitar, sang." Pete paused and looked at Missy. "Then there's the tragic past that makes him a little bit mysterious, a little bit dangerous. He left town years ago on a Harley, but his legend lives on."

"Ooh," Holly grinned, "I can see the appeal."

Michael laughed. "You really do need to lock up your women when Chance hits town. Dan's the only one that's safe."

Dan was surprised by that. Michael gave him a small nod and a friendly smile. How about that? Dan smiled back, relieved that he didn't need to worry about Chance, or Michael.

"I don't need locking up," said Emma. "I'm perfectly happy with my own cowboy, especially if he'll dance with me?"

Jack grinned as he got up from the table. "Want to come scoot some boots, bro?"

Dan stood and looked down at Missy. "Does the little lady want a turn around the floor?"

Missy nodded happily and followed him. Out on the dance-floor, Dan curled an arm around her waist, glad for the excuse to hold her again.

"I didn't realize you were such a dancer. You surprised me with the Latin stuff at Em's bachelorette party, then ballroom at the wedding, now you're a country boy too?"

Dan smiled. "You never asked." He loved to dance. It was a skill Jack had shared with him in his junior year of high school. Missy gave him a mischievous grin. "Seems I need to start asking about your many hidden talents, don't I?"

He held her a little closer. "You can ask, or I'm sure I'll get around to showing you soon enough."

~ ~ ~

Missy's body reacted to his words, even as her mind struggled to believe them. She was enjoying seeing more of his true personality. She was used to him being quiet, but was beginning to realize that he wasn't really shy. He said what he wanted to, and what he meant.

"I'll look forward to that." She rested a hand against his chest.

He covered it with his own, his eyes twinkling down at her. "Not as much as I will."

The band launched into a new song and his hands dropped to her waist. He pulled her hips against his so she could have no doubt what he was talking about. The feel of him pressing against her like that sent shockwaves coursing through her. It had been a long time. She panicked and looked around. She shouldn't be feeling like this. He wasn't free yet. What would the others think? She tried to break away from him, but he only held her closer.

"Dan! We shouldn't. I can't. Everybody's looking."

He dropped his head to bring his mouth next to her ear. The feel of his breath on her neck, his lean body pressed against her, it made her feel dizzy, her breath shallow. She closed her eyes and leaned into him, panic forgotten as he overwhelmed her senses.

"It doesn't matter who's looking, Miss." He stroked her hair away from her ear. She trembled all over as his lips touched her ear when he spoke again. "You've gotta dance like nobody's watching." He rested his lips against her hair. She kept her eyes closed, giving herself up to him and all the sensations he filled her with, as he moved her body to the music. All she could do was cling to him. If this was what dancing with him did to her, she could only hope to survive if they took it any further.

When they returned to the table, Missy caught a few raised eyebrows, but none of them looked disapproving. And why should they? She and Dan had done nothing wrong. Yet.

Emma was sitting in Jack's lap. "What do you think, Miss? We're all going to head back up to North Cove. Do you want to come?" she asked.

"No thanks, Mouse. I'm about ready to keel over. I'm going to call it a night and head home."

"Lightweight!" said Michael. "What happened to my little hell-raiser?"

"Life. Motherhood. Bills. Responsibilities. Need I go on?"

Michael's teasing smile vanished. "No, sorry critter. I guess not."

She felt bad; she hadn't meant to shoot him down. "No apology needed. I think I'm just a bit worn out around the edges. You know how cranky I can get."

Dan stood at her side. "Want me to walk you back?" he asked quietly.

Oh, the things that voice did to her! She met his eyes. It may not be the best idea to let him come back with her, but the shivers running down her spine tried to convince her that it was. "Yes, please."

Missy was pretty sure there were more than raised eyebrows around the table after they left, but so what? Nothing was going to happen. She was just going to enjoy his company a little longer as they walked home. There was nothing wrong with that. She and Dan had been hanging out for months now. He'd stayed at her place plenty of times. Granted, Scot had always been there too, 'til tonight.

Dan put an arm around her shoulders as they walked across the square. He didn't need to say anything. Just like when he'd sat so close to her on the bench earlier, he was silently letting her know he was there for her. She slipped her own arm around his waist. He might not be as tall or as big as Jack or Pete, but he was perfect for her. She fit neatly under his arm.

"Thanks, Dan. I'm so tired right now, I'm not sure I'd even make it home under my own steam."

He squeezed his arm tighter. "Gotta take care of ma lil' lady," he drawled.

Holly was right; it *was* damned sexy when he talked like that. It did funny things to her stomach—and other places too. "Well the little lady appreciates it, very much."

"No worries. We'll get you to bed. You look like you need it."

She caught her breath and looked up at him. Was he saying...? The smile playing on his lips told her he was at least thinking about it.

"I mean like you need the sleep," he clarified.

She knew she shouldn't feel so disappointed. "I do." They walked on in silence.

For the second night in a row, he stood close behind her as she unlocked her front door. She let them in and went through to the kitchen. He followed, but hovered in the doorway.

"Do you want a drink?" she asked, then tried to stifle a big yawn.

He leaned against the doorframe, arms folded. "I'd love to, but I think you need to get some sleep."

She nodded. She really was exhausted, but she didn't want their time alone together to end so quickly.

"Hug goodnight?" he asked, holding his arms out to her. She went to him and he wrapped them around her. She leaned her head against his chest. He felt so good. She chuckled.

"What?" he asked.

"This is our first fully clothed hug."

He rested his chin on top of her head. "Yeah, I considered whipping my shirt off again."

She laughed at that, wishing he had. He brought his mouth to her ear. "I have to keep it on though, Miss. I think, tonight, if the shirt went, everything else would soon follow it."

She brought her arms up around his neck and looked deep into his eyes. Her heart fluttered in her chest. She was so tempted to take him upstairs, right now. Even though she knew it was wrong. He stroked his fingers all the way up her spine 'til they caressed the back of her neck. She sighed. If he wanted to, she would happily go with him, no matter how wrong it might be.

"Miss, if I don't stop now, I'm not going to be able to."

She let out a moan as he held her against his arousal. He was so hard. She was already past the point of being able to stop.

She wanted him so badly. She'd fantasized about this moment for months. Her phone brought them both back to their senses, the Star Wars theme tune slicing through the tension that had been building. Scot's ringtone. Dan smiled and let her go. She rummaged in her purse.

"Hey, Scotty!"

"Hey, Mom. Sorry it got so late."

"It doesn't matter. How are you doing? Tell me all about it?" She watched Dan lean against the doorframe, crossing his arms. She wasn't sure if it was regret or relief she felt at the timing of Scot's call. Either way, the most important thing was that he had called.

"I'm good." He gave a big yawn into the phone.

She laughed. "Sounds like it! You going to tell me about it?"

"Yeah. It's awesome. We made finals, but they're not 'til tomorrow afternoon. We get the morning to work on repairs and mods."

"That's great. Are you excited?"

"Yeah. I'm tired though." He yawned again. "You mind if I go now, Mom?"

"Course not. I'm glad you called. Have fun sunbeam."

"Mom!"

"Sorry, honey, but no-one can hear me. Good luck for tomorrow. Enjoy yourself."

"Thanks, Mom."

"Love you, Son."

"Love you, Mom. G'night."

"G'night, honey."

He hung up. At least he'd called and he was happy. Dan smiled at her. "How's our little champ doing?"

"You know more than I do. That was just the obligatory, 'I'm good, we're doing well, yawn, yawn, bye!'" She rolled her eyes. "He called though."

"You are such a wonderful mother, you know."

Her heart leapt at that. She tried her best to be, but she wasn't at all sure she succeeded most of the time. "You really think so?"

He looked stunned. "I don't think so, I know so. You can't seriously doubt it?"

"I wonder sometimes. It's not always easy to know what the right thing is, but I always try to do it."

"You're the best mother I've ever known."

That warmed her heart. "Thanks, Dan." She had to stifle another yawn.

Dan smiled. "And on that note, I'm going to go."

"Go?"

"Yeah. I'm going to sleep in the RV."

"You don't need to do that."

"I do, Miss. I think I just proved I can't be trusted. Nothing but Scot could have stopped me just now."

Missy nodded. She felt the same. If Dan slept in the guest room, she didn't think she'd be able to stay in her own bed. She wanted another hug, but as she stepped towards him, he shook his head. "I can't do it, Miss. If I hug you now, it'll be game over. I'll see you in the morning."

She followed him to the door. He stepped outside and walked to the corner of the house before he turned around. He cocked his head to one side and blew her a kiss. "Goodnight, Miss. It'll be worth the wait."

She blew him a kiss back and watched him disappear down the side of the house. She stood there, half tempted to go after him. She jumped when his head popped back around the corner. He grinned. "Go get some sleep, beautiful. And do us a favor?"

"What's that?"

"Make sure you lock all the doors...and windows!"

She laughed as he disappeared again. She went back inside and only hesitated a moment before locking the door behind her. He was right. It would be worth the wait. She'd waited this long. Though when they would ever have the house to themselves again, she didn't know. She yawned as she made her way up the stairs. She wouldn't have to worry about lying awake thinking about what they could be doing. She needed sleep too badly. She got ready for bed and was asleep minutes after her head hit the pillow.

~ ~ ~

Dan fired up his computer. He needed to distract himself. All these feelings—physical and emotional—were driving him crazy. All he could think about was Missy. Missy laughing. Missy calling him hero. The longing in her eyes when he'd talked about getting her to bed! All he could feel was Missy. Her little arm around his waist as they'd walked home. Her hand on his chest as they'd danced. The length of her body pressed against him in the kitchen just now. He'd wanted to bury his face in her hair when he'd whispered in her ear. He'd wanted to bury himself deep inside her when he'd felt her breasts crushed against his chest. He wanted her so badly it hurt. It hurt in his chest and it hurt in his pants—he had a raging hard-on. It would have been so easy to give in. Even after she got off the phone with Scot. They could have been back to the point of no return in minutes. But it would've been wrong. He didn't feel he owed Olivia his loyalty. Hell, he was fairly certain she hadn't shown him any. Nevertheless, he had his own sense of honor. He didn't want to taint what he had with Missy by starting out like that either. Like he'd told her, it'd be worth the wait.

For now though, he needed to lose himself in his code. While he waited for the program to load, he set the alarm on his watch. When it went off he would go to bed and get some sleep. He didn't want to work all night and then sleep all day. He wanted to be awake tomorrow, with Missy home alone.

~ ~ ~

The sun almost blinded him when he parted the shades to peek out. He scrunched up his eyes, then slowly opened them, adjusting to the bright light. He peered at the house. The kitchen curtains were open. Good. He took a shower in record time and pulled on his shorts. He rifled through the drawers. He needed to bring more clothes up here—or wash some. He grinned when he found one of his workout shirts. Hey, he'd worked hard to get in the shape he was in now, why not? He pulled it on and looked in the mirror. It looked good. He shook his head, wondering what the jocks from high school would think if they could see him now. He didn't really care though. He was more interested in what Missy might think. He left the RV and walked through the back yard. He could see her in the kitchen. Her hair was mostly up in a ponytail. She wore a short, blue robe, belted at the waist and clinging to her round backside. Maybe this was a bad idea? He already had the beginnings of a major hard-on. Before he could change his mind, she turned and saw him. The bulge in his shorts grew bigger as she ran her eyes over him. Seemed she liked his choice of shirt.

She waved and pointed to the door. He hurried around and drew in a sharp breath when she opened it. If the robe clung to her backside, it did even better with her full breasts, showcasing her cleavage and doing nothing to disguise the fact that either she was cold or she was quite pleased to see him too. He only realized he was staring when he heard her laugh.

"G'morning, hero. And by the way? I'm up here!"

Oh, no! He bit on his lip as he raised his eyes to meet hers. "I'm sorry, Miss. I...."

She laughed again. She didn't seem angry at all. "No, problem, honey. I take it as a compliment, not an insult."

He grinned, relieved. "Oh, it's definitely a compliment. They're...."

She cut him off. "Alright! Don't push it. Come on in and have some coffee. But, when you speak, just remember, up here." She pointed at her eyes with a grin.

She was amazing! So easy going. He followed her into the kitchen and sat at the table. He couldn't help but admire her ass while she poured two mugs of coffee. She put one in front of him and sat down.

"I didn't expect to see you up and about this early."

He grinned. "I didn't sleep too well."

"Me neither."

"Aw, Miss. You needed to."

"Tell me about it. But someone left me wanting and I kept having all these dreams." The look on her face was half teasing, half serious.

"Want to tell me about them?" He raised an eyebrow and took a sip of his coffee. He'd love to hear about her dreams.

"No chance!" She grinned. "Maybe next weekend."

He wished they could fast forward to next weekend. Olivia would be history by then. "Fair enough."

She sipped her coffee, looking at him over the rim of her mug. "What are you doing today?"

"Not much. I'm just sticking around to see Scot when he gets back." And hoping to spend some more time with Missy. And delaying seeing Olivia—he wasn't looking forward to that. "I was wondering if you want to hang out? I was going to go to the store for the papers and get some breakfast at the resort. If you want, you could come, or I could bring them back here?"

"You'd do that?" She looked thrilled.

He knew she liked to read the Sunday morning papers and usually made a big breakfast whenever they didn't eat at the restaurant. "Course I will."

"Oh, Dan! You really are my hero. I was thinking I'd give it a miss this morning. I just need to laze around here and do nothing, not even go into town."

He grinned. "Then why don't you do that? Put your feet up and I'll go get us papers and breakfast." He stood up and she joined him, throwing her arms around his neck. Oh, man! He couldn't help it. He buried his face in her hair. She smelled like the beach and sunshine. She felt soft and warm through the silky robe. He ran his hands down her back 'til they closed around her ass cheeks. They felt just as good as they looked, round and firm. He ground his hips into her and heard her sigh. He needed to.... No! He shouldn't. He lifted his head. She looked up at him, her breath coming fast as she clung to his shoulders. It was obvious she wanted him as much as he wanted her. Disappointment spread across her face when he brought his hands back up to her waist.

"We shouldn't, should we?"

He shook his head sadly. "We could, but we'd regret it, and I'd hate that."

She nodded and stepped away from him. "Me too." She seemed to sway, then braced herself against the wall. He was back at her side in an instant.

"Miss, are you alright?"

"I think so."

He led her back to her chair and she sat down. She gave him a weak smile. "You made me all dizzy."

He frowned. "I don't think it was me. You look pale. Do you feel okay? Should I get a doctor?"

"No, honey. It's nothing. I'm fine now. You know sometimes how it feels when you stand up too quick? It was just like that."

"Are you sure? Can I get you anything?"

She smiled. "I'm sure. No need to worry. I'm fine. The only things I need are the ones you already offered to get, breakfast and the papers. I just need a good rest and that is what today is all about."

Dan wasn't convinced. "Will you be okay if I go out?"

"Of course I will."

"How about we at least get you comfortable on the sofa, instead of sitting here?"

"Look at you! I'd never have guessed you were the caregiver type."

"If I'm going to be your hero, I need to get my act together and figure out how to do this kind of thing."

He was surprised when she frowned. "You don't have to figure anything out. I like you just the way you are!"

He didn't know what to say to that, so instead he asked, "What would you like for breakfast?"

She didn't even pull him up for the abrupt change of topic. "I'd love a full Boathouse breakfast, the works. That should give me my strength back."

Dan laughed. "Do you have hollow legs? I have no idea how someone your size can eat that huge breakfast mountain, but you always manage it."

"It's not hollow legs, I keep it all in the trunk, as you just noticed."

He grinned. "In that case, please don't ever stop eating those huge breakfasts."

~ ~ ~

Dan jogged down the street. When Jack had sent him that home gym as a birthday present, he'd thought it was a bit of a joke. He wasn't exactly the sporty type. But he'd really gotten into it and he'd started running again too. He'd run cross-country as a kid and had forgotten how much he enjoyed it. It gave his life another dimension, which he had to admit, he'd needed. This morning's run wasn't about staying in shape though. It was about getting back to Missy as soon as possible. He was concerned. She'd looked so small and pale when he'd left her on the sofa. Even though she smiled and reassured him, he'd hated to leave her like that. He would have driven if he'd had his Jeep here. That was the only drawback to flying up—it left him without transport.

As he ran, he took in the neighborhood. It was a great little town. Being here was like going back in time. Neat little yards fronted the sidewalks, lawn mowers buzzed, people walked dogs, kids played ball in the street and zoomed by on bicycles. Most of the houses were like Missy's; small and modest, but well kept. As he neared the center of town and the resort, the houses were larger. When he turned onto Main Street, the waterfront homes that lined the lakeshore looked beautiful. Set back at the end of long driveways, with beautiful sweeping lawns leading down to private docks on the lake.

He stopped to catch his breath before he entered the convenience store for the papers. From there he ran across the square to the Boathouse. He'd called ahead and hoped their order would be ready to go. He spotted Ben sitting out on the deck and ran up the steps.

Ben grinned at him. "Run, Forrest, run!"

Dan laughed. "Very funny. How you doing?"

"I'm good. Just catching some peace and some sunshine before the day kicks in. You?"

"Yeah. I'm good."

Ben raised his eyebrows. "I saw a breakfast order with your name on it. I'm guessing I know who the Boathouse is for?"

Dan shifted from one foot to the other. "You do."

Ben smiled. "Hey! I'm just busting your balls, buddy. I think it's great. I was wondering how long it would take the two of you."

Dan met his eye. "It'll take us a little while longer, yet. I still have to officially end it with Olivia."

Ben nodded. "But it must have been over for a while, really? I mean, you're here every weekend and she never came with you."

"Yeah," said Dan. "I don't even remember the last time we went out."

"Then kick her to the curb and move up here, like everyone else is doing!" Ben grinned.

"I'm seeing her tonight to finish it."

"Good."

"I need to get that breakfast and get back."

Ben raised his eyebrows with a grin.

Dan bit his lip. "No. I'm worried about her. I think she's more than worn out, Ben. I know she's been working a lot, but I think she might be sick. She keeps going really pale, and this morning she was all dizzy."

"That doesn't sound good. Do you want me to call Michael?"

What the hell did Michael have to do with anything? Dan was going to take care of her himself!

Ben laughed out loud. "Jesus, Dan! Don't look like that. He's a doctor. Didn't you know?"

Dan felt foolish. "No, I didn't. Still, I don't think she'd be too happy if we did that. Would you text me his number, just in case, though?"

"Will do, bud. Let's go find you that breakfast so you can get back to her."

Running back down Main Street, Dan spotted a For Sale sign in the yard of one of the waterfront homes down at the end of the road. He ran on, clutching the insulated delivery bag Ben had put the food in. *Move up here, like everyone else is doing.* That's what Ben had said. How could he do that though? He had to go into the office everyday. He didn't really though, did he? That was one of Olivia's rules. She made him and Steven go in every day—just like she made him shave—because that was how *she* thought things should be. He and Steven could work anywhere they could get online. Why had he been allowing her to dictate everything? For that matter, why had Steven?

He slowed to a walk as he turned onto Missy's street. He knew why. Both he and Steven had been allowing it because it was easier than standing up to her and arguing with her. He'd always thought he was being wise, taking the path of least resistance. Right now he was starting to think that what he'd actually been was cowardly—and not very wise at all.

~ ~ ~

Missy opened her eyes when she heard the front door open. She must have drifted off. She struggled to sit up when Dan poked his head into the living room.

"Don't get up. You stay right there. I'll get us some plates."

She nodded. Her limbs felt like lead. She sank gratefully back down, hoping she'd be able to muster the strength to sit up by the time he came back. She'd never felt this tired before—and she'd always known what an honest day's work felt like. She smiled, listening to Dan bang around in the kitchen. He'd find whatever he was looking for eventually. She sat up against the arm of the sofa and pulled a cushion towards her. Scot used a cushion as a lap tray whenever she let him get away with it. Time for her to take a lesson from her son. Dan came back and put a fresh coffee on the end table beside her. He handed her the newspapers and some napkins.

"Thanks."

He nodded, his face full of concern. He went back into the kitchen and returned with her breakfast. Hash browns, scrambled eggs, bacon, sausage, beans, and toast were all piled high on the plate. It was a ridiculous amount of food, but she almost always managed to finish it.

He grinned as he handed it to her. "Dig in. I know you like to save the pancakes 'til last, so I left them in their carton to keep warm."

How did he know she always ate the pancakes last? She'd never understood when people ate them along with everything else. She considered to them to be dessert. "Thanks, hero."

His beautiful smile lit up his face as he disappeared to get his own breakfast.

~ ~ ~

Missy sipped her coffee. She was stuffed! Dan had cleared the dishes away and was sitting on the floor beside the sofa, looking up at her. He still looked concerned.

"Do you feel any better?'

She nodded and yawned. "Sorry. Much better. Now I'm just full and sleepy."

"Why don't you go back to bed, get some rest?"

"Mm. I would if I thought I could make it up the stairs." Before she knew what he was doing, he'd stood and scooped her up off the sofa. She nestled in his arms. "Are you going for super-hero status?"

He smiled. "I don't think I'll ever make that."

He already had, in her eyes. He tightened his grip and carried her up the stairs and into her room. She let go of him reluctantly as he gently set her on the bed. She couldn't help but tease him. "You really only brought me up here to sleep?"

He met her gaze. "Close your robe and get under the covers, so I can say yes!"

She looked down and realized her robe was gaping open, almost completely exposing her breasts. She looked back up to find him staring determinedly at her face, a tight little smile playing on his lips. "I daren't look down, Miss."

She laughed and got into bed, pulling the covers up to her chin. "There. We're safe now."

He cocked his head to one side. "Damn!"

She turned on her side and patted the other pillow. "Stay with me a while?" She watched the struggle on his face. "Just 'til I fall asleep? It won't take long."

He lay down facing her. With a little smile he tucked the covers tighter under her chin. "Just to keep you safe."

He was so sweet! He ran his fingers down her cheek, his callused fingertips so very gentle. "Go to sleep beautiful. Hopefully you'll feel better after a good rest."

Her eyelids were heavy and her stomach was full. She wanted to lie there for hours, get lost in those big brown eyes, but she was already drifting away.

Chapter Five

Dan sat in the minivan and looked across at the group of parents standing, talking in the parking lot. Occasionally, one of them would glance over at Missy's van. Each time they did, he quickly occupied himself with his phone so they wouldn't catch his eye. As so often happened, his determination to avoid unnecessary social interaction was helping his business. While he sat there, he'd discovered that the new text-to-voice app was really buggy. He'd need to spend some time this week working on the digitized voice production. When he typed the word 'set', the digital voice said 'sex'. 'Asset' sounded even funnier. He smiled to himself. Perhaps he shouldn't try to fix it, but work instead on how to get it into the hands of teen-aged boys. It was bound to go viral if he did.

He couldn't wait to see one teenaged boy. The bus should be here soon. Scot had called earlier, talking at a hundred miles an hour about how they'd won. Dan had put his phone on speaker and sat next to Missy on the sofa, knowing she'd want to hear all about it too. They'd listened to him for a good twenty minutes before he'd run out of steam.

"So, anyway. We should be back at school by five, Mom. Can you pick me up?"

"I will," Dan had answered quickly. "Your mom's tired and I want to see you before I have to leave."

"Awesome! Thanks, Dan. See you then."

Missy had been grateful, not mad at him like he'd feared. She'd had a good few hours' sleep, but she still looked tired and pale. "Thanks, Dan. You'd probably better take the van though. Scot won't thank you if you make him walk home."

So here he sat. In Missy's van. Waiting for Scot to get back. He'd take him home and go get them an early dinner from the Boathouse. Then he really should leave. He needed to call Smoke an hour ahead of time, so he could file a flight plan and have the plane ready to go. He enjoyed using Jack and Pete's plane. He was enjoying it so much that he and Steven had talked about investing in one themselves. Of course, Olivia didn't approve, but then that shouldn't matter. She had no real say in the business. She was a minor partner. It was just that he and Steven had let her walk all over them. Dan was starting to realize just how stupid he'd been when it came to her. He hoped he could make Steven see it too. Over the last couple of years she'd changed the shape of their business, and their lives. She'd changed things in her own best interests, not theirs. Though he wasn't looking forward to the conversation he needed to have with her tonight, he was very much looking forward to being on the other side of it. He'd be free, free to explore whatever might happen with Missy, and free to start re-arranging his life, and his work, to suit himself.

The minibus pulled into the parking lot and a group of tired, but happy-looking kids piled out. Dan spotted Scot and got out of the van. Scot high-fived a couple of his friends, then hitched his backpack higher and came to Dan, a big grin on his face. Dan was surprised when the kid wrapped his arms around his waist and hugged him. Dan hugged back. This was a new development.

Scot let go. "Thanks, Dan."

"My pleasure, champ. I wanted to see you before I have to go."

Scot stood close and leaned against him as a couple of his friends walked by.

"See you tomorrow, Scot."

"Yeah, see ya."

The mothers smiled and nodded at Dan as they passed, curious eyes darting between him and Scot.

"Bye, Mrs. Miller." Scot waved at them.

"Come on," said Dan, getting back in the van. "Let's get you back to your mom."

"I'm surprised she let you come for me. She usually likes to stand and yack with all the other moms."

Dan grinned. No doubt all the other moms would be yacking about him, wondering who he was and where Missy was. "She's really tired, so I persuaded her to let me come."

"She must be beat. You can't normally keep her away."

"Listen, champ. Will you take care of her? She really is beat and I'm not convinced that she's not sick, too."

Scot turned big eyes on him. Big gray eyes, just like his mom's. "She's sick?"

"Not bad sick, just tired out. She needs a rest." Shit! He hadn't meant to scare the kid, just to make him think to look out for her. "I just think maybe you can help her out a bit, you know? Look out for her."

Scot nodded, his face solemn. "Can you stay and help?"

Dan had thought about it, but he figured he should get out of the way now Scot was home and would be back at school in the morning. He'd often come on Friday, or left on Monday over the summer, but he knew Missy liked to stick to a routine when Scot was in school. He didn't want to mess that up. Plus, he was supposed to meet Olivia at eight. On the other hand, he didn't want to leave if Missy wasn't feeling any better.

"You'll be fine, champ. She's probably better by now."

Scot didn't look convinced. Dan didn't feel so sure either. He'd make the call when they got back to the house and he saw her.

~ ~ ~

Missy sat on the sofa waiting for Dan to bring Scot back. She still felt totally exhausted. What she couldn't figure out was why. She'd slept for hours, but she still felt like she could sleep for a week. Her body felt heavy and lethargic. She didn't feel ill though. Well, maybe a low-grade headache, but she'd had that on and off for weeks. She'd felt dizzy a few times, but she did get that way when she'd been overdoing it. She just hoped a good night's sleep would set her straight. She had a lot of work lined up for tomorrow. She covered her eyes at the thought. She had no idea how she would manage it all if she still felt like this.

She smiled when she heard the van pull in to the driveway. Scot bounded in to the living room.

"Hey, Mom!" He flung himself on the sofa and wrapped his arms around her. "Are you okay? I missed you."

Missy's heart overflowed. "Hey, sunbeam. I missed you too!"

Moments like this were the highlights of her life. Much of the time she wondered if he even knew she was there. It was hard when he was engrossed in his computers, or his robots. When he didn't even hear her speak. When he forgot to call her. It was so very hard, but she knew he was doing what he needed to for himself, to become his own person. If she waited long enough and didn't push, he gave her what she needed, too—a show of his love, like this one right now. She hugged him tight and he snuggled up, resting his head on her shoulder.

"Are you okay? Dan said you were tired."

"I'm fine, honey. Now, what do you want for dinner? You can tell me all about it while I fix us something."

Dan cleared his throat. He was standing in the doorway, watching them.

"Can you stay for dinner?" She knew he'd have to leave, but she didn't want him to.

His eyes searched her face. "I should go. I can go get dinner for you both before I leave though. Save you having to make anything."

"Great!" said Scot. "Can we get pizza?"

Missy gave him a stern look. "On a Sunday?" His face fell.

Dan grinned. "I think after winning State Championships, a guy should be allowed a celebration dinner. Don't you, champ?"

Scot grinned back at him and nodded. "Yeah, Mom. Don't spoil my victory."

Missy laughed. She wasn't going to win when the pair of them teamed up on her like that. Besides, Dan was right, it should be a celebration dinner. "Okay then. Pizza it is, but you don't need to go for it. I'll call Giuseppe's for a delivery."

"I'll call it in," said Dan. "You want the usual, champ?"

"Yes, please."

"How about you, Miss. Want your lasagna?"

"Yes, please." She was surprised again. He knew she saved her pancakes for dessert. He knew she always got lasagna when they ordered from Giuseppe's. He was turning out to be full of surprises. All good ones too, so far. She snuggled with Scot on the sofa while he called in their order.

"Should be here in half an hour. I'll eat with you, but then I'll have to get going."

Missy nodded. He'd be cutting it fine if he was supposed to meet Olivia at eight. She wasn't going to say anything though. It was none of her business. She was just glad he was staying a little while longer.

Scot wriggled off the sofa. "Dan, Dan, Dan, did you see the files I left you?"

"I sure did. I think we're making progress."

"Will you show me what you've done? Come on, let's go see before the pizza comes?"

Dan looked at Missy.

"Go on," she smiled. "Don't make him wait 'til next weekend."

Dan nodded and followed Scot out to the RV. Missy got up. She would have to wait 'til next weekend for what she wanted to do with Dan. She was glad for Scotty's sake that he didn't have to. She made her way into the kitchen. She could get the table ready for when the food arrived. She felt a little unsteady on her feet and leaned on the table for support. After a few moments she straightened up, hoping it had passed. That was when everything started to spin. And went black.

~ ~ ~

Dan was laughing with Scot as they came back into the house. Missy was gone from the sofa. He went into the kitchen. She was sitting on the floor, looking dazed.

"Miss! What happened?" He was at her side, picking her up off the floor.

She tried to focus on him, but looked woozy. "I'm okay," she mumbled.

"Mom!" Scot's eyes were round and scared. "Are you okay?"

"She's going to be just fine, champ." Dan's voice didn't sound like his own. It sounded calm and soothing. Inside he felt anything but calm. His heart and his mind were racing. "Do you think you can call Uncle Ben and ask him to send Michael over here?" He hoped Scot would fare better if he had an important job to do. Dan carried Missy back into the living room and sat down with her still in his arms. She looked more with it now.

"I'm okay, hero." She gave him a weak smile.

"Jesus, Miss. What happened? You scared me."

"I blacked out." She gingerly touched at her forehead, where he could see a bruise and a big lump starting to form. "I think I gave myself a doink on the way down too."

"Looks like you did. That's going to be a doozy."

Scot came in, putting his phone back in his pocket. "Uncle Ben's going to call Michael. He said he'll come himself later, too." Dan knew he'd done the right thing when Scot asked, "Can I do anything else?"

Dan was proud of the kid, trying to be the man for his mom. Dan knew what he probably needed most though. "Actually, there is. Can you swap places with me while I get some ice to put on her head?"

Scot looked at him as though he'd gone completely nuts. "You're going to put ice on her head? Why?"

He felt Missy shake in his arms as she started to laugh. He had to laugh with her at the incredulous look on Scot's face. "He means an icepack, honey. I bumped my head when I fell." She lifted her hair with her hand to show him.

"Oh! Ouch. I get it." He came and sat on the sofa and stroked his mom's shoulder. "You'll be okay," he reassured her.

Dan slid out from under Missy and went into the kitchen. He leaned his forehead against the fridge, his head filled with memories. Fetching ice packs for his own mom's bruises and black eyes. Telling her she'd be okay, hoping it would be true. He shook his head to clear it, and opened the freezer. Did anyone ever eat frozen peas? Or were they just kept in every freezer for moments like this? He pulled a bag out and wrapped it in a dishcloth. With a smile he opened the freezer again and squeezed three ice cubes out of the tray. He put them in a dish and took it back to the living room. Missy looked less ashen. Scot, with his arm around her, less scared.

Dan knelt on the floor at their feet. Taking an ice cube from the dish, he winked at Missy and placed it on top of her head. Scot's eyes grew wide again. Dan took another and put it on top of Scot's head, trying hard not to laugh as the kid's eyes almost disappeared into his hairline as he tried to watch. He took the third ice-cube and put it on top of his own head. "There, she'll be fine now. It's an old Texan ritual to heal the sick."

Scot looked at him as though he really had gone crazy.

Missy burst out laughing. She definitely looked a bit better. "He's teasing you, honey!"

Dan grinned and held out the frozen peas. "This is the more conventional treatment though." He gave them to Missy.

Scot rolled his eyes and laughed. "You ass...tronaut! I thought you'd lost it!"

They all laughed now. Dan was pleased Missy didn't call Scot out on his language. He had been scared out of his wits for a minute there. She obviously had something going on with her, but it wasn't anything imminently life threatening. She smiled gratefully at him as he plucked the ice-cube off her head and tossed it into the dish along with his own. He grabbed Scot's and pressed it against the kid's nose for a second.

"Eww!" Scot swatted at him, laughing.

"How are you feeling?" he asked Missy.

"No worse than I did this afternoon. Except now I have a big lump on my head."

He smiled at her. "Well, your friend, Dr. Michael is on his way to give you the once over."

"Thanks, but I'm fine, really."

"I'll be happier when I hear him say that."

The doorbell rang. Dan went to answer it. He took the pizza and gave the guy a huge tip because he didn't want to wait for change. As he turned to go back in he heard a shout. "Hang on, Dan." Michael came hurrying down the street carrying his bag.

"Thanks for coming so fast."

"What happened?"

"She blacked out and keeled over. Gave herself a good knock on the head, too."

Michael frowned.

"You know how tired she's been? Well, today she started to get off balance, feeling dizzy. Come on in, she's in the living room. He took the food through and dumped it on the kitchen table before following Michael, who squatted down next to the sofa.

"What you been up to, critter?"

Dan watched her smile at Michael. He didn't feel any of his earlier jealousy, just gratitude that Michael had come so quickly.

"You know me, causing trouble as usual. Do you think I'm going to make it, Doc?" she asked as he strapped a blood pressure cuff to her arm.

"Hold still and we'll see." After he'd taken her blood pressure and her pulse, he gently pulled her lower eyelid down. "Have you been eating properly?"

Dan smiled when she looked up at him. "Yessir. You can ask Dan."

"I can vouch for quantity consumed," he said. "I don't know about nutritional value. What are you thinking, Michael?"

"I'm thinking anemia. Symptoms are classic, but we'll need a blood test to make sure."

"Is that just iron deficiency?" asked Dan.

Michael stood up. "It can be, or it can be a couple of other things, too. Decreased volume of blood itself, which would account for the low blood pressure, or a decrease in red blood cells. Which is why we'll need that blood test. Miss, can you come in and see Dad in the morning?"

"I can't. I'm at work. I could stop by later?"

Dan shook his head. "You're not going to work, Miss."

Michael nodded his agreement. "No chance, critter. I'll meet you at Dad's office at nine, okay?"

Missy looked from Dan to Michael and back again. "I have to go to work." She sounded desperate.

Dan hated to see her like that; she looked pale and defeated. He didn't know what the problem was, but it couldn't be anything they couldn't work out. "You have to get yourself sorted out first."

She rested her head back against the sofa. "Okay."

Michael looked at Scot. "Will you help Dan keep an eye on her and make sure she comes in tomorrow?" Scot nodded. "Okay. I'll leave you guys to it then."

Dan walked him to the door. "Thanks, Michael."

"Not a problem, but you might have to drag her into the office in the morning." He lowered his voice. "And make sure she knows it's my favor, not an official visit, so no charge."

That puzzled Dan. "Doesn't her insurance cover office visits?"

"It might, if she had any."

"What?"

"Shh! I shouldn't know that. You sure as hell shouldn't know that. My dad's been the town doc for years. You can't help but know who has which insurance, who's self-pay and who tries to stay away. Point is, you need to bring her in in the morning and that's only one of the reasons it'll be hard to get her there. Good luck. I'll see you tomorrow."

Dan watched Michael walk up the path, then closed the door. He stood in the hallway, trying to assess the situation. She said she had to go work. It must be for the money. There was no way she could, though. She needed to get the blood test and he knew she wouldn't go if he didn't take her himself. He went back into the living room.

"You hungry, champ?" Scot nodded. "How about you, Miss?" She nodded too. She was getting a little color back in her cheeks, but now she looked worried.

After they'd eaten, Dan cleared the dishes. Scot came to join him. "She's fallen asleep," he said.

"Good. She needs the rest."

"Want to go in the RV and go through that code?" asked Scot hopefully.

Dan grinned at him. "I'd love to, but do you think maybe we should stay in the house and keep an eye on your mom?"

Scot nodded.

"What do you usually do on Sunday night?"

"Get my backpack ready for school."

"You want to do that while I see to the dishes?"

"Okay." Scot didn't look thrilled.

"You got any homework you need to do?"

Scot pulled a face.

"I'll take that as a yes?" He couldn't help but smile as the kid nodded reluctantly. He remembered only too well how it felt to have to write boring essays about irrelevant dead people when there were programs waiting to be written and systems waiting to be designed, or hacked. "If you get it done quickly enough, we can maybe see if you can beat my high score before you have to go to bed."

Scot brightened at that. "Okay, I'll be quick."

Dan laughed. "Not too quick! Get it done properly, okay?"

"Okay," sighed Scot. He picked up his backpack and headed upstairs.

Dan peeked in at Missy. She was fast asleep on the sofa. He went back to the kitchen and closed the door behind him. Sitting down at the table, he pulled his phone out and called Ben.

"Hey, man. Hang on." It sounded like the restaurant was busy.

"Okay. I can hear you now. How's Miss? What happened?"

"She fainted, but she's fine now. Thanks for getting a hold of Michael."

"No problem. I'll come over when I get a minute."

"No need. She's sleeping."

"Alright then. It's crazy in here tonight. What did Michael say?"

"He thinks she's anemic. Wants me to bring her in for a blood test in the morning."

"You sticking around then?"

Oh, shit! Dan had completely forgotten that he was supposed to be leaving. "Yeah." He looked at his watch. It was almost seven thirty already. "Listen though. She can't work 'til she gets sorted out. She needs to rest. Do you know what she's supposed to be doing this week?"

"She's got a crazy schedule. I've got her on the cabins all week."

"She can't do it. I don't want her working at all this week, but I'll cover it."

Ben laughed. "You offering to clean cabins?"

Dan laughed with him. "You've seen the RV, I don't think you'd want me on the cleaning crew. I mean I'll pay you whatever it costs to find cover for her."

"You don't need to do that. I can take care of it."

"I want to. Seems like Miss needs the money, so I need you to pay her whatever she would have made this week. I'll pay you to actually get the work done. I may be able to get her to stay home tomorrow, but I can't stay all week. There's no way she'll rest up if she's losing money."

"You've got a point, but we could split it?"

"No need. You're going to have to hustle to find someone to do the work. I get the easy part and just hand over the money."

Ben laughed. "True. I'd happily trade with you. Listen I'd better get on it. See who I can find to fill in. Tell her I'll stop by tomorrow?"

"Will do, and I'll have my checkbook ready."

"Okay, bud. See you tomorrow."

"See ya."

Dan hung up. That was the easy phone call done. Now for the not so easy one. Olivia. He chewed the inside of his lip, and remembered he needed to text Smoke.

Sorry. Change of plan. Not leaving tonight. Call you tomorrow?

He stared at the phone. It buzzed almost immediately with a reply.

OK. C U 2moro.

Now there were no more excuses. He searched his contacts for Olivia and listened to it ring.

"Hello, Daniel. I hope you're not going to be late."

He rested his head in his hand. "Hello, Olivia, Yes, I'm fine thanks. How are you?"

"Ugh! What's the matter Daniel?"

Why did she insist on calling him that? "I'm not coming."

"What? I canceled other plans because you said you wanted to see me!"

"Yeah. Sorry."

"Sorry's no use, is it? Why aren't you coming?"

"I'm still in Summer Lake and I'm not coming back tonight. Maybe not tomorrow either"

She tutted loudly. He hated when she did that. "You spend far too much time with that boy!"

"His name is Scot."

"Whatever. And you better come back tomorrow. You need to be in the office."

Dan had had just about enough of her telling him what he did and didn't need to do. "I don't know what I'm doing yet."

"Well, I'm telling you what you're doing, Daniel. You're going to get back here as soon as you can and get yourself in the office in the morning. I have the people from Systech coming and I need you to talk to them."

What the hell? "Olivia, I'll come in whenever I'm ready. I've told you, I'm not going to talk to the pricks from Systech. I don't want anything to do with them, and neither does Steven. I do not want them in the building. Do you understand me?"

She was quiet for a long moment. When she spoke again her tone was much softer. "I'm sorry, darling. I'm just trying to look out for you. I know you can't see it yet, but this will be a great deal for us. You need to talk to them, then you'll see."

Dan didn't trust himself to reply, just waited for her to continue, as he knew she would.

"I'm sorry I was snappy. I was looking forward to seeing you tonight. It's been too long."

Her wheedling tone made his skin crawl. It was so obvious she was simply trying to get her own way, and would use any tactics she thought would work.

"I'm sure if you left now, you could be here by bedtime. We can talk. You can spend the night."

Dan shook his head at the thought. He hadn't slept with her in months. Even on the few occasions they'd gone out, he hadn't been able to muster any desire for her. He'd just kept thinking of Missy instead. He let out a deep sigh. "I told you. I'm not coming back tonight. We'll talk when I see you."

"But Danny, I want to see you. I want you."

That did it. She was a manipulative bitch! He'd told her once, in the early days when he was still quite flattered by her interest in him, that only the people who loved him had ever called him Danny. She tried to use it on him whenever she was determined to get her own way. "*I* don't want to see *you*. We're done. Through. Finished. I wanted to tell you face to face, but now you know."

"You don't mean that, Danny."

She was still wheedling! He took a deep breath. "Yes, I do, Olivia. Goodbye." He hung up. *Damn!* He'd wanted to do the decent thing. Tell her to her face. But she was so damned pushy! He was sick of her telling him who he was, and what he thought, and what he wanted. She didn't know, or even care, what he really thought, or really wanted. He seriously doubted now that she ever had. She wanted the money and the control that came with Prometheus. He took a beer from the fridge. Well, it was done now. He'd no doubt have to face her—and her anger and pouting and wheedling—once he went back, but at least he'd told her. The worst of it was over. He hoped.

Chapter Six

Missy opened her eyes. She felt a little groggy. She couldn't figure out why she'd been sleeping on the sofa. Dan sat in the chair, his legs slung over the arm. She closed her eyes and opened them again. Was she still dreaming? No, it came back to her. Passing out in the kitchen. Dan taking care of her. He was working on his laptop. Seemingly engrossed as he tapped away at the keyboard. He would pause occasionally to chew on his thumb as he stared into space, then start tapping away again. He was gorgeous! That muscle shirt he wore showed off a lean, muscular torso that he usually hid under baggy T-shirts. What she would like to do to him, if she could find the energy! But she had to find some energy from somewhere. She had to go work tomorrow, no matter what he said, or Michael for that matter. She caught her breath. What was Dan still doing here anyway? He couldn't make her go to see Doc Morgan in the morning because he needed to get back to San Jose. She looked at the clock. It was past ten! She sat up, making herself dizzy. Where was Scotty? He had homework to do.

"Whoa." Dan appeared at her side. "You shouldn't get up so fast."

"It's late. Where's Scot? I need to make sure he does his homework, and gets his bag ready, and...."

Dan put an arm around her shoulders. "Slow down, Miss. It's all taken care of."

She looked at him in disbelief.

"Seriously. We went through his schedule and made sure he has everything he needs for tomorrow. He did his math homework, no problem. Then I think we did okay with his history."

Missy continued to stare at him. "You? You helped him get it all done?"

Dan lowered his eyes. "Yeah. I tried. I think we got it all covered."

"Oh, thank you, hon! You really are turning out to be my hero." She watched his smile spread as he slowly raised his eyes to meet hers.

"I just wanted to help out. He and I are both supposed to be pretty smart. We managed to figure it out between us."

She wrapped her arms around him. "Thanks, Dan!"

He hugged her to him and she nestled close, enjoying the feel of his arms around her. The living room door opened and Scot stared at them. Dan made to let go of her, but Missy clung on to him.

"Are you guys...like...." Scot's eyes bored into her, then he looked at Dan and back at her. "Like getting together?"

Missy smiled. She didn't like to hide anything from him, certainly not this, though none of them knew what 'this' was yet. She wrinkled her nose. "We're thinking about it." She smiled at Dan. "We're testing out hugs first, to see how they go. "What would you say if we were to go on a date?"

Scot grinned and punched the air. "*Yes*! I'd say yes!" He looked at Dan "And I'd say, what took you so long?"

Dan laughed. "Timing is everything, champ."

"Then I hope it's time now," said Scot.

Missy smiled. "It's time for bed now, young man. That's what it's time for."

He pulled a face at her, but didn't argue.

"Have you got everything ready for morning?"

He grinned. "Yeah. Dan helped." He came to the sofa and put one arm around Missy, the other around Dan. "Group hug, guys!"

Missy hugged back, enjoying the feel of two very different arms around her.

Scot stood back and grinned at Dan. "I think you need to sleep in Mom's room in case she gets dizzy in the night."

She saw a touch of pink color Dan's cheeks. Bless him. "Scot!" She frowned at him.

"Well! If you need to pee in the night and you fall down again, you need someone there." He tried to look serious, but he was laughing.

She smiled. "I'm fine now. Go on. Off to bed with you." She kissed his cheek. "Love you, sunbeam. G'night"

"Love you, Mom. G'night, Dan,"

"G'night, champ. See you in the morning."

Once Scot had gone, Dan put his arms around her again. "So, how am I doing in these hug tests?"

"You pass with flying colors."

He grinned. "That's good to know."

A big yawn came out before Missy could stop it. "Sorry."

"No problem. You need sleep and if you're anemic, you need the oxygen too."

She looked at him questioningly.

"I was reading about it while you were asleep. I won't bore you with what I learned, but tomorrow I'm going to get you some iron pills, and some suitable groceries."

She had to laugh. Only Dan could seriously call groceries 'suitable'. "Now this I have to see. Do you even know where the grocery store is?"

He shrugged and gave her his gorgeous smile. "I'm a smart guy, and besides that's what GPS is for. Right now though, you need more sleep. Think you can make it up the stairs?"

She probably could, but she didn't want to. She wanted him to hold her again. She looked into his eyes. "Take me?"

He scooped her up off the sofa and smiled at her. "You know, until today I always thought it was kind of cheesy when guys picked women up and carried them around."

She looped her arms around his neck and rested her head against his shoulder. "And now?"

He held her closer to his chest. "Now I get it." He grinned. "I really get it." He climbed the stairs easily and took her into her room, where he gently placed her on the bed. "Are you going to be okay?" He asked.

"I do feel better."

"Good. I'll say goodnight then. I'll sleep in the guest room, so knock on the wall if you need me."

She held her arms up to him. "Stay with me 'til I go to sleep?"

He looked back over his shoulder. "What about Scot?"

She didn't want him to go yet. "He rarely comes out of his room at night. He wouldn't mind anyway. You're only taking care of me."

He bit his lip. Poor guy. She was probably being cruel, asking him to lie in bed with her when there was nothing they could do about it, but she couldn't help it. She just wanted to feel him close as she went to sleep. He made her feel better. He made everything feel better.

"Okay. But I'm going to wait in the guest room. Tap on the wall when you're in bed." His eyes twinkled. "And make sure you've got the covers up to your chin before I come back in here, okay?"

"Okay."

By the time Missy had brushed her teeth and got undressed, she was exhausted. She crawled into bed naked. She'd thought she should find something to put on, but didn't have the strength. She tapped on the wall and smiled when Dan tapped back. He slowly opened the door.

"Are you decent?"

"Yep. All covered up."

He came in and closed the door behind him. Tired as she was, her body came alive as he sat on the edge of the bed and pulled his shoes off. He lay down face-to-face with her and smiled his gorgeous smile. She reached an arm out of the covers to stroke his face, loving the feel of his stubbly beard under her fingers. His eyes were like pools of melted chocolate, achingly beautiful. She ached for him. She had thought her body had forgotten what desire was, but it remembered all right. He covered her hand with his.

"Now that's not fair. You're supposed to stay covered up. I can see naked shoulder and you have no idea what you are doing to me."

"Tell me?" She needed to hear that he wanted her.

"I'll show you." He brought her fingers to his lips and kissed them. Then he touched them to the pulse in his throat, it was beating wildly. "You're doing this," he murmured. He drew her hand to his chest, to feel his heart hammering. He took her hand lower still and placed it over the front of his pants. She could feel the heat of his erection. He was hard as a rock, quite a big rock too! "This. This is what you're doing to me, beautiful. It's what you always do to me. Have done since the first time I saw you. And now you want me to lie here and watch you go to sleep? Okay, I'll watch you. It will almost kill me to watch and not touch, but it's what you want, so it's what I'll do. I'm showing you what your body does to my body, but I want you to understand something else, too. Miss, who you are, the woman you are, has the same effect on who I am, the man I am. I want to know you, to learn you, to explore you. You make me a better man." He smiled and pressed her hand against the bulge in his pants, "You make me a bigger man, and all of that is before we get to anything physical. You're turning me upside down and inside out, Miss. Please, for now, hurry up and go to sleep. So I can go back to wanting to take care of you, and stop wanting to do less honorable things to you."

Missy felt tears prick behind her eyes. How could he be so incredibly sweet and so incredibly sexy all at the same time? "You're turning me upside down and inside out too, hero. I want you. Right now I want nothing more than to get you under these covers with me and start exploring those less honorable things." She stroked him through his pants and watched him close his eyes and let out a deep breath. She reluctantly withdrew her hand. "Soon, Dan. Soon you'll be a single man and hopefully by then I'll have the strength to misbehave with you."

His eyes flew open. "I am a single man! I called Olivia while you were sleeping. She was giving me all kinds of grief, Miss. I told her. We're done."

"Oh." Missy was filled with a rush of emotions. He was single? Then they could? She struggled to free her arms from the covers and wrapped them around his neck. "Then what are we waiting for?"

He pulled back. "We're waiting for you to be well." She pressed herself against him through the covers, but he shook his head. "You're not going to seduce me now. It wouldn't be right. We can wait 'til you're feeling up to it."

She wrinkled her nose at him. "More excuses? I'm starting to think you don't want me." He caught her hand and brought it back down to the front of his pants.

"There's your proof that that's not true." He gave her a mischievous grin. "It's just that you'll need all your strength. You *will* be worn out by the time I'm done with you." She caught her breath as he ran his fingertips down her bare arm. There was nothing shy or sweet about the way he was looking at her now. Her insides melted. "Please go to sleep before I have to show you what I'm talking about?"

She nodded. "Kiss goodnight?" She asked hopefully. She'd been longing to kiss him, to feel his lips on hers.

He shook his head sadly. "We both know it wouldn't end with a kiss. Go to sleep, Miss, please? You need the rest."

"Okay then."

She turned over and pressed her back against him. He put an arm around her and pulled her closer. How was she supposed to go to sleep when she could feel his hard-on pushing at her through the covers? When she could feel his warm breath on her neck? Impossible as it seemed, she could feel her eyelids starting to droop.

~ ~ ~

Dan sat in the kitchen, nursing his second cup of coffee. Missy had still been asleep when he came downstairs. He'd hardly slept, just lain there holding her close all night, fighting the urge to get out of his clothes and under the covers with her. He'd known that if he did, there would only be one outcome. He wanted so badly to make love to her. Had wanted her for months. At first he'd thought it was just a fantasy, a physical attraction, albeit stronger than any he'd known before. But as he'd gotten to know her, spent more time with her whenever he came to see Scot, his feelings had grown stronger, and deeper. He knew now he wanted to make love with the woman, not just have sex with her body. He'd waited this long. He knew now that it would happen, and sooner rather than later. The obstacles to their being together were being dismantled one by one. Olivia was out of the picture. Scot knew the score and was happy about it. They'd both vowed to not let it affect him. Now, if she could get this anemia addressed, get herself back to full strength, there'd be nothing to stop them. He shook his head at the ever-present pressure in his pants. That part of him didn't understand the logic or the reason in waiting. It had one desire, and in the early morning hours, it had almost convinced him that he really shouldn't wait any longer. That was when he'd had to get up and come downstairs.

He'd worked on his laptop for a while. Now he was a little concerned about what time Scot would need to be up, and if he should wake him—or Missy. He fixed himself a fresh coffee and sipped it, trying to decide what to do. The decision was made for him when he heard what could only be Scot coming down the stairs. The kitchen door flew open.

"Mom, Mom, I...." Scot froze when he saw it was Dan and not his mom sitting there. He hung his head. "Morning," he mumbled.

Dan was a little surprised by the sudden change in him. Then he noticed the front of Scot's pajamas appeared to be soaked. Ah! How to handle this without making it worse for the kid? "Morning, champ." He rubbed his eyes. "I'm nearly awake. How about you?"

"Yeah." Scot was still looking at the floor.

"Do you have coffee?"

"Orange juice," he mumbled.

Dan got up and poured him a glass of juice. "What about breakfast?"

"No thanks. I have to.... Is Mom awake?"

"Not yet. What do you need, bud?"

Scot lifted his head just enough so that Dan could see his eyes. His brows knit together. "I...." He lowered his gaze again and stood there, clutching his glass in both hands.

Poor little guy. Like so many of the things Scot went through, Dan remembered how this felt too. "Listen, bud. When I used to do it, Jack would make me go take a shower while he stripped the bed and put the sheets and jammies in the washer. You think we should try that?"

Scot looked up at him. "You used to pee in the bed too?"

"Yup, sure did." Dan nodded solemnly. "Sometimes I would do it when I wasn't even asleep."

"You did?"

"Yup. You know how the real world fades away when you're coding? Sometimes I'd be so into what I was writing that I wouldn't notice that I needed to pee—or even that I had peed! I think it's the way our minds work. We get so involved with the interesting stuff, we don't always pay as much attention as we should to the everyday stuff."

Scot nodded. "I used to do it when I was awake too. I don't anymore though."

"Me neither," said Dan with a smile. "What do you think, you want to go shower while I strip the bed?"

Scot smiled and nodded. "Thanks, Dan."

"No worries, champ. We smart guys have to stick together right? Not everyone else gets us, do they?"

He held his fist out and Scot bumped his own against it. He followed the kid upstairs into his bedroom. "Throw your jammies out to me before you get in the shower and I'll stick them in the washer with the sheets. And be quick so we can have some breakfast."

~ ~ ~

Missy came out of Dr. Morgan's office and smiled at Dan, who sat in the waiting room looking uncomfortable, surrounded as he was by gossiping women and coughing kids. He jumped up when he saw her and followed her to the door.

"So, what did he say?"

"That you and Michael are right. I need some good food and some iron pills."

Dan raised an eyebrow and gave her a knowing look. "And some rest?"

"Yeah, that too."

"So what caused it? Did he know?"

"Umm, a couple of things. It's kind of hereditary. My mom was always on iron pills."

"What else?"

Missy wasn't sure she wanted to tell him.

"*What*, Miss?" He looked so concerned it would be easier to tell him than to leave him worrying it was something serious.

"Heavy blood loss."

He looked horrified. "Heavy blood loss? How? When?" Oh, the poor clueless man! She couldn't help but laugh. "Dan, you're supposed to be a smart guy. If I tell you that the answer to when is a few days every month, I think you can probably figure out the how!"

"Ah." He gave her a shamefaced grin. "I didn't think of that. Sorry."

She laughed. "Not a problem. It makes it easier for me to ask you to take me to the pharmacy."

He held up a hand. "No need to tell me anything more. I don't understand, but I don't need to."

She smiled. Hopefully, at some point he might be interested to know that Dr Morgan had put her on the pill. Not for the sake of any sex life she might be hoping for, but in an attempt to help with the anemia by moderating her period. "Okay, I shall say no more."

"Thank you." He opened the passenger door of the minivan for her. Before she got in, she reached up and kissed his cheek. "No, Dan. Thank *you*. I don't know what I would have done without you this weekend." She sat in the van. "Or this morning, getting Scotty ready and off to school. Getting me here. You've done so much. Thank you."

"I'm glad I was here. Very glad."

While he went around to the driver's side, she knew that, as much as she loved having him around, she needed him to leave soon so she could go to work. It would be a struggle. She still felt exhausted, but she still had five cabins to clean today.

Once he climbed in she said, "I know that you've stayed longer than you meant to already. Do you want to call Smoke and I'll drop you at the airport?"

He looked across at her and cocked his head to one side. "You really think I'm that clueless?"

She was shocked. "What do you mean?"

He rolled his eyes. "You think you're going to get rid of me and then head up to the resort and start cleaning cabins, don't you?"

She didn't say anything. She hadn't realized she was so transparent, and she hated to admit that she had indeed been trying to get rid of him. Yes, he was wonderful, she loved being around him, but her priorities had to revolve around making ends meet, not spending time with a gorgeous man.

"Not going to admit it?" he asked. He didn't look angry, she wasn't sure what the look on his face meant.

She let out a big sigh. "Okay, I admit it. Don't think it's because I want you to leave though. I really don't. It's because I have to work. I need the money. I have to do this to pay the bills. I know it's not something that occurs to the rest of you, but it's a huge factor in my life, Dan."

"That's not fair, Miss. You know where I come from. I know all about struggling to get by."

She did know that. He and Jack had grown up dirt poor with an abusive alcoholic for a father. She nodded. "Yeah, but it's not a factor for you anymore is it, Mr. Tech Genius? You've made boatloads of money with your software. It's not like you have to go out and scrub other people's toilets so you can feed your kid, is it?" Oops! She hadn't meant to bite his head off. It wasn't his fault. His gaze softened as he looked at her.

"You don't have to either. Please. At least for this week, stay home. Rest. Get better?"

"I can't!"

"You can. You'll still get paid. I talked to Ben last night. You'll still get a week's sick pay."

How could that work? She wasn't employed by some corporation. She didn't get any benefits, let alone a week's sick pay.

"Think about it, Miss. It makes sense. It's better to pay you to take one week off to get better now than it would be to lose you for several weeks, or more, if you keep pushing and make yourself worse."

She frowned. What he said made sense, but it didn't make sense that Ben should pay her to stay home and still have to find and pay someone else to do all the work that she wasn't doing. He started the van and pulled out while she was still trying to figure out what to think, say, or do. "Where are we going?"

"I'm taking you home and you're not going to argue."

"You mean you hope I'm not!"

He laughed. "Nope. I'm *telling you* you're not. You're going to be a good girl and do as you're told for once. You're going to go home and take a nice little nap while I go get iron pills and groceries."

She smiled. "Suitable ones?"

"Yes, suitable ones."

How could she argue with him? "Okay, you win and I do appreciate it, Dan. But seriously, don't you need to get back yourself?"

He shrugged. "I don't want to."

She laughed. "Now you sound like Scotty!"

He grinned. "Maybe so, but I don't really need to either. Plus, I need to make sure you're not going to go sneaking back to work as soon as I leave."

"And how are you going to make sure of it?"

He shot her a quick look. "I could tie you to the bed."

Yep. Her body sure did remember what desire was! "But if you did that, I hope you wouldn't leave?"

"No, ma'am. No way I'd be leaving." He reached over and gave her hand a quick squeeze. "See, that's another reason you need to take the whole week off. We can't start misbehaving 'til you're all rested and better."

She looked at him. He was looking way too pleased with himself. "Hmm. That could be a persuasive argument."

"I could be even more persuasive and say we can't start misbehaving until you've taken five full days at home to rest—and don't think I won't know. If you do decide you're all better and go back to work, you'll be delaying our date. And everything that goes with it."

Her stomach fluttered at the thought of everything that might go with their date. "You drive a hard bargain, hero."

"I guess I do for a clueless geek, don't I?"

She laughed. "You're no clueless geek! You're my hero!" She'd call him hero all day every day if she could, just to see the way he smiled when she did. "You win. I'll stay home all week and rest, but you'd better come back and take me out on Friday night."

He squeezed her hand again. "It's a date."

Chapter Seven

"Sorry I haven't been over sooner, bud."

Missy smiled. "That's okay, you've sent enough minions over with food. You didn't have to do that, you know. I'm not a complete invalid. I can cook for Scotty and me. I feel bad enough that you're paying double to get the cabins cleaned."

Ben shrugged. "Just smile and say, thank you, huh?"

"Thank you. But honestly, you don't need to have every meal sent over here. Make it stop now."

"Sorry, Miss. No can do."

"Why the hell not? I'm asking you to stop it."

"I'm under orders to ignore any requests from you that would mean you do any work of any kind, cooking, cleaning." He grinned. "Lifting a finger, if it can be helped."

Under orders? What did that mean? It dawned on her that there was only one thing it could mean. "Dan?"

"Yep."

She felt the fluttering in her stomach. "He asked you to do this?"

"No, not asked. I really am under orders. He might seem like a mild mannered nerd on the surface, but I'm telling you, Miss, there's a man of steel under the quiet exterior. And he is most concerned about your well being. I like him. It's obvious he likes you. A lot!"

"I like him too, Ben." Missy wrinkled her nose. "A lot. We're going out on a date on Friday."

"Only if you keep your word and don't go back to work between now and then."

"He told you?"

"Yep and he asked me to snitch on you if you weren't getting your rest."

She smiled. "That was sneaky of him."

"I wouldn't say sneaky. He cares that you should rest up and get your strength back. And I'd say he has a vested interest in your being well enough to go out with him on Friday night."

He also had a vested interest in her not being too tired by the time they got home on Friday night, too. Not that she was going to tell Ben that. "Between restaurant deliveries for every meal and the fact that I'm not working, I feel much better already." She did feel better, less tired than she had at the weekend, but she still wasn't anywhere near one hundred percent. "I do feel bad about you paying double to get the cabins cleaned though."

Ben shrugged. "Don't worry about it."

"No, I can't let you do it. I've been thinking, once I'm back to work you can add an extra one here and there and not pay me for them 'til we're even. And don't go saying no." She grinned at him. "I've decided, and you know you can never win an argument with me."

Ben looked uncomfortable.

"What?"

He looked at her, but didn't say anything.

"Okay. What's the problem?"

"I can't do it. You don't owe me anything."

"Yes, I do."

"No, Miss. You don't owe *me* anything."

Oh, no. He wasn't saying.... "Not Dan?"

Ben nodded. "Yep. He already had it figured out before I even knew what was going on with you. He told me what we were going to do. I didn't have any choice. Not that I would have let you work, had I known." He gave her a shrewd look. "But if it weren't for Dan, I doubt I would have known at all, would I?"

Missy frowned. She was filled with conflicting emotions. She took care of her own business. She may struggle sometimes, but she got by. She wasn't one to ask for help from anyone, and she was proud of that. Dan had stepped in without being asked. She wanted to feel angry with him, but she didn't. She felt cared for, and that was a new one for her. She felt like she shouldn't, but she liked it.

"And, Miss? I wouldn't give him a hard time over it, if I were you."

She smiled. "Don't worry. I won't. And don't think I'm turning into a weak and needy damsel in distress, or anything, but I kind of like it."

Ben laughed. "I could accuse you of many things, but I would never accuse you of that. You're the strongest woman I know. Seems to me you and Dan bring out each other's hidden qualities. He brings out your soft side. You bring out his strong side. It's kinda cool."

"And when did you get so smart about that kind of thing? You never date anyone who's going to be here more than two weeks." She wanted to deflect the attention back onto Ben. He'd hit the nail on the head about her and Dan and she needed some time to think about it.

Ben shrugged. "I've seen too many people ruin their lives, standing by a commitment that no longer works for them. I choose to keep my own relationships short and sweet. I watch people all the time get entangled in things that I can tell aren't going to work out, I'd rather not do that." He smiled. "Seems there's been a run of good luck around here lately though. I don't deny that good relationships happen too and I can spot 'em a mile off. I knew Jack was what Em needed as soon as I saw them together. I knew Pete had met his match when Holly came up here. I believe you and Dan are headed down the same road. You're good for each other."

Missy shook her head. "No. It's not like that. We're just going to date for a while. I really like him, but I'm under no illusions. We're at different places in life. He's like the others—he's at the beginning of his life story. He'll find a woman and settle down and have kids, all that good stuff. I'm already half way through my life story. I am settled down, my boy's ready for high school. There's no way I'd ever start back at diapers now."

"I'm not going to argue, Miss. I'm just saying I think you're good together."

Missy smiled. "I hope so."

~ ~ ~

Dan hit the snooze button and pulled the covers over his head. He didn't want to be awake. He wanted to get back to his dream. He didn't want to be in his own bed. He wanted to be back in Missy's bed, his hands full of her wonderful, round ass, his face buried in her breasts. He wanted to feel her willing little body beneath him, opening up to him when he finally.... His phone rang. Damn! Without opening his eyes he patted

around the nightstand 'til his hand closed around the phone.
He brought it under the covers to his ear.

"Hello?"

"Good morning, Daniel. What time will you be in the office? I
think we need to talk, don't you?"

Olivia's voice grated on his nerves, but at least it ensured he
wouldn't have an uncomfortable boner to deal with. She'd
turned his morning wood into morning wouldn't. He bit back
a laugh at the thought.

"Can you hear me?"

Unfortunately. "Yes."

"So. What time?"

"Whenever the hell I'm ready. What do you want to talk
about?"

"Us."

"Olivia, there is no us. I was serious. We're done."

"We'll see about that when you come in."

Jesus! Where did the woman get off? He supposed he did at
least owe her a conversation. He wasn't going to let her push
him around though. Not anymore. "You can come to my
office at eleven thirty. Bye." He hung up quickly. That would
give him plenty of time to shower and take care of some things
around the apartment. He wanted to go in and set up remote
access to a couple of his programs anyway. He could talk to
Olivia while he was there. After that, he wanted to pick up
some textbooks for Scot. The kid had taught himself a bunch
of programming languages, but he'd picked up some bad
habits by learning everything online. He didn't want to point
them out. He wanted Scot to own the knowledge. Dan knew
he'd devour the textbooks if he left them lying around the RV.

He smiled to himself—as long as he made them look used first.

He went into the kitchen to make himself some coffee. Uh-oh. He'd forgotten he'd used the last of it before he left for Summer Lake. He checked the fridge—empty. Oh, well. He'd pick up coffee and pastries from the coffee shop in the lobby before he showered. He wasn't going to run around like an automaton doing whatever Olivia had programmed him to do anymore. He pulled on some sweatpants and a T-shirt and headed for the elevator.

~ ~ ~

"So. We really need you on board, Danny."

He sat at his desk and stared at her. What had he ever seen in this woman? She was good looking. Kind of. Attractive might be a better word. But she was harsh, both in her personality and her looks. Even her hair was cut in straight lines. There was nothing soft about her. He bit his lip to try to stop the smile that came at the thought. Nothing soft and round, like beautiful little Missy. Olivia must have thought the smile was for her.

"So. You agree, then?" Her own smile was smug, not at all appealing.

"No. I don't. I told you when you first raised the idea. I don't like Systech. I don't respect them. I don't respect their work. And I don't want anything to do with them. Why you chose to pursue it is beyond me. I will not work with them."

"You'll have to." Now the smile was condescending. "When we merge with them, you'll have no choice. We need you to toe the line so it all goes smoothly, Danny."

"First of all, stop calling me that. Second, we are *not* merging with them."

"But we are. Had you bothered to come in yesterday, as I asked you to, you would have been part of the discussion. But since you chose to hang out with your little friend instead, we went ahead without you. The decision is made."

"You have no authority to make any decisions about Prometheus, let alone something like this." He was stunned by how out of control she'd gotten."

"I know that, Danny. But Steven and Corey do and they've agreed to it. With both of them on board, you're outvoted. The merger *will* go ahead."

How the hell had she talked them into it? Actually, he could imagine how. Steven was the weaker twin; he usually ended up doing what Olivia wanted. As for Corey, Dan had suspected for a while that Olivia had been using her 'charms' to win him over. It looked like she had succeeded. He needed to talk to them both—without Olivia around. She smiled at him, as if she expected him to meekly accept her hijacking the company he and Steven had built from nothing.

"I thought we could have dinner tonight. Just the two of us and, you know, *celebrate*." She gave him what he supposed what meant to be a sexy look. It left him cold.

"No, thank you. I told you on the phone. We're done."

"Don't sulk, darling. It'll all work out, you'll see."

He gave her a grim smile. "Oh, it'll work out alright." Just not the way she was hoping. Dan stood and headed for the door. "Excuse me." He left her staring after him and went in search of Steven.

~ ~ ~

"Either you buy me out, or I sell my shares direct to Systech, then." Dan couldn't believe what was happening. Steven was standing firm that merging with Systech was the right move.

His sister apparently had some hold over him, but he was denying it. He had admitted that Olivia had been sleeping with Corey for weeks. The only feeling that aroused in Dan was disgust. While he and Missy had resisted temptation, while he had refused to even kiss a woman he really liked, Olivia had been screwing a guy she had often made fun of, calling him ugly and dorky, just to get the deal she wanted. He almost felt sorry for Corey. Almost. Except Corey was supposed to be his friend, and he had been screwing the woman who was still supposed to be his girlfriend.

Steven was blinking at him through his thick glasses. "No! We do this together, Dan, like always." He looked horrified.

Dan shook his head sadly. "No. Not this. I don't know how Olivia is controlling you, or why you're letting her, but she's not controlling me. Not anymore. We always said we wouldn't merge with anyone. Not unless we both agreed. Now Corey and Olivia both have a say, but I didn't think that mattered, that it'd always be the two of us making the big decisions together. But this? Systech? You have to be kidding me? No way. If you're really committed to this, then it's the end of the road. I'm done."

"You don't understand, Dan."

"Damned straight, I don't! And you're not going to tell me, are you?"

"I can't."

Dan sat down opposite his old friend. "Steven, you can. Whatever she's got on you, you can tell me. We can work this out if we stick together, you and me, like we've always done."

"I wish we could Dan. But she's my sister, and our parents support her in this."

"In what? Will you at least tell me what this is all about?"

"I can't."

"So you're telling me you're going to go ahead and merge with Systech?"

Steven nodded.

"Even though it will mean the end of our partnership?"

He nodded again.

"Okay, then. I'm out. Do you want to buy me out, go into the merger stronger? Or should I just sell to them?"

"I'll have to ask Olivia."

"Jesus, Steven! Really? I'm done. We can handle this through attorneys." Dan stood up. "And I'll be using Leanne."

"Leanne is the company attorney. Prometheus' attorney, not yours."

"We'll let her decide that, shall we? And I'll be keeping the name too. You won't need the Prometheus identity once you're taken over by Systech." He didn't point out that Steven was losing his own identity as his sister took him over. Dan had been in danger of succumbing to that fate himself.

Dan handed his keys to the valet. It still amused him that the guys in the parking garage took it in turns to have a chance at driving his car. It was the one thing he was grateful to Olivia for. Without her encouragement, he would never in a million years have paid more for a car than many people paid for a house. The black Lamborghini had been his dream car as a kid. He'd had a poster of one on his side of the bedroom. Jack's side had been covered with football players, cheerleaders and city skylines, but Dan just had the Lamborghini. He'd told Olivia about it once, in an attempt to talk about himself and his childhood. All she'd been interested in was the fact that he liked an expensive, fast car. She'd insisted that he owed it to himself, to his image and to the company, to indulge his childhood dream. So he had. He still felt a little self-conscious about it, but he wouldn't deny he loved it.

"You're home early, Mr. Dan." The valet grinned as he took the keys.

Dan returned the grin. "Yeah, it's time to shake things up a bit, Billy."

When he emerged from the elevator in the lobby, the concierge greeted him. "Afternoon, Mr. Dan, how's things?"

"Changing for the better, I think, Herb. How about you?"

"Doing great, son. It's good to see you smiling. I'd say a smile like that has something to do with a lady?" Herb raised an eyebrow.

"Two ladies, Herb. Getting rid of one and hoping to get to know another."

"Well, damn, son! Good for you. Sorry to say it, but I never could warm to that Olivia."

Dan smiled. "I know. It took me way too long, but I finally understand why. I'm done with her. I'm free. I think it's going to cost me my business, but you know what? Even that may turn out to be a good thing."

"Cost you your business?"

"Yeah, but that's okay. I can build another, or do something different."

Herb shook his head in wonder. "You're not like the rest of 'em, are you?"

"I hope not, but I think for a while there, I was starting to be."

Dan noticed one of his neighbors enter the lobby. "Looks like you're about to get busy."

The lady was bustling toward the desk with a list in her hand. Herb rolled his eyes. "Wish me luck?"

"Yeah, looks like you'll need it. Good luck."

"You too, Dan." Herb shot him a grin before turning away to deal with Mrs. Emmersley.

Dan let himself into his apartment and looked around. He wondered what Missy would make of this place. It was the penthouse of one of the most prestigious buildings in town. Again, Olivia had been the major influence in him buying it. He didn't love it like he did his car though. The stark white walls and high ceilings just emphasized how empty it was. How alone he was. Now there was a novel thought! Being alone was one of his priorities. He craved solitude most of the time. When he was with people he couldn't wait to get away from them, back to his machines, to his code, to a world that made sense to him. That had changed lately, though. He'd always enjoyed being around Jack. Spending time with his brother had never been the challenge spending time with other people was. Since Jack had asked him to come up to Summer Lake to work with Scot, he'd discovered that he didn't mind, in fact he enjoyed, spending time with the people there. He'd liked Pete since he first met him. He must have been about fifteen then—no wonder he felt like another brother. Ben was becoming a real friend too, as was Smoke, the Phoenix pilot with whom he'd been spending quite a bit of time. Even the women up there were cool. Jack's new wife, Emma was great, and Pete's fiancée, Holly was fun. They didn't make him feel uncomfortable like most women did. They weren't bossy or gossipy. They made sense.

He chewed his thumb as he walked over to the plate glass window that rose twenty feet to the ceiling. As much as he liked everyone up there, it was Missy that changed everything. The beautiful, little Missy. As he rested his forehead against the cool glass, he realized that it wasn't just that he didn't mind being around her, he actually missed her when he wasn't. He thought about her much of the time, and Scot too. He couldn't remember to buy coffee for himself, but he had remembered to stop at the bookstore to get the textbooks for Scotty. That was why this place felt so empty now, when it never had before—it was because they weren't here with him. He felt alone because he wasn't there with them. He wandered into the bedroom to change into his workout gear. He hadn't told Jack, but he'd added a bike, a rower, and a full weight bench to the home gym birthday gift that had started it all. He needed to think clearly, and the endorphin rush from a good workout would help. All the parameters of his world were shifting. He needed to figure out how best to arrange them to suit the man he was becoming, and the kind of life he was starting to want.

Chapter Eight

Missy pulled the sheets from the dryer and dumped them into the laundry basket. She'd get Scot to help her with them in a little while. She hated folding sheets, so the two of them made a game out of it, dancing around the kitchen. She smiled, remembering the look on his face when he'd helped her fold his sheets on Monday. He'd told her how Dan had taken care of his wet bedding and pajamas that morning, before he'd walked with him to the bus stop. She'd been so pleased. Pleased that Dan had helped him out with his little accident, and that he qualified as cool enough to be seen with in public. *She* wasn't allowed to accompany Scot to the bus stop under any circumstances.

Lindy Miller, Jarret's mom, had called her to ask about the hot guy who had picked Scot up after the robotics trip. Apparently Dan had caused quite a stir. She felt the now familiar fluttering in her stomach at the thought of him. She could see why people called them butterflies. She couldn't wait for tomorrow night. For their date. They hadn't even talked about where they would go, but she didn't care. They'd probably go to the Boathouse, it wasn't like there were many other options around the lake. As long as Ben left them alone, and the whole gang didn't come down to join them, it would be fine. She wanted to be alone with him, have him all to herself for an evening. She was excited just to be going on a date—it had been a long time. She'd dated some over the years, but it was hard with Scot to think about. Most guys didn't get it. She'd never met anyone she'd felt was worthy of being around her son. She'd certainly never met anyone like Dan before. On the surface he didn't make any sense as a guy for her. He was so damned smart. When he and Scot talked computers—or robots, or physics, or even math for that matter, they may as well be talking Arabic for all she understood. She had common sense and life smarts, but all that techno stuff fried her brain when she tried to grasp it. Apart from being so smart, Dan was also quiet. She had thought he was shy, but she wasn't so sure about that now. It wasn't that he was afraid to talk to people, he just didn't bother with mundane chatter. If he was interested in the conversation, he joined in. If he wasn't, he didn't see the point in talking for the sake of it. She, on the other hand, could chatter away with the best of them. She usually saw the funny side of things, and liked to share it. She loved to make people laugh and was never afraid to speak her mind. It shouldn't make any sense that Dan liked talking to her and she liked listening to him, but she was glad of it.

She threw another load in the washer, wondering what she should wear tomorrow night. He must have seen every outfit she owned by now. She wanted to look good, but she couldn't exactly afford to go out and buy something new. She mentally ran through her wardrobe. The doorbell interrupted her musings and she went to see who it was.

"Hey, Miss!"

"Hey, you two! This is a nice surprise." Emma and Jack stood on the doorstep. "Come on in." They followed her through to the kitchen.

"How are you feeling?" asked Emma.

Missy grinned. "I'm fine, honestly. Almost back to full strength, just like I told you this morning." Emma had called everyday to see how she was doing. "You'd think there was something really wrong with me, the way you've all been carrying on. Though it is kind of nice to know you care. Have a seat, do you want a drink, or anything?"

Jack sat at the kitchen table. "Not for me, thanks. I've got to run over to see Ben, so I'll leave you ladies to visit a while."

"I'll have an orange juice," said Emma, "but I'll get my own." She was at the fridge before Missy could move. "Do you want one?"

"Yes, please, but I'm not used to being offered a drink in my own home. I was a bit tired, not at death's door!"

Jack laughed. "You're just not used to having people looking out for you, Miss, but now that we're up here you're going to have to get used to it, okay?"

"I don't know." Missy smiled. "I mean, it's nice to feel cared for, but damn! I'm not allowed to do anything. I haven't been to work all week. I haven't even cooked a meal. You're right, I'm not used to it. At least I've still got Scotty to take care of, otherwise I'd feel completely useless!" Emma and Jack exchanged a look. "What? What are you two scheming?"

Jack laughed. "You don't miss a trick, do you?"

"Can't afford to in my world, hon. Now tell me what you're up to?"

"We came to see if Scot can come up to North Cove tomorrow night and stay with us?"

Missy frowned. "Why?"

"Because," said Jack, "the gang is all coming up there for dinner. Michael is bringing Ethan and we thought Scotty would enjoy it."

She wrinkled her nose at them. "Why do I feel like you're all taking over my life?"

Jack looked concerned. "We're not trying to interfere, Miss. It was just an idea."

Emma laughed. "Yes we are. We're interfering because we know you're going out with Dan tomorrow night, okay?"

Missy nodded. "Yeah, that's more like it."

"So we're all staying out of town. Even Ben is taking the night off and coming up to our place. That way you two will have the run of the town all to yourselves. And Ethan has been dying to see Scotty."

Missy shook her head. "Oh, the joys of small town living."

Jack nodded. "You know what they say—the worst thing about it is that everyone knows your business, and the best thing about it? Is that everyone knows your business!"

"Ain't that the truth!" agreed Missy. "And thanks, guys. It is sweet of you to do that. I'm sure Scot would love it. He was going to go to my dad's, but he wasn't too keen on the idea."

Emma smiled. "Well, ask him, to make sure, but I'll bet I can seal it with the offer of pizza and pie."

Missy laughed. "With that offer, you'll probably get Dan up there too!"

"No chance!" said Jack. "Who do you think suggested getting Scot and Ethan together? He wants to take you out, but not unless he knows Scot gets to do something fun too."

Missy smiled. Dan was so thoughtful, and it wasn't as if he was just doing it for her. She knew how much he cared about her son. Now she wouldn't feel guilty about not only usurping time Scot would normally get to spend with Dan, but adding insult to injury by packing him off to Poppy Jim's. Scot loved his grandpa, but there was no internet connection at his place. Her dad would have come to her, but he'd expect to see Dan leave before he left himself. Missy was hoping that Dan wouldn't be leaving at all. She realized Jack was watching her.

"I'm hoping you two will have a good time, Miss. I've never seen him like this."

Missy didn't want to say too much. "I'm hoping so too."

"And on Saturday," said Emma, "Scot and Dan can get their time because, if you feel up to it, you, me, and Holly are going to LA to get our costumes."

"In that plane?" asked Missy warily.

Emma laughed. "Yes, we're going to go hurtling through the skies in our very own tin can again. But don't worry, I've asked Smoke to stock extra champagne to take the edge off your nerves."

That plane really did make her nervous. It was kind of cool to be able to just pop to LA or San Francisco for a day's shopping, but still. "Okay." she said. "I'll be brave."

Jack laughed. "That's the spirit, Miss. Now. I'd better get over to see Ben. I'll be back in an hour, Mouse, okay?"

"Yes, say hi to Ben for me?"

"Will do." He stood and gave Emma a quick kiss. He hugged Missy. "See ya."

Missy hugged him back. Jack was a good guy; she was glad he'd been so determined to earn Emma's trust. They were good together. "Bye, Jack."

"Do you feel like packing a bag?" asked Emma once he'd gone.

Missy laughed. "Why? Are we planning on skipping town?"

"No!" Emma laughed with her. "My running days are over. Jack's been so good to me. I'm over myself and being scared. These days he's the only place I want to run to."

"Good," said Missy. I'm glad to hear it, but if we're not running away why do I need to pack a bag?"

"Because we might stay at my apartment when we go into the city shopping. And don't worry, if we do Scot can stay with Dan and Jack. Since you're not supposed to lift a finger, I thought I should help you pack your bag now."

"Seriously, Em? It's not exactly a big job."

"Just humor me, would you?"

"Fine. Come on then." They went upstairs and Emma sat on the bed while Missy packed an overnight bag. "There," she said once she was done. "Happy now?"

"Um, I will be in a minute." Emma went into the closet and came out holding a little black dress.

"Team Slinky?" asked Missy. It was the dress she had worn for Emma's bachelorette party. Emma, Holly and Laura had all worn exactly the same that night.

Emma laughed. "It's best to be prepared for anything." She folded the dress and put it in the bag and closed it up. She grabbed the bag and ran down the stairs with it."

"Where are you going?" laughed Missy as she followed.

Emma went out of the front door and ran down the path. She slid open the minivan door and put the bag in the back. Missy stood at the bottom of the stairs watching.

Emma came back in and grinned. "Just making sure you won't forget it."

"Sometimes I worry about you!"

"No need," said Emma with a sweet smile. "I'm not as crazy as I make out."

"I hope not." Missy turned and looked back up the stairs as Scot emerged from his room. "Hey, Scotty. Want to come down and say hi to Auntie Em? She's got something to ask you."

~ ~ ~

Dan stared out of the window, not seeing the city below. He rarely noticed the view from his apartment. It was illogical to pay a premium for something that others coveted yet he barely noticed. He recognized now that many aspects of his life had become illogical over the last couple of years. He did things that should suit a person in his position, but that didn't actually suit him. He'd never really liked San Jose, but it was logical for Prometheus to be here. If he was going to sell his share of the company, it wouldn't make sense for him to stay here. He felt no emotion about what had happened. His partnership with Steven was over. The company they'd started in a garage and grown to be worth hundreds of millions of dollars, was about to be subsumed into a huge—and to him, distasteful—corporation. Everything that had been his life here was ending and he felt nothing. Well, perhaps that wasn't true. He felt no negative emotions, but he did have a sneaking sense of relief, of freedom. In the early days Prometheus had been fun, building, coding, striving, even persuading venture capitalists to invest in them; that had all been fun. He'd loved it, felt alive. The last few years though, it had all grown stale. The only highlights had been developing new programs, but they'd just been more of the same. He hadn't done anything truly innovative in two or three years. As he'd told Herb, this might turn out to be a good thing. It wasn't like money was an issue.

He had more than enough to live out several lifetimes in style, and that was before he sold his share—to Steven, or Systech, or whomever, he didn't particularly care. He just wanted out. He didn't know what he was going to do next. He did know it would be something he wanted to do, something he could enjoy and find value in.

The intercom buzzed. He went to answer it. "Yes?"

"Hey, Mr. Dan. It's Herb."

"Hey Herb. What's up?"

"You have a visitor. A Mr. Ryan Brady."

"Ryan? Jesus, send him on up, Herb. Thanks."

Dan went to the door and waited, watching the elevator lights flicker their way up to him. What the hell was Ryan doing here? The elevator doors opened and there he was. Even in a suit, Ryan looked rough around the edges, menacing even.

"Hey, nerd!"

Dan laughed. "Ryan! What the hell brings you out of the jungle, or the desert or wherever it is you hide these days?"

Ryan grinned and clasped Dan's shoulder. "I could tell you, but then I'd have to shoot you, and it'd be a shame to lose my favorite nerd."

"Well, come on in," said Dan. "I've got some beer if you want one?"

Ryan followed him into the penthouse and looked around. "Damn! Looks like tech town's been good to you."

Dan shrugged, "I wouldn't say it's been good to me, but I have made a shitload of cash."

"It's got you in shape too, by the looks of it."

Dan felt a little self-conscious as Ryan looked him over. He did have more muscle, was in better shape than he'd ever been, but standing next to Ryan he felt like a Whippet next to a

Rottweiler. They were equal in height, but Ryan was probably twice as wide, and solid muscle. His neck was probably wider around than Dan's thigh. "I did finally get around to working out, like you always told me. And you were right, I do love it."

"Good on you, it suits you. Now, where's that beer?"

Once they were settled at the kitchen island with their beer, Dan asked. "So what brings you? I know I'm your favorite nerd and everything, but I don't normally warrant an in-person visit."

Ryan nodded. "I'll cut to the chase. I need some help with security and can't think of anyone better than you."

Dan laughed. "I may have been working out, but I don't think I'll ever be much use for your kind of security." He didn't even know what Ryan really did. He worked for some government agency, spent most of his time overseas. The last time Dan had seen him had been about eighteen months ago, Ryan had been back stateside on forced R&R while he recovered from a gunshot wound to his shoulder.

"I'd sooner take you into the field with me than the kids they're sending me these days. But no, I mean cyber-security, not physical security. I've still never met anyone who can do what you do."

They had first met at Berkeley. Dan still wasn't sure what Ryan had been doing there. They'd only shared one cryptography class, and Ryan had been gone after that semester. They'd formed and maintained a close, if unlikely, friendship though. Ryan would pop up out of the blue like this after months, sometimes years of silence. Dan was never surprised, and always glad to see him. Right now, he was intrigued. "What kind of cyber-security?"

"I need someone to hack our systems. The agency's nerds have come up with a new system that they claim is unhackable, impenetrable. Before I take a team into the field with our lives depending on that, I want to be sure. When I kicked up a shitstorm, they gave me the budget to hire an independent contractor to test everything. Course you're the only man I'd trust to do it. I never forgot when the whole world was saying your systems were impenetrable and you told me they weren't, that no system ever truly could be. When the agency guys started claiming that this new system of theirs is unhackable, I knew they were more invested in their egos than in my team's safety. I want, and need, the best nerd there is, and that's you. And I've got the budget to pay for it. So, what do you say?"

Dan's mind raced. He'd just been thinking that whatever he did next would have to be something he enjoyed and valued. Getting the chance to hack government systems in order to expose their weaknesses, and to keep Ryan and his team safe, fit the bill on both counts. The timing couldn't be better, which made him pause. He frowned and looked at Ryan. "And what makes you think I'd have the time to do it? I have a company to run."

"Not for long you don't. Word travels fast, Danny boy."

How the hell could he know?

Ryan waggled his eyebrows, apparently understanding what Dan was thinking. "It's probably best not to ask. But I know you, you don't actually need the money, but I'm sure you'll find some use for it. I do know you need the challenge. It'll save you from sitting up here playing video games and dreaming about getting laid by a real woman instead of that Olivia. So, say you'll do it."

Dan laughed. Ryan disliked Olivia immensely and loved to tease him about her. "Okay. It sounds good. What needs to happen?"

"First we'll have to get you a security clearance. That shouldn't take too long, we can expedite it. Then we'll get you read in. You'll have to work remotely, get in past all the firewalls and shit from the outside, just like a malicious hacker would."

Dan grinned. It seemed this might be a good fit for the plans he was starting to make. He'd be able to work from wherever he wanted, and he was beginning to think he knew exactly where that was.

"Sounds good," he said. "I've been talking to my attorney about this merger and my selling out of the company, this should tie in nicely."

Ryan's face was expressionless. "Your attorney?"

Damn! Why hadn't he thought before he opened his mouth? "Yeah. Leanne."

Ryan nodded, a faraway look in his eyes, then his grin returned as if the moment had never happened. "I always knew we'd end up working together someday, nerd!"

Dan nodded, he had hoped they might. He just wished he hadn't mentioned Leanne.

Ryan left that subject behind as he continued, "What do you say, want to get some dinner? Maybe afterwards we'll see what we can do about finding you a real woman." He grinned, "I'll be your wingman, see if we can't get you laid."

Dan shook his head. Ryan had always busted on him about women. Ryan himself seemed to attract them like bees to honey and he worked his way through the adoring crowds, one after the other—ever since Leanne. "There's no point trying to find me a woman," he said.

"Don't tell me you've given up trying, nerd. Never give up! We'll find you one, I'll help," he mocked.

"I've not given up, asshole! I've done it all by myself, I've found one." He rubbed at his face and gave Ryan a look. "And I think she's *the one.*"

Ryan rolled his eyes and laughed. "Don't go talking like that nerd, there's no such thing as *the one.* There's just this one, then that one, then another one, and another one. You get it?"

"I get that's how it works for you these days, but not for me, you know that."

Ryan was serious now. "I do know that. I just don't want you to escape from Olivia only to have some other bitch getting her claws into you, sucking the life out of you."

"Missy's not like that, Ryan. She couldn't be less like that if she tried."

"We'll see." Ryan looked skeptical. "And we will see. She'll have to be checked out as part of your security processing."

Dan didn't like the sound of that. "Why?'

Ryan shrugged. "Pillow talk."

Dan bit his lip.

"Don't worry about it, nerd. Come on, let's go get some dinner. You still got the Lambo? Gonna let me drive?"

Chapter Nine

"Hey, hero!" Missy couldn't help the big grin on her face as she answered the phone. Dan had been texting all week, but they hadn't spoken since he left on Monday.

"Hey, beautiful. How are you feeling?"

"Better! I'm all better, I promise."

"Did you get a good rest?"

"I did. Not that I had much choice with everything you arranged. There was nothing left for me to do but rest. Thank you."

"You're welcome. And it was for me as much as for you. I wanted to take you out tonight, but we couldn't do it 'til you were better."

"Well, I am now, so where do you want to go?"

"It's a surprise."

"I like surprises." She couldn't think of anywhere too surprising around the lake, but she appreciated the thought.

"Good. I should be there by six. Would you mind meeting me at the airport?"

"Of course. Ben's picking Scotty up at five thirty to take him up to North Cove."

"I know."

"You do?"

"Yeah, I talked to him earlier. Wanted to make sure he's okay with it all."

Missy loved that he had a relationship of his own with Scot, one that wasn't about her. "Thank you."

Dan laughed. "I'd say you're welcome, but I didn't do it for you."

"I know, that's what I like best about it."

"Good. I'm glad you don't mind that he and I have our own thing."

"Mind? I love it!"

"Me too. I've got to go now though. I'll see you at six, okay?"

"Yep, see you then."

"I can't wait."

Shivers ran down her spine. "Me neither."

Missy hung up and looked around the kitchen, the big silly grin still plastered across her face. Finally, it was here. She was going out on a date with Dan! She really did feel better too, maybe not back to a hundred percent, but the tingly excitement more than made up for any lingering tiredness. She went upstairs and knocked on Scot's door.

"You nearly ready to go, son?"

"Yep. I've got everything in my bag."

"And you really don't mind spending the night at Auntie Em's?"

"Are you kidding? I can't wait to see Ethan. And besides, it means you get to go out with Dan! I'd stay at Poppy Jim's so you could do that, Mom."

She gave him a hug. "Thanks, I am looking forward to it."

"You really like him, don't you?"

She smiled. "So do you."

"Yeah, but I wouldn't date him!"

She laughed at that. "I'm glad to hear it. I don't think I could handle the competition."

"You've got no competition. He really likes you, too."

She raised an eyebrow. "What makes you say that?"

Scot grinned. "Guy talk, Mom. Don't worry about it. Is it okay if I take my Xbox? Me and Ethan can play while the rest of them yack."

"Course you can, but please turn it off and go to bed when Auntie Em says"

"Sure. Auntie Em's cool."

~ ~ ~

Dan sat in the right seat next to Smoke. He loved to sit up front, and watch and listen as Smoke flew the plane. He enjoyed it so much he was starting to think about getting his pilot's license. They'd taken off twenty minutes ago and would be up at Summer Lake a little before six. He couldn't wait to see Missy. He hoped she would like the surprise he had in store. That it wouldn't be *too much* of a surprise. Smoke grinned across at him and spoke into his headset.

"You've got no need to look so nervous. She's into you in a big way. I can tell."

"You reckon?"

"I do. It was obvious at Jack's wedding. I kept comparing you and her to Ben and Laura."

Dan cocked his head. "Why?"

Smoke laughed. "Because I was trying to reassure myself that Laura wasn't into Ben!"

"Ah! I forgot you like my cousin."

Smoke nodded and returned his attention to flying the plane. He had programmed the autopilot, but ATC had just asked him to adjust course for traffic. When he was done he looked back at Dan. "I do, and seeing the way Missy was dancing with you compared to Laura with Ben, made me feel much better. Thank you."

"Hey, the pleasure was all mine."

"Looked like it, too. Where did you learn to dance like that anyway?"

Dan grinned. "Now that's a long story. Jack taught me."

"Really?"

"Yep, really. Maybe I'll tell you someday.

Smoke nodded.

It wasn't a story Dan wanted to share right now, so he changed the subject. "Have you seen anything of Laura since the wedding?" He hadn't talked to her in weeks himself, but he hoped she would come up for Missy's birthday party.

"No. We tried a couple of times, but either her schedule changed or mine did, mostly mine though. We've never quite made it work." He shot Dan a quick look. "I think she thinks I'm jerking her around, but I'm not. You know yourself how my schedule can change on short notice."

Dan had a horrible thought. "Please don't tell me you were supposed to see her last Sunday?"

Smoke pursed his lips, but said nothing.

"Shit! I screwed you over by not leaving 'til Monday, didn't I?"

Smoke shrugged. "It goes with the job."

"Oh, man. I'm sorry."

"No, don't be. It is what it is."

Dan didn't like it. He'd talked to Laura about Smoke. He knew she liked him and was hoping they might go out together. She'd be madder than hell with Dan if she knew he'd cost her a date with 'her pilot'. Then again, she wouldn't, because she'd understand why. He'd only changed his plans so he could take care of Missy and Scot. Still, he would have to figure out a way to make it up to them. For now though, his own date was most important. He'd had a busy week, despite mostly staying away from the office. He'd met with Leanne a couple of times about how best to deal with the sale of his shares. As he'd expected, she'd dissociated herself from the company and was acting as his attorney. He smiled; she hated Olivia with a vengeance. She'd been excited to hear that he was finally taking Missy out and had wished him luck for tonight. She'd even suggested he wear the black shirt and slacks he had on. He felt good in them, he just hoped Missy would like them.

~ ~ ~

Missy turned the ignition off and sat in the minivan when she arrived at the airport. She had to wipe this silly grin off her face before she went in there. She hugged herself and took a few big, deep breaths. "Get with it, girl!" she muttered to herself. She got out of the van and smoothed herself down. She'd decided to wear jeans and a red top. They were her nice jeans, and the top was dressy enough, with a cowl neck that slid off one shoulder, but it was nothing too over the top for the muted nightlife of Summer Lake.

As she walked across the parking lot, she saw the plane coming in to land. There were no commercial flights that came into the resort, just private light aircraft. Pete and Jack's plane was probably the biggest of them and easily recognizable, even to her. She quickened her step as she watched it taxi towards the FBO building.

The girl at the desk nodded to her. "Hey, Miss."

"Hi Rochelle." Rochelle had been a couple of years ahead of her at school and had kids a couple of years younger than Scot.

"Are you here to meet Papa Charlie?"

The fact that they all called that big hunk of metal such a silly name always made her smile. "I am."

Rochelle grinned. "I *love* that plane! It delivers hot men to Summer Lake every time it comes. And you never know which one it's going to be. Doesn't matter though, they're all gorgeous, even the pilot." She looked out of the window as Papa Charlie's steps came down and Dan appeared at the top of them. Rochelle gave a little squeal. "Ooh! This one! He's my favorite. He's like the strong, silent type, you know?"

Missy had to laugh. "Yeah. This one's my favorite too!" She went to the door and watched Dan stride across the tarmac. There was no question in her mind. He was, for sure, the hottest of all the hot men that traveled in that plane. He spotted her and that beautiful smile spread across his face. She was glad he hadn't shaved off his scruff. He was gorgeous! Dressed all in black. She went out to meet him and caught her breath when she met his twinkling eyes. She felt like she might explode with the excitement, happiness, and desire, which all mingled to fill her with that wonderful tingly feeling. He strode right to her and wrapped her in his arms. She reached her own arms up around his neck and smiled at him. "Hey, hero!"

His gaze softened as he smiled back at her. He lowered his head until his lips touched hers all too briefly. When he straightened up, he lifted her off her feet, pressing her body to him as she clung to his neck. "Hey, beautiful! Are you ready for this?"

"You'll have to tell me what *this* is, but yes, I'm ready. Where are we going?"

He put her down, his eyes shining even brighter. "My place."

"What?"

"We always hang out here. I thought you might like to come see where I live, too?"

Missy was stunned. "You mean, go? Now? Fly back to San Jose tonight?"

"Yeah, I do." He cocked his head to one side and fixed her with his big brown eyes. "Please say you'll come, Miss?"

How could she no to that? "But what about Scotty?"

Dan grinned. "I told you. I talked to him. He's cool with it. We'll be back in time for you to see him before you go shopping with the girls."

"You mean, not come back 'til tomorrow?"

For the first time his smile faltered. "We could get you back later, if you want. But," he brought a hand up to stroke the back of her neck, making her sag against him as desire rushed through her, "I was hoping you might want to stay with me."

"I do." She wasn't going to lie. She'd hoped they would spend the night together, but in her bed, not his! "But, I'd have to bring some things. My toothbrush...." Well. That sounded stupid! But she was trying to get her head around this.

His smile was a lot cockier now than she'd ever seen before. "Why don't you just grab your bag from the van?"

She stared at him, not understanding. Then she remembered. Emma! She'd put her overnight bag in the back of the van. She started to laugh. "You mean, you...?"

"Yep." He grinned as he nodded.

She tightened her arms around his neck and reached up to peck his lips. "Well, aren't you full of surprises? How could I say no?"

He looked way too pleased with himself. "I was hoping you wouldn't find a way to. Let's go get your bag and lock the van up. Smoke is having the plane refueled and then we can go."

They went through the building and out to the van. Missy reached for the bag in the back and Dan took it while she locked up. She grinned to think how sneaky Emma had been yesterday, with her sweet smile and her, *I'm not as crazy as I make out.*

Missy was torn between wanting to thank her old friend and wanting to tell her off. As she turned back to Dan, she knew she wanted to thank Emma, and her lucky stars, that she was flying away with this beautiful man. That she would get to spend the night with him, at his place, in a city a couple of hundred miles away from here.

"Ready?"

She nodded and he shifted her bag to his other hand so he could put an arm around her as they walked.

"I want to show you my life, Miss. Take you out for dinner." He smiled down at her. "Take you back to my place, so you can see it."

Her stomach fluttered madly at the thought of going back to his place. As they walked back through the building, Rochelle caught her eye and gave her a big grin and two thumbs up.

~ ~ ~

Missy buckled herself in and gripped on to the arms of her seat.

"Are you okay? We're not even moving yet," said Dan.

She let out a little laugh, but didn't loosen her grip. "I'm fine. I'm just a big old weenie about flying."

Dan looked puzzled. "You do realize that, statistically, it's much safer than driving?"

"Maybe, but I'll bet those statistics aren't much comfort when you're falling out of the sky!"

He laughed. "Don't worry. Smoke's a fantastic pilot. Little hops like this are just like popping round the corner for him. We'll be there in no time."

"I know, I'm fine really. It's just the taking off and landing that get to me. I don't understand how it's possible to get a big hunk of metal up in the air in the first place, or how it can hit the ground at a hundred miles an hour without smashing itself, and us, to pieces."

"Ground speed is around sixty-five miles an hour, I think, when we touch down and...." Dan stopped himself and smiled.

"You don't want to know, do you?"

"No, thank you. I do not!"

He pried her hand off the armrest and held it between his own. "Then how about you hang on to me 'til we get there?"

Now that was an idea she could go for. "Okay. Thanks, hero."

As they thundered down the runway, Missy held on tight and closed her eyes. When she opened them, he was smiling at her.

"There. See? We're up."

She let go of his hand and he rubbed it. "Sorry."

"That's okay. You've got quite a grip."

She nodded. "Yeah. Sorry."

He touched her cheek. "Please don't be. I liked it. It makes me feel like I really am your hero. You can hold on to me whenever you're afraid."

Wouldn't that be something? To have someone to hold on to when life got scary. Especially if that someone were Dan. Dan with his big, brown eyes fixed on her. She reached out and touched his cheek, loving the stubble under her fingers. "Thank you."

He lowered his head towards her, sliding his hand around the back of her neck to draw her closer. She closed her eyes and felt his warm, soft lips meet hers. He ran his tongue across her bottom lip. She kissed him back. His tongue met hers and explored her mouth slowly, gently, driving her crazy. He drew back, gently nipping at her lips. Her breath was coming fast. She wanted more.

"I've wanted to do that since the first time I saw you on the deck of the Boathouse," he murmured.

Missy unbuckled her seatbelt and slid across into his lap. "Me too, and now we've started I don't plan on letting you stop any time soon." She slid her arms up around his neck and brought his head back down to her. His arms closed around her and she clung to him as their lips met once more. Everything faded away except the feel of him. His lips, his tongue, her breasts pressed against his chest as he held her to him. She could feel him growing hard as she sat in his lap. She could feel herself getting wet as he ran his hand up and down her back, stroking her neck when it reached the top and her ass when it reached the bottom. They may be making out like a couple of kids, but the desires he awakened within her were the adult-only type. She slipped her hand inside his shirt. She needed to touch him, his warm skin, the lean muscles of his chest. He moaned through the kiss as she slid her hand lower. His arms closed around her, holding her against his erection. She wriggled against him, wanting more.

He lifted his head. "Jesus, Miss! We have to stop."

She grinned at him and wriggled some more, knowing she was tormenting him. "I don't want to stop, and besides, we're hardly getting started."

He groaned. "We can't get started because I won't be able to stop. I've waited too long already."

"That's okay, because I don't want you to." She brought his face down to her and started to kiss him again.

He pulled back. "We have to though. We're going out for dinner, then if you're not too tired I thought we could go to the club, dance?"

Missy wrinkled her nose. "What if I said I'm too tired for all that and I need to go to bed? Would you take me straight to bed? Or would you think I'm a slut?"

All the humor left his face. "Don't use that word. You could never be one of those."

She was taken aback by the force with which he said it. "Sorry, hero. I was only joking."

His face softened. "I know, but no one, not even you, gets to call my beautiful, little Missy that horrible name. You're so sweet, so soft, you smell so good, you feel so good, I want you so badly. I'd take you straight home, straight to bed in a heartbeat. It's all I've been able to think about. But I'm afraid I'd never let you out again. There'd be no dinner, no dancing, just your body and mine, lips, arms, legs tangling 'til morning. I'm not even sure I'll be able to let you go then."

He was melting her with his words. She didn't want dinner, or dancing, just his body tangling with hers. "Take me home, Dan. Please?

He nodded and drew her back into that kiss.

~ ~ ~

A golf cart met them on the tarmac at San Jose and took them to the FBO building.

"That was quick, Mr. Benson," said the guy behind the desk. "Want me to bring your car around?"

Dan shook his head. "I've got it, thanks." Normally he would indulge the guy, let him have a quick drive, but right now all he wanted to do was get Missy back to his place. All his plans for a memorable evening, the dinner, the club, were forgotten. He just had to get her to his place. To his bed. He'd been proud of himself last weekend, of the restraint he'd shown. But she'd been ill. Now she wasn't and he had no self-control left. He wanted her, and she made it so clear she wanted him too. Nothing else mattered. He held her hand as they walked out to the parking lot. His car beeped and flashed when he pressed the remote. The doors swung up into the air and he threw her bag in.

Missy stood stock still and stared at him wide-eyed. "This is your car?"

He nodded, waiting for her to get in. Then it dawned on him that it wasn't exactly an everyday kind of vehicle, and she was always making quips about her old minivan. He shrugged. "It was my dream car as a kid and my one big indulgence when Prometheus took off."

She grinned at him. "I keep calling you hero. I might have to change that to Batman. This is like the damned Bat-mobile!"

He laughed and came to stand behind her, running his fingers down her arm. "I'm glad you like it. If you'll get in it, I'll take you to my bat-cave. Unless you want me to take you out first?" He wasn't sure how he'd survive if she did, but he'd wanted tonight to be about much more than sex. He was relieved when she smiled up at him.

"I told you, the only place I want you to take me is home, to your bed, or your bat-cave or whatever you call it."

He grinned. "Then can you get in the car and let's go?" As they drove away from the airport Dan thought how perfect she looked, sitting there in the passenger seat. He'd love to drive her around, but that would have to wait for another time.

Right now he was taking her straight home, as fast as he could get there. When he pulled into the parking garage, Billy came to meet them.

"Hey, Mr. Dan."

Dan pulled Missy's bag out and threw the keys to him. "Hey, Billy." He didn't want to hang around, Billy was a talker when he got started. He guided Missy to the elevator, which luckily was there at the parking level.

When they were inside she looked at him. "You live here?"

He laughed. "Yep. You don't think I'd waste time taking you anywhere else at this point?" The elevator stopped at the lobby and they got out. Dan wished it connected the parking levels with the rest of the building. They'd have to cross the lobby and waste precious minutes. He spotted Herb at the concierge desk. Hopefully this wouldn't take too long.

He pressed the button to call the elevator before he said, "Evening, Herb. I'd like you to meet Missy. The lady responsible for my happy face these days."

"Evening."

Missy looked up at Dan, then left his side to go shake hands. "Nice to meet you, Herb."

Herb grinned. "It's very nice to meet you too, Missy."

Dan loved that Missy did that. Olivia had never spared Herb more than a quick nod. The elevator doors opened behind him and he stepped inside. "Come on, Miss. Goodnight, Herb."

"Goodnight. I hope to see you again soon, Missy."

"You too," she said. As she turned away from him, Herb smiled over her shoulder at Dan and nodded his head approvingly.

Dan smiled back, he'd known the old guy would like her.

Once the elevator doors closed, he pulled her to him. "Almost there, beautiful." She smiled at him, but she looked nervous now. That wasn't what he wanted. "We can go dump your bag and go out for dinner if you want?"

She smiled again, but still said nothing. He wasn't used to her being nervous—or quiet. The elevator stopped and the doors opened. His was the only door up here. He opened it and ushered her in ahead of him. He put her bag down and took her hand. "So, what do you think?" He'd wondered what she would make of the place. Now she was here. She looked so small and unsure of herself.

She looked around the huge, open plan space. "I feel like the country mouse come to visit the big city! And we may need to have a talk about false advertising."

He cocked his head, not understanding.

She laughed. "Just last weekend you were feeding me the 'I'm just a poor, dumb, country boy' crap!"

He held up his hands. "I am! Well, I never claimed dumb." He slipped into his Texan drawl, "But jus' a good-ole, country boy done good."

She smiled. "By the looks of your car and this place? You done real good!"

"Do you like it?" It mattered to him what she thought. He'd trade this place for her house any day. Her place may be small, but it was full of life, full of her and Scot. It was a real home, something he'd never known as a kid, and couldn't imagine he'd be able to create for himself. He wouldn't know how.

"I love it," she said. "It's just...." She frowned.

"What?"

"Well, it's just not *you*, is it? Or maybe I'm wrong. Maybe this is you and I don't know you like I thought I did."

He put his arms around her. "Miss, you're right. This isn't me. You already know me better than most people do. This isn't me at all. It suits the life I somehow slipped into, but it doesn't suit me, the man I am. The kind of man I want to be."

She looked up into his eyes. "What kind of man do you want to be, Dan?"

"I want to be the man I am when I'm around you. When I'm with you I know what to do. I know what I want. I can see what you need and I can see what Scot needs, and I can make it happen."

She clung to him now. Her little hands on his shoulders. "Can you see what I need now, Dan?"

He nodded. He could, and he was damned sure going to make it happen. He scooped her up and carried her through to the bedroom.

She smiled. "So you don't think this is cheesy anymore?"

He shook his head. "I do not. I think it's a great way to get you to what you need that much quicker." Instead of placing her on the bed, he climbed on himself and lay down with her in his arms. "Are you sure about this?" he asked. "This is your last chance to change your mind, because I guarantee you I'm not going to be able to stop anymore." The look in her eyes told him all he needed to know.

"You'd better not even think about stopping, hero!" She was already unbuttoning his shirt.

Chapter Ten

Missy's hands trembled as she unbuttoned Dan's shirt. She'd waited so long for this. Hoped it would really happen someday. Now she was here, in his place, in is bed, looking into those big, brown eyes, now glazed with desire. She got his shirt undone and pushed it off his shoulders. He shrugged out of it and threw it. His warm mouth came down on her neck. She sighed as his hands found their way inside her top. His callused fingertips felt deliciously rough as they moved up over her ribcage. At the same time his tongue burned a trail down her neck, over her collarbone. He filled his hands with her breasts as his lips worked their way down between them. He mouthed at her nipple through the fabric. She had no clue how, but within seconds her top and bra were gone. His hot wet mouth came down over her bare flesh, teasing the hardened peaks with his tongue. She moaned and squirmed as she fumbled with his belt, needing to get him out of his pants. She sighed as his mouth left her breast, but it soon covered her own.

There was nothing slow or gentle about his kisses now. His tongue plundered her mouth while his hands unfastened her jeans and pushed them down over her hips. She struggled with his belt, then his button and zipper. He broke the kiss to get rid of his pants and pulled her jeans down and off. He rolled her onto her back and knelt above her.

"You are so damned beautiful, Missy."

She reached up to run her hands down his sides. His cock jerked at her touch. She wanted to know about the tattoo, but not now. "So are you." She licked her lips. She'd wanted this for so long, but now she was nervous. He looked so big.

"Are you okay?" His voice and his gaze were so soft, he made her wetter.

She nodded. "Just be gentle with me? I'm out of practice at this."

He nodded and came down to kiss her again. He slid his hand between her legs, making her moan. He barely touched her, tracing his rough finger over her opening, circling her with the slightest touch. She lifted her hips, wanting him to touch her fully, wanting the pressure of his hand on her, inside her. He was driving her crazy. She stroked her hand down over his abs, then closed it around him. He throbbed in her hand. He was so hard and thick—what was she supposed to do with all that?! He slipped the tip of his finger inside her. She writhed on the bed, wanting more. She stroked him from base to tip, but he pulled away from her hand, working his way down, covering her body with little kisses 'til his face was between her legs. He spread her thighs with his hands and gripped them tight as he trailed his tongue over her. She yelped and tangled her fingers in his hair as he repeated the motion then closed his mouth around her and sucked. Oh, god! He had her at the edge already. She tugged at his hair. She wanted to feel him inside her.

He came back up to lie beside her, his breath coming fast. "You taste so good, don't make me stop."

She closed her hand around him. "I want you, Dan. I want to feel you."

He nodded and opened the drawer in the nightstand to get a condom. He tore the wrapper with his teeth, but Missy took it from him. Her hands trembled as she rolled it onto him. She lay back and looked up at him. His body was amazing, lean and well-defined, narrow hips coming down towards hers. He settled himself between her legs, big brown eyes so tender.

"We only get one first time, Miss."

She nodded; she'd waited long enough for it already! Her need was almost feverish now, she couldn't speak, couldn't even think straight. She put her hands on his shoulders and spread her legs wide. He pushed at her opening, the very tip of him pressing inside her, opening her up. He reached down and stroked her, looking deep into her eyes as he did. She was desperate now for the moment he would enter her. The look in his eyes and the touch of his fingertips filled her with hot waves of pleasure. Then he plunged deep and she felt as though she was spinning away into outer space, his hard cock the only thing pinning her to reality as every thrust stretched and filled her. She wrapped her legs around his as his mouth sought hers. She gave herself up to the rocking of his hips, thrusting into her, carrying her along. All she could do was cling to his shoulders as their bodies melded into one and her orgasm shook her. All the tingly excitement he'd filled her with for weeks burst in a thousand tiny explosions as he laid claim to her body.

When she regained control, he slowed his pace, slowly, sensuously pulling almost all the way out then just as slowly filling her so deeply that it seemed he filled her soul as well as her body, becoming a part of her in every way. His smile had never looked more beautiful as he lifted his head and looked into her eyes.

"Come with me, Dan?" she breathed. She'd never had an orgasm anything like he'd just given her, but she wanted to share with him, go there together. He thrust deep and hard and buried his face in her neck as he picked up his pace. Missy was powerless as he swept her along, he owned every single cell of her body and filled every last one with pleasure. She grabbed his ass, hoping to take him with her as the mounting pleasure began to explode again. She felt him tense, his thrusting harder and deeper still. He found his release, taking her to new heights as he pulsated inside her, their bodies soaring together.

Finally he slumped down. She rested her cheek against his.

"Jesus!" she muttered when she could catch her breath.

He turned his head and smiled. "Nope, just me."

She wrapped her arms around him, loving the feel of his lean, naked body. "Yep, just my hero."

He grinned. "Like I told you, call me anytime you need a hero."

"Oh, I'll be calling you! Every day if this is what I get when I do."

He rolled to the side and got rid of the condom, then pulled her to him, pressing his face into her hair. "Told you we'd be worth the wait."

"You did and you're not often wrong, but that may have been an understatement." She pressed closer and kissed his soft lips. "That was unbelievable!"

His eyes twinkled. "Then we'll have to keep doing it 'til I make a believer out of you."

That sounded good.

His hand closed around the back of her neck and she closed her eyes as his lips came down on hers. The way he kissed her did funny things to her insides. He made her heart race and her stomach flutter. She clung to him as she kissed him back. His hand was firm around the back of her neck. She loved the feel of it. It felt like he was in charge, like he had her where he wanted her, but that wasn't scary or smothering, because it was where she wanted to be. Eventually his lips left hers. He rubbed his nose against her own with a smile, his fingers still stroking the back of her neck.

"You okay, beautiful?"

She nodded. "So much better than okay. When you hold my neck like that, I feel like a little kitten."

He grinned.

"You know how mother cats pick up their kittens by the scruff of the neck and they just go limp? That's me. I just go limp and you can do whatever you want with me. I might even start purring, I'm that happy right now."

He closed his hand tighter. "Whatever I want?"

She nodded happily.

"In that case." He reached into the drawer and pulled out another condom. "Would you help me with this?"

Her eyes widened. "Already?"

He tore open the package and gave it to her. "You tell me."

She rolled it on to him. "Not just already, but more than ready!"

He lay on his back and pulled her on top of him, closing his hand around the back of her neck again. "Whatever I want, right?"

She nodded, her breath coming hard as she lay on top of him, supporting herself with her hands. His hands closed around her ass and drew her down as he thrust up inside her. "Oh, God, Dan!"

He rocked his hips slowly. "Is this okay?"

She bit down on her lip and nodded. She hoped it was, he was so big! She could feel him throbbing. He drew her down so her breasts were in his face. He teased her nipples with the tip of his tongue. At the same time he grasped her ass tight, holding her still as he pumped up into her. Oh, God! What was he doing to her? His mouth closed around her breast, sucking hard. His fingers dug into her ass, squeezing and kneading as he held her against his rocking hips. His cock thrust deep, stimulating the bundle of nerves between her legs. The sensual friction in so many places had the tingly pressure building inside her again. She may be on top, but there was no question he was in charge, taking her exactly where he wanted her—to another mind-blowing orgasm! She could feel him getting closer, his thrusts and his cock harder as he squeezed her ass tighter and his tongue tormented her breasts. The heat in her belly exploded into an orgasm that had her gasping. His mouth on her breasts sent electric currents shooting through her to connect with his pulsing cock. She moaned as the sensations kept rolling through her. He came hard, straining into her.

"Oh, God, Dan," she moaned, and collapsed onto his chest.

He brought one hand up to caress her neck, the other still holding her ass, rocking her against gentle thrusts that had her quivering and moaning as aftershocks shook her. She gasped as he clamped her ass with both hands and rolled his hips one last time.

"Daaan!" she screamed as the last few explosions had her seeing stars.

He kissed her neck. "Yes, beautiful?"

"What are you doing to me?"

He wrapped both arms around her, holding her tight to his chest. "Whatever I want, just like you said I could."

She slid off him and lay there spent. "I had no idea you'd do something like that!"

He turned and put his arm across her waist, nuzzling his face into her neck. "We're just getting started, beautiful. That was the warm up. I told you you'd need all your strength."

She turned to look at him. That was more sex than she'd had in years, and better sex than she'd had in...well...ever! And he was saying they were just getting started?

His eyes twinkled. "But you can have a break before we get to the real thing if you like?"

She nodded; she needed a break after that.

He tightened his arm around her waist and kissed her cheek. "You're so beautiful, little Missy. So perfect."

She shook her head. "I'm far from perfect, Dan."

"You're perfect for me. You can't say we don't fit together perfectly."

She couldn't. Despite her concern when she'd first seen him without his pants, he did indeed fit perfectly. "We do."

He stroked his hand up over her rib cage and circled her nipple.

"I thought you were going to let me have a break?" His touch felt so good, but she needed a little time before she'd be ready for more.

"Sorry. I did, didn't I?" He didn't look sorry at all, but he did stop stroking her breasts. She wished he hadn't. "Do you want anything? I have some beer and there's pizza in the freezer." His face fell. "I was going to take you to this great little Italian place. I'm sorry. We could still go?"

She wrapped her arms around him and kissed his lips. "Don't you dare be sorry! There is nowhere on earth I would rather be than right here, in your bed with you. You can't seriously think there's a single restaurant in the whole world that would have been better than this? Let's have a beer and some pizza, and we won't have too far to go after our break?"

There went that smile again. "That's what I love about you, Miss. You're so easy going. Thank you. Come on, I'll get us that beer."

She watched as he opened the fridge and took out two beers. He popped the tops and handed her one.

"Thanks." He opened the freezer and she laughed when she saw it stacked full of pizzas and not much else. "Is that really all you eat?"

He gave her a sheepish grin, "No, but it's all I cook. We can order something better if you like?"

She shook her head. "You, beer, and pizza are all I want."

He put his hands on her shoulders and smiled down at her. "Then you can have everything you want and as much of it as you'd like. What kind of pizza?"

"Whatever you prefer. I like them all."

He smiled. "Unless they've got olives on them."

He really had been paying attention. "I can pick 'em off if they're there. I don't mind."

"Shall we go with a Hawaiian?"

She smiled and nodded, it was what she usually ordered. While Dan got the pizza out, she wandered around the place—it was huge. Stark white walls rose at least twenty feet to the ceiling. A wall of glass looked out over twinkling city lights. The whole place had a minimalist feel. The kitchen had a large island which divided it from a huge living space with enormous black sofas, steel tables and the biggest TV screen she had ever seen. The place was...what was it? She could imagine it in the pages of a magazine, or as the reception area of some fancy office building. It was impersonal, that was it. She couldn't imagine Dan living here. It didn't feel like anyone lived here. It was beautiful. Expensive. But soulless.

She went back to the kitchen where he was setting the timer on the oven.

"Do you like the place?"

She wrinkled her nose. "It's beautiful."

"But you don't like it?"

"It's not that. It just doesn't feel like a home." Oh no. What was that look? She hadn't meant to offend him. "But then what do I know?" she continued quickly. "My home is furnished from the thrift store. It's full of Scot's junk, and mine. I'm the wrong person to ask."

"No, Miss, you're right. This is more like a hotel room than a home. Your place is a real home, I just don't know how to make that happen. I never really had one."

Missy came to him and slipped her arms around his waist. "You and Jack had it rough growing up, didn't you?"

He nodded. "Jack had the worst of it. He shielded me. At home and at school. I was pretty clueless." He smiled. "Still am, I suppose. There was never any money. Mom worked. Dad drank whatever she earned. Neither of them were around much. Jack raised me and fed me. When Dad was there, he used to beat whichever one of us got in his way. Usually it was Mom, but when she wasn't around it was me. Jack tried to stop it whenever he could, but he worked too. He couldn't always be around."

Missy looked up at him. He was so matter of fact. She could imagine him at Scot's age. So much like Scot—super-smart in some ways, clueless in others. Her eyes filled with tears for the boy he had been.

"Hey, I wasn't going for the sympathy vote. Don't look so sad, it's all a long time ago. All I meant was that I envy the home you've made for you and Scotty. A home isn't made from a building, or the furniture inside it, it's made from the people and the love that fill it. You and Scotty are both such amazing people, and the way you love each other is so very special. Your home is such a wonderful place because of that. It's something I've never known, that's all."

The tears brimmed now, ready to fall. Dan rubbed his thumb under her eye. "Don't cry for me, beautiful, teach me." He lowered his face to her, big brown eyes open and honest. They seemed to be pleading with her, but for what, she didn't know. His lips met hers in a slow, deep exploration. She kissed him back, hoping her lips could tell him that, whatever he was pleading for, she'd willingly give—if she just knew what it was.

~ ~ ~

Dan held her tight against his chest. Standing naked with Missy, kissing her in his kitchen, he was baring himself to her in so many ways. He wasn't afraid, though. He trusted her completely. He viewed trust a little differently than most people. In his experience when people talked about trusting someone, it meant they expected that someone to do what *they* wanted them to, conform to what *they* believed was right. Dan didn't expect anyone, especially not Missy, to conform to his ideas. For him, trust meant seeing and admiring a person for who they really were, and knowing that they would stand true to their own beliefs and what they thought to be right.

When he lifted his head from that kiss, her eyes still shone with tears. He rubbed his nose against hers and smiled. He wanted her to smile again. Not to feel sad for the boy he had been, but to feel happy with the man he was now. He held out his beer bottle in a toast. "I'll be honest, Miss. I'm hoping this is the first of many evenings we'll spend together. Perhaps over time you can teach me, have a little of your ways rub off on me?" She was so beautiful, smiling up at him as she touched her bottle to his.

"I hope it's the first of many too, but I think you've got more to teach me than I have you. I'm just a dumb hick-chick that never even went to college, remember?"

It seemed to bother her that she hadn't gone to college. "You didn't go because you were too busy doing something much more important. You were raising your son, and doing an awesome job of it. Do you know how many supposedly 'well-educated' people ruin their kids' lives because they fail miserably as parents? College is just about a piece of paper. What you do is so much more important, it's about shaping a life. Scotty is a fine young man, and that's down to you."

Missy shrugged. "He is a good kid. I think it's more about nature than nurture, though. I got lucky. When I look at some of his friends, I don't know how I would cope."

Dan shuddered, some of Scot's friends baffled him. "I think it's nature *and* nurture, and I think you know it." He brought his hand up to cup the back of her neck and smiled when she let out a big sigh and relaxed against him. "So, little kitten. No more false modesty. You are the best mom I've ever known, but for this evening we don't need to talk about how good you are with your boy. I want you to keep showing me how good you are with your man."

She looked into his eyes, searching, questioning. He drew her closer, surprised how possessive he felt, how in control. He *was* her man and she was all his. He closed his hands around her waist and lifted her to sit on the island. Standing between her legs he hugged her to him.

"*My* man?" she whispered.

Sitting up here her eyes were level with his. He gazed into them as he rubbed his nose against hers. "I want to be. What do you say?"

"I say I'd like that, too." Her smile didn't just light up her face, it lit up the whole room. Hell, it lit him up! He was hard again, very hard.

"Hold that thought." He practically ran to the bedroom for a condom and had it on by the time he returned to his position between her legs. He scooted her to the edge of the counter-top and dipped his head to taste her. She was as ready as he was. Her hands met in his hair and she tugged. He slid a finger into her but she tugged again.

"*You*, Dan. I want *you*."

No way could he resist that. He stood and held her to him, spreading her legs as he nudged at her, needing to be inside her once more. Her skin was flushed, she was so wet and willing as he thrust his hips, impaling her. She gasped as he plunged deep and hard. Her arms came up around his neck and she wrapped her legs around his. The feel of her full breasts against his chest spurred him on, her warm soft body yielding to him, her inner muscles tantalizing as they closed around him. She was so tight he'd feared hurting her, but she was so wet he penetrated her easily, her heat surrounding him, drawing him deeper. He felt her growing tighter, increasing the delicious resistance. As he drove deeper she gave him more of herself. He let himself go, needing to fill her, to possess her. His own climax took her over the edge, she gasped and clenched around him, their bodies becoming one in a blinding shower of pure ecstasy that pulsed through them.

His legs were weak as they breathed hard on each other's shoulders. When he could finally speak he brought his lips to her ear and whispered, "Your man, Miss. And you are my lady, my beautiful, perfect, little lady."

She brought her hand to his cheek and landed a kiss on his lips. He wanted to be the hero that could chase away the doubts that still lingered in her eyes.

Chapter Eleven

Missy rubbed at her nose, it was tickling. Then it was her cheek. She ran a hand across her face without opening her eyes. She wanted to sleep on. Now her chin tickled. She swiped at it then yawned and stretched; her bed felt so much more comfortable than usual this morning. Oh! Now her nipples were tingling. That felt so good. For a moment she enjoyed the sensations radiating out, settling as heat between her legs. Then her eyes flew open. Dan was smiling down at her, still rolling her nipples between his fingers and thumbs. The heat between her legs intensified as she took in his hard, naked body.

"I thought this might get your attention." He smiled and squeezed harder, drawing a gasp from her at the exquisite discomfort.

"Morning," she mumbled. "You definitely got my attention. Now what are you going to do with it?"

He covered her body with his own, awakening every nerve ending she had. She shivered in anticipation. He kissed her lips, but she pressed them shut, horrified at the thought of her morning breath. He grinned, seeming to understand and instead buried his face in her hair as he buried his hand between her legs. He stroked her, intensifying the tingling heat that filled her whenever he was close. He slid a finger inside her and nibbled her neck. How could she be this close to orgasm within seconds of waking?

"I want you, Dan."

As soon as she breathed the words, his hand was gone. She watched him stretch a condom over himself. There was no question that he was awake and ready. He rested between her legs and looked deep into her eyes.

"Ready?"

She nodded, then caught her breath when he guided himself with his hand until he pressed into her. She spread her legs wider as he slowly slid deeper and deeper. He was so thick and hard. Last night his thrusts to plunge inside had been momentary pain that filled her with pleasure. This slow, steady, building pressure was something else. It felt impossible, yet it was happening, he was stretching her, filling her. The tiny explosions around the place where they joined threatened to combine into one. Once she'd taken all of him, he lost his restraint, picked up his pace and she came undone. The tiny explosions ignited a wild fire that tore through her being, searing every part of her. When the fireworks behind her eyes began to fade she felt him stiffen; his release demanded her response and she was carried away again, clinging tightly to him as he clung to her and moved her body with his own.

When they finally lay still she pressed her cheek against his. "Way to say good morning, hero!" She felt him shiver as an aftershock rolled through him and into her.

"I was hoping you'd like it. I think we should start every day this way."

If only. She'd already accepted she'd probably only ever see him on the weekends he could come to the lake. Still, she'd happily make the most of any days they could start this way.

~ ~ ~

While Missy was in the shower, Dan ran down to the coffee shop to get them some breakfast. He knew she liked vanilla cappuccino, but wasn't so sure about pastries. He'd seen her eat Emma's muffins, so got some blueberry ones, and banana ones. He needed to get it right though, so he had them fill up a box with more muffins, and scones, and Danish. He had them add a couple of chocolate croissants, just in case. He dashed back through the lobby. He slipped into the elevator unnoticed, not wanting to waste any time getting back to her.

He let himself in to find Missy sitting at the island with a glass of water. She looked so tiny, sitting there. He hated to admit it, but she was right about being a country mouse. Her shoes were pretty, but well worn. There was a patch on her jeans where he remembered her tearing them a few weeks back. She'd said something at the time about needing new jeans anyway, but she'd fixed these instead.

"Hey, hero!" Her smile really did light him up. He felt like he *could* be a hero when she said it. He wanted to take care of her, make life better for her, easier for her, in so many ways.

"Hey, beautiful. I got us some breakfast."

"Thanks." He handed her the huge cappuccino. She took a sip and grinned. "Have you been taking notes on everything I like and don't like?"

He nodded. "Pretty much. I can't help but notice. Though the notes are only mental ones." He put the box of pastries on the counter in front of her and opened it up. "I didn't have enough data about your pastry preferences, though. So I tried to cover all the options."

Missy laughed. "Did you clean the place out? Looks like you bought everything they had."

He gave her a sheepish grin. "Sorry if it's overkill. We can give the rest to Herb and the guys in the garage, but I needed to make sure you get what you want."

She held her arms out to him and hugged him tight. "I already have what I want, and that's you. Plus you got my breakfast favorites. These little chocolate thingies? I love them, and I can only ever get them when I come here, or go to the city."

Dan was thrilled by her response. He was also intrigued. "I don't know why, but I assumed you hadn't been to San Jose before."

Her happy smile faded. "Oh, it's been a couple of years now. I was looking at schools, but it never worked out."

"What kind of schools?"

She sighed and took a bite of her croissant. Dan climbed onto the stool beside her and sipped his coffee as he waited for her to reply. She took a gulp of cappuccino, then said, "Don't laugh, but for the longest time I was trying to figure out how I could go to school to become a guidance counselor." She laughed as though the idea was silly somehow.

"I don't get it. Why would I laugh and why didn't you do it?"

"I thought you might laugh, because you are smart and logical, and I'm sure you can see how the logistics wouldn't work."

"What logistics are you factoring in? It seems like a great idea to me. I think you'd be an awesome guidance counselor."

"Maybe, but first I'd need to get my Bachelor's degree, then my Masters. I could do all my placements at the high school in Summer Lake, I checked, but I could never find a Masters program that didn't have an on-campus element. I could never spend that kind of time away from Scotty, so eventually I let go of the idea."

The look on her face said she'd never really let go of it, just resigned herself to the fact that she couldn't make it happen. Dan's mind began working through the options. It seemed logical and fairly straightforward to him. "So why don't you work on your Bachelor's degree online for now? That would take a couple of years. By the time Scot's ready to go off to college himself, you'll be ready to do your Master's."

Missy nodded. "That's the conclusion I reached too."

"But?" He could see there was some obstacle to it in her mind, but he didn't understand what it might be.

She smiled at him. "But nothing, hero. I'm getting there. Now. Would you pass me another of those chocolate thingies? They are wonderful."

Dan passed the pastry, knowing she'd deliberately avoided answering, but not wanting to push for an explanation she didn't want to give. Was it the money?

~ ~ ~

Missy let go of Dan's hand once the wheels touched down on the runway at Summer Lake. His eyes twinkled, even as he rubbed his fingers to encourage the circulation to return. "Sorry." She gave him a shamefaced smile.

"No problem. That's what heroes are for." He cupped his hand around the back of her neck and drew her face towards him. "I know you don't like flying, but I'm glad you braved it to come with me." He rubbed his nose against hers. "I'm hoping you'll get used to it over time."

Missy hoped the same. She'd had such a wonderful time with him last night, and this morning. She hoped they'd be spending more time together. She didn't really care where and if it meant she had to fly in this scary plane to see him, then she'd do it. It was a small price to pay. "I don't know that I'll get used to it, but I'll keep braving it. I know I can't expect you to come here all of the time."

There was a definite twinkle in his eyes now, and she could only describe his smile as mysterious. She didn't get chance to question him though as Smoke's voice came over the intercom.

"Here we are folks. The FBO guys tell me the others are waiting. So, it'll be a quick refuel and then we'll turn around and get you ladies to the city."

Dan grinned. "Are you looking forward to shopping?"

She nodded. "It'll be fun. I need to see Scotty before we leave though." She gave him a quick kiss. "And I wish I'd still have your hand to hold on the way." She really never had seen such a beautiful smile.

"Well, I can't hold your hand on the way, but I can be here waiting when you get back, okay?"

She nodded, "I'd like that."

"Me too. And you know Scot will be fine with me. We've got big plans of our own for today."

Missy's heart filled up. She still couldn't believe how lucky they were. Dan was wonderful for Scot, and she was starting to realize how wonderful he was for her too.

Dan followed Missy down the steps onto the tarmac. Despite the fact that they hadn't gone out for dinner, or gone dancing, or done any of the things he'd planned, it had been a great night. He grinned, the best night. Having Missy over to his place had reinforced everything he was starting to believe. All those things that were supposed to make him feel good about himself really didn't. The success, the company, the apartment, the car.... Hmm, maybe the car, but all the rest, none of it made him feel good. Missy did. Being here did.

Scot burst out of the building and came running towards them as they got off the golf cart. Missy smiled and held her arms out, but he ran straight past her, barreling into Dan and wrapping his arms around his waist.

"Dan, Dan, Dan, I beat your high score! I did it!"

Dan laughed and ruffled Scot's hair. "Way to go, champ!" He looked at Missy, afraid she'd be hurt at being bypassed, but she smiled happily at the two of them. "I guess we're going to have to battle it out now, then?"

Scot grinned up at him. "Nah. We don't need to play today. I want you to help me with code, remember?" He stuck his tongue out. "Let me stay champion for a while, 'til you knock me off the top spot again?"

"Hmm, I suppose." Dan grinned. He loved spending time with Scot, and although all this hugging was a new development, he was liking it, too."

"Erm, hello?" said Missy. "Any chance I could get one of those?"

"Oh. Sorry." Scot gave his mom a quick hug. "So." He looked from her to Dan and back. "Did you guys have a good time? Are you going to start seeing each other, for real?"

Dan caught Missy's eye. "We did and we are. As long as that's okay with you?"

"Okay?" Scot's eyes were wide. "I've been keeping my fingers crossed all night!" He gave Missy a playful grin. "She can be a bit annoying sometimes, but she's pretty cool, for a girl."

Missy laughed indignantly. "Thanks! I think!"

"She's very cool for a girl," said Dan. "Most of them don't make much sense to me, but your mom's different. I like her." As they walked into the building he placed a hand on the back of Missy's neck and squeezed gently. "I like her a lot," he said, as she leaned against him.

~ ~ ~

Dan and Scot stood with Jack and Pete after they had waved the girls off on their shopping trip. Dan wished Missy could buy herself a whole bunch of new clothes instead of just an angel costume. He had no idea how to broach that subject though, so hadn't gone anywhere near it. Maybe over time she'd let him buy her things, as gifts? It was nearly her birthday. She was beautiful, no matter what she wore, but it had made him feel sad to see her with Emma and Holly. They both wore logos of expensive brands even he recognized, while she was in her worn and patched jeans. She deserved so much more, and he wanted to give it to her.

Jack snapped his fingers in front of Dan's face. "You coming, little bro?"

Dan shook his head, attempting to catch up with the present. He turned to Scot. "What do you say, champ? Want to get some brunch with the guys before we get to it?"

Scot grinned. "Pancakes?"

"Sure, pancakes."

"Okay then, yes please."

Dan smiled to himself. Missy always reminded Scot about his manners, yet as soon as she was out of earshot, the kid's manners were impeccable.

"Come on. We can take your mom's van so we can come get her tonight."

~ ~ ~

Dan looked around the table. Ben had joined them at what he'd come to think of as *their* table on the back deck over the lake. He'd never felt at home in a group of men, but he did here. Had for months now. Of course, it helped that these were all men he liked and respected.

"I have to ask." Jack grinned at him. "Do I need to add you and Missy to our table at the dinner next month?"

Dan pursed his lips. Jack and Pete hosted a huge fundraiser every year. Jack always tried to talk him into going, but Dan squirmed out of it by making a large donation instead. For the last couple of years he'd also paid for his attorney, Leanne to attend. She loved those kinds of events whereas he just felt uncomfortable and avoided them whenever possible. But this might be different. He looked around the table. "Do you think she'd enjoy it?"

"She'd love it!" Pete and Ben both spoke at the same time.

"Believe me," said Ben. "Miss absolutely loves any chance to get all dressed up and go out. It's not like she gets many opportunities, but when she does...man!"

Dan looked at Jack. "In that case, I guess we're in."

Jack grinned. "Excellent! You'll enjoy it, little bro. You really will."

"As long as Missy does. That's what matters." He looked at Ben. "Do you usually go?"

"It depends. I probably won't this time. It's no fun at a table full of couples and I don't have a pretty lady tucked away anywhere."

"Well, if you'd be interested in escorting a stunning lady, that could be arranged."

He had Ben's full attention now. "Describe stunning."

Dan laughed.

"Leanne?" asked Jack.

"Yep," replied Dan.

Jack looked at Ben. "She'd eat you for breakfast, bud."

"Yeah, but you'd die a happy man." Pete laughed.

"I say again, describe stunning," said Ben.

"Okay. Long blonde hair, big blue eyes, she's curvy in all the right places, beautiful face, beautiful person."

Ben looked puzzled. "And you're not interested?"

"God, no!" Dan pulled a face. "I can see that she's technically beautiful, but I don't feel it. To me she's a study buddy. We met in college. Two misfits together. We weren't cool enough for the cool kids or geeky enough for the geeks, so we stuck together. She's the company attorney." He stopped himself. "Well, I guess she's my attorney now. She'll no doubt be up here over the next few weeks. I'll introduce you."

Ben nodded. "I'll look forward to it."

Dan's train of thought went back to Missy, though. "Is it black tie?"

Jack laughed. "Yeah. Same as every year. Why?"

"What does that mean for women?"

He was surprised that, of all of them, Pete was the one who understood what he was thinking.

"Don't worry about it, we'll talk to Holly. Clothes are her thing." He grinned ruefully. "Especially expensive dresses!"

Dan laughed. "Great, thanks. I'll talk to her."

Ben's phone rang. He checked the screen and sighed. "Sorry, guys. I need to take this, I'll be back." He walked away to take the call.

"Have we got any plans for tonight?" asked Jack.

Dan didn't know what Missy thought, but he hoped they'd be spending it together.

"Holly had suggested that we all eat here when they get back," said Pete. "They're usually worn out after shopping in the city." He grinned. "I'm seeing dinner here, a hot tub and an early night on my horizon."

Jack laughed. "I promise I won't disturb you this time, partner. How about you?" he asked Dan. "Do you two tech guys have any plans to come up for air?"

"I'm going to Ethan's tonight," Scot piped up. "If you don't mind taking me?"

Dan frowned. "Does your mom know?"

"Err, I thought you could tell her?"

"How about you call and *ask* her? If she says it's okay I'll take you."

Scot grinned. "Okay, but you know if I go, you have to keep her company, right?"

"I think I can manage that." He'd look forward to it.

Ben returned to the table looking agitated.

"S'up, buddy?" asked Pete.

"Ah, nothing. You know the old DeWinter place at the end of Main?"

"That's the one at the very end, with the big dock?" asked Pete.

"Yeah, that's the one. When Mrs. DeWinter passed on last year, her kids sold the place. The people who bought it thought it was a straight, by the numbers investment. They put it in the rental program with the resort. I did tell them it's not a guaranteed program, but they're disappointed with the return they made over the summer. They want to sell it on before the quiet season. I've told them they're asking too much, especially if they want a quick sale at this time of year. But of course they don't want to hear it. They call every couple of days. Drive me nuts!"

Dan pictured the beautiful, big house he'd spotted on his breakfast run last weekend. "Does it have a For Sale sign?" he asked.

"Yep," said Ben. "The only place on Main with a sign in the yard."

It *was* that house then. "How much are they asking?"

"Way too much," said Ben.

"How much is too much?" asked Jack with a gleam in his eye. He was looking at Dan and apparently seeing every thought in his head. He'd always been able to do that. "House prices are a little different here than they are in San Jose."

Dan smiled.

"Six-fifty," said Ben.

Dan's smile spread into a huge grin. "Is that all?"

"I know that's peanuts in your world, but up here it just won't sell for that," said Ben.

"I'm guessing it might," said Jack with a grin.

"Can I give you a call this afternoon?" Dan asked.

"Sure." Ben's phone rang again. "I'll catch you later," he said as he stood up.

"So what are you thinking, little bro? Want to talk about it?" asked Jack.

"You know me," replied Dan. "Think first, talk later. How about I call you and we'll meet up before the girls get back?" He looked at Scot, who had finished his pancakes and was starting to get fidgety. "I think we need to be getting to work, huh, champ?"

"Yep. Let's go. Laters Uncle Jack, Uncle Pete." Scot scampered off while Dan reached for his wallet.

"I've got this," said Jack. "But make sure you call me later?" He raised an eyebrow. "We need to talk."

Dan smiled and nodded. He did want to talk to his brother. He thought Jack would be pretty happy about what he was thinking.

Chapter Twelve

Emma emerged from the dressing room rolling her eyes. Missy had to laugh.

"Err, I don't think so, Em!"

"Tell me about it! I'd be okay in a school nativity, but it's not quite the look I was after for your birthday party." Emma had tried on an angel costume that would indeed be more appropriate in a school play.

"You could be the fairy godmother?" suggested Holly.

"Shut up!" laughed Emma. "You're just too smug because you already found the perfect costume. It's easy with your figure, though."

Holly did look amazing in the short silvery shift she'd found to go with glittery little wings. Missy was enjoying herself immensely. She'd tried on a quite a few costumes, but she and Emma were finding the same problem. They were both shorter and curvier than Holly. Most of the costumes Missy had tried made her feel like she belonged on top of a Christmas tree. What she hoped to find was a costume that made her feel like she belonged in the arms of a tall, dark, handsome cowboy. She smiled to herself, knowing Dan's arms fit the bill perfectly.

"I'm going to try this one," she said.

Holly looked skeptically at the dress she held up. "If you say so, but I think it's another dud."

"We'll see," said Missy and drew the curtain behind her. This outfit didn't look like much on the hanger, but she had a feeling it might just work. It was sheer netting, covered in tiny golden sparkles. As she wiggled into it, she thought she might need something in a larger size. It was figure hugging, for sure. And short. *Damn!* It barely covered her ass. She looked in the mirror. *Wow!* It clung to her. *Well, double damn!* She grinned as she took in the halo, it was completely lopsided—that seemed appropriate considering the effect she hoped it would have on Dan. She twirled in front of the mirror. This was it! She felt like a million dollars and sexy as all get out. Not something she was used to, but she liked it.

"Ta-dah!" she cried, flinging the curtain back.

"Oh, my God!" squealed Holly. "Who are you and what have you done with Missy?"

Emma clasped her hands together. "Oh, Miss! You're so beautiful! There won't be any mistaking whose party it is. You'll be the belle of the ball."

Missy grinned. She was used to taking a backseat to her friends when it came to dressing up. She didn't have the looks or the wardrobes they did. But boy! This costume did great things for her and she knew it. "Isn't it wonderful?" she asked. "For once I won't feel like the dowdy old aunt around you two."

"What?" cried Holly. "Sweetie, you cannot be serious that you ever feel like that?"

Missy laughed. "No need to be kind about it, hon. You're Miss Long and Lean, the hottie. Then we've got Blonde and Bubbly Barbie here." She nodded her head towards Emma. "I know

I'm just the tag-along usually. My point was that in this get-up I do feel like the birthday girl and not the poor relation for once."

Holly looked stunned. Emma less so. Emma had been one of her best friends since they were kids. She knew how Missy felt.

"But, sweetie," said Holly. "You are soooo beautiful! You have to know this? And your figure? Damn, girl! In the right clothes you have more to show off than the rest of us put together. As that costume is proving. Just look at you!"

Missy did glance at the mirror, and had to smile. "It is wonderful, but it's a one-off birthday thing. The rest of the time, while the two of you swan around in your designer labels, the only names I do are Lee and Levi. Don't get me wrong, I'm not complaining, just stating the obvious."

"But...." Holly seemed determined to continue with her argument, but Emma cut her off.

"There's no point arguing with her. I've been telling her for over twenty years. If our Miss is anything, she's stubborn. So just be grateful she's admitting how amazing she looks in that costume." She grinned at Missy. "And I can't wait to see Dan's face when he sees you. The poor guy won't know what to do with himself!"

Holly laughed. "The poor guy never knows what to do with himself. He's so sweet and so quiet."

"Oh, he knows what to do with himself alright!" Missy spoke before she thought about it.

Emma laughed. "And by the looks of that smile, he knows how to do it very well too, right?"

Missy nodded happily. She'd managed to avoid most of their questions this morning, but Holly saying Dan didn't know what to do with himself had triggered a defensiveness in her. He may come off as quiet and shy, but she knew better.

"So?" asked Holly. She and Emma looked at her expectantly.

"What?" she asked, knowing that big, silly grin was plastered on her face.

Emma laughed. "If I know you.... You're not going to say much, but your face is giving it all away, Miss."

She nodded. "Let's just say, I think he's wonderful."

"And seeing the two of you together this morning, I'd say that feeling is mutual," said Holly. "Which is weird. You two are the least likely couple I can think of."

"Why's that?" Missy felt defensive again, this time about herself. "You mean because he's so smart?"

Holly shook her head. "Come on, sweetie. You know I don't mean that. I mean he's so quiet, while you're so outgoing. You're the life of the party, while he rarely says much. You're practical, while he's intellectual. If someone gets out of line you tell it like it is, while he walks away and says nothing. You're so cute together, though. You bring out the best in each other. He talks more when you're around." She grinned. "And when he talks, you actually shut up and listen!"

Missy smiled. It was all true. "Yeah. It doesn't make any sense, does it? But he's wonderful! You know what I'm like. I always felt the need to compete with the guys. I have to shout Pete down when he starts. Show them I'm just as strong and capable as they are. But Dan feels so different. I just relax around him. I feel like it's all okay, just because he's there." She smiled as she remembered the feel of his hand on the back of her neck. She'd never wanted, or believed she needed, a man to take care of her, never understood how her friends could turn into helpless little women when a big, strong man entered the picture. Now she was starting to understand it—and to like it.

Emma smiled at her knowingly. "I'd still lay odds on you becoming my sister-in-law. I've never seen you like this."

"Em, honey. He's wonderful. I admit it. I'm smitten with the man, okay? But that? No! Even if I wanted to." Which she wasn't going to admit she had considered. "It wouldn't be fair to him. He needs to meet someone he can marry and have kids with. You know how good he is with Scot. He needs to have kids of his own. I'm past all that. I'm a couple of years older than him, but it's not about the age, it's about where we are in life. He's got it all ahead of him. I've got most of it behind me."

Emma frowned at her. "Does he even want kids?"

"I don't know. Why would he not? Look at the rest of you. That's what you're all planning, plus it's the standard thing to do at our age. I'm the non-standard one."

"I'd hardly describe Dan as standard," said Holly. "Maybe you should talk to him about it?"

Missy rolled her eyes. "And say what? Dan, honey, I know we've only been on one date, but what are your thoughts on babies and a family? I don't think so. We're just going to date for a while. You have to remember that he lives hundreds of miles away and has a business there too. He'd never leave all that, and you know I'd never leave the lake. It doesn't have to be about forever, just about enjoying it for now." She didn't want to think about it ending, about it not being forever. "Now, can we get back to admiring my ass in this costume? Because I've gotta say, I'm looking pretty damned hot!"

Emma nodded, the look she gave Missy said she understood, but she went along with the change of subject. "You're not just hot, Miss. You are sizzling! I am suitably jealous and I still need help finding something that will make me look even half as good as you do."

~ ~ ~

"So, tell me about these angel costumes," said Pete. He had an arm around Holly's shoulders, grinning at her lecherously. "Did we decide to go with slutty angels?"

Holly laughed. "You'll have to wait and see, Bigshot, though I doubt you'll be disappointed. Now, *you*...." she looked across the table at Dan, "*You* I can guarantee will not be disappointed. Our little birthday angel over there...." She waved her glass towards Missy, who sat beside him. "Damn! When you see her costume, you'll think you've died and gone to heaven!"

Dan smiled at Missy and cocked his head to one side.

She wrinkled her nose. "It is a pretty cool outfit, if I do say so myself."

"Cool?" asked Emma. "There's nothing cool about it. It's hot, hot, hot!"

Dan was liking the sound of this.

"Is yours hot?" Pete asked Holly.

"Never mind me, how about you, Bigshot? Have you found anything that's going to make you look enough of a cowboy to distract me from Missy's brother?"

Dan laughed as Pete spluttered his drink. While the others teased Pete about not being cowboy enough, Dan edged a little closer to Missy. She leaned against him to look up at him.

"Any chance of a sneak preview of my hot little angel?" he murmured. He loved the way the gray of her eyes lightened when she was happy.

"I don't think so, hero. I want to save it for my birthday."

"By the sounds of it, it'll feel more like my birthday!"

"I hope so."

Ben returned to the table. They'd finished eating a while ago and Ben had been taking care of some problem behind the bar. "So, Dan," he said. "They just got back to me and you can go over any time you like tomorrow." Dan nodded, but said nothing. He'd wanted to talk to Missy in private about this first, not let her hear about it along with everyone else. As happened so often, Jack sensed his discomfort and stepped in to rescue him.

"Speaking of tomorrow, is everyone up for breakfast? I'm ready to take my bride home now, but we'll be in town in the morning if anyone, or everyone, wants to meet up?"

Holly looked at Pete. "We were planning on it, weren't we?"

"We were," he agreed.

"How about you, Miss?"

Dan had been hoping that they might get to the papers and breakfast at her place. He liked hanging out with the gang, but he wanted her all to himself sometimes too.

She looked up at him. "Yeah, we'll come, won't we?"

He nodded. The way she'd included them as a *we* almost made up for not being able to keep her to himself.

"Well, you know I'm going to be here," said Ben. "And I'll give you the key then, Dan."

Dan nodded as Missy looked up at him enquiringly.

"Okay." Pete rose from the table. "We're outta here."

Holly joined him. "G'night guys. See you tomorrow."

Once everyone had left, Dan walked with Missy across the square to where they'd left her minivan. "How tired are you?" he asked.

"I'm okay, why?"

"I wondered if you'd like to walk home? It's a beautiful evening, and we could get the van in the morning. But only if you're not too tired."

She smiled happily. "I'd love that. I love walking this town. It's even nicer when I get to walk with you."

He put an arm around her shoulders, pleased that she wanted to walk. Even more pleased that she was so straightforward with him. She told him what she liked and what she didn't, he never needed to puzzle her out. Being with her felt so easy. So right.

As they walked down Main Street, the moon shone on the lake. It was so beautiful here. So peaceful. "Have you ever thought about living anywhere else?" he asked.

"No. This is my home," she said. "I love this place. I've thought about moving houses, but I wouldn't go far."

"Would you go this far?" He swept his arm out to indicate the large waterfront homes they were passing.

She laughed. "Only in my dreams. When I was a little girl I used to dream about living in one of these places. But you have no idea how much they cost. They're ridiculous. I love to walk down here, but that's as close as I'll ever get." She grinned. "How tired are you?"

"Not at all. Why?"

"There's a little waterfront park at the end of Main. Most folk don't even know it's there. I used to take Scotty to the swings when he was small. Do you want to see?"

Dan nodded. He did want to see, but there was something else at the end of Main he wanted her to see. And to talk to her about. He felt a little uncomfortable about her comment though, that the house prices here were ridiculous. He thought so too, but to him they were ridiculously low. As they neared the end of the street he could see the For Sale sign looming. His mind was spinning, wondering how he could bring it up. She did it for him.

"This house is my absolute favorite in all of Summer Lake," she said.

"You know it?"

"Yeah. I spent a lot of time here as a kid. The DeWinters were lovely people. They had a grandaughter who used to come from England every summer. You know what I'm like, when I heard there was a little girl here with no one to play with, I came and introduced myself. We became great friends. We still write. I hoped she might buy the place when the family sold, but some city people bought it as a moneymaker. It's such a shame. It's a family house. It should be a home, not an investment."

Dan took a deep breath. She was giving him the perfect lead in, but still he hedged. "What do you think will happen to it now?"

"No doubt more money people will buy it. They're the only ones that can afford it, and they won't be interested in making it a home."

Here it came. "I can afford it, and I'm interested in making it a home...especially if you'll help me?"

Her eyes widened. "You? But you live in San Jose! Your home is there!"

"As you pointed out last night, it's not really a home. It's just where I live, and I don't want to live there anymore. I want to live here."

"But what about your work?"

"I know we haven't talked about it, but I'm selling out. I'm done. I'm starting a new chapter. I want to start a new life.

Here, in this place. A life that has Jack in it, that has real friends in it. Most of all, a life that has you and Scotty in it."

Her mouth was open, but no words came out. It seemed that, for the first time since he'd met her, she was speechless. He felt his stomach drop. Perhaps she hated the idea? Didn't want him here? He stared at her, hoping she'd put him out of his misery. She didn't. This wasn't going like he'd hoped. "Sorry," he mumbled. "I didn't mean any pressure or anything. I...I just...well...." He had to pull it together! "Sorry." It was the only thing he trusted himself to say.

She reached her arms up around his neck and planted a kiss on his lips. "No. *I'm sorry*, Dan. You surprised me. I had no idea. I thought this was a strictly weekends place for you. I didn't imagine you'd ever move up here."

Dan frowned. He felt like he'd been kicked in the gut—and it hurt! "And you don't want me to? Am I a strictly weekends guy for you?" He closed his arms around her and held her tight, maybe a little too tight, against him. He didn't want to let her go, in any way.

She looked directly into his eyes. "Well, yeah, I suppose. I thought that's all you were offering."

"It's not. It's not all I'm offering and it's not all I'm asking either."

Her eyes searched his face. She looked confused; confused and perhaps a little afraid? She felt tense, rigid in his arms. He could feel her heart battering against her ribcage. He brushed his lips over hers and felt her relax a little. Keeping one arm tight around her waist, he brought his hand up to the back of her neck. He gripped, gently but firmly, holding her still for his kiss. He didn't know what to say to make her understand, but he knew he could tell her so much more with a kiss. She sagged against him and kissed him back. What started out soft and sweet, soon became heated. He couldn't express how he felt about her, what she meant, without including the physical need. The feel of her soft body made his own body hard. The kiss stoked a desire that had to be fulfilled before they'd be able to address anything else. All he wanted now was to get her home.

It appeared she felt the same. She tugged at his hand. "Take me home?"

Her gaze was soft. Almost pleading. It aroused him even more to know she wanted him that badly. They set a brisk pace back to her place.

Chapter Thirteen

Missy fumbled with the key as she tried to open the door. Dan was right behind her on the step. She could feel him so close, his musky scent invading her senses. She managed to turn the key and stumbled inside. Dan followed and closed the door behind him. He took her hand and led her up the stairs. Her mind was a mad jumble. He wanted to move here? Buy the DeWinters place? He wanted more than weekends?

He led her into her bedroom. She closed the door. It felt strange, even though Scot wasn't here. She turned to find herself trapped between Dan and the door. He leaned his weight against her, pinning her there. He kissed her deeply, a sensuous exploration of her mouth, while his hands seemed to be everywhere at once. In seconds she stood naked, while he was still fully dressed. She tried to unbutton his shirt but he caught her hands and led her to the bed. He pushed her down on it and held her waist in his hands as he kissed her stomach. The now familiar tingles filled her. His hot, wet mouth working its way up over her body had her moaning. She gasped as his grip on her waist tightened and he laved at her sensitive nipples. She tried again to undo his shirt, but he moved away, trailing his tongue back down over her stomach.

Her breath caught in her throat when his mouth closed over her heat and his hot tongue snaked inside.

"I want you, Dan." His mouth felt wonderful, but she wanted to feel all of him, his body moving with hers as he entered her. This time though, he didn't comply. His hands left her waist to spread her thighs. "You'll have to wait," he said, rolling her nub between his finger and thumb. She writhed as the first tiny explosions began. When his tongue returned to its work, she grasped the sheets beneath her as it thrust deeper.

"Please, Dan," she begged. She wanted him to make love to her. "You're going to make me come."

He lifted his head and gave her a predatory smile. "I am. I'm going to make you come, and come, and come."

Just the look on his face took her closer to the edge. Then his mouth was on her again and she felt her muscles tense as the explosions began. "Daaan!" she screamed as he slid his fingers deep. Only her heels and her shoulders remained on the bed as he worked her mercilessly; true to his word he carried her through wave after wave of an orgasm that she thought might never end. When he let her catch her breath she sagged back down onto the bed, ragged breaths still coming fast. She knew it was only a small respite as he knelt above her, unfastening his shirt and throwing it to the floor. There was something incredibly sexy about watching him unbuckle his belt and unfasten his jeans. She felt that little shiver of trepidation when he freed his cock from his pants and kicked them off. That tattoo ran down his side, over hard muscle down past his hipbone.

He took his cock in his hand and held her open, stroking himself against her swollen flesh, tormenting her. She didn't need him to tease her, she needed him to make love to her.

She grasped his ass in her hands and lifted herself up to him. She moaned as he plunged deep. He was so hard, he felt so good, better than ever, and different somehow. He rocked his hips in an insistent rhythm that carried her inevitably towards another mind-blowing orgasm. She moved with him, giving herself up to him. He felt so damned good! She could feel him straining, his cock pulsing as he grew hotter and harder with each thrust.

"Missy!" he cried as he let himself go. She felt him explode, his release shooting hot and deep inside her. Even as her body trembled and the fireworks exploded behind her eyes, she finally understood what felt so different—they'd forgotten the condom!

As they lay recovering, her mind raced. It had only been a week since Doc Morgan had given her the pills, was that enough?

Dan wrapped her in his arms and pulled her close. "I hope that was as good for you as it was for me, beautiful?"

"Unbelievable!" It was true. She couldn't believe they'd forgotten.

He pressed his face into her hair. "Good, then I get to keep working on making you a believer." He propped himself up on one elbow and looked down at her. "Would you really have a problem if I moved up here to work on it? You seemed upset back there."

His expression was troubled. He looked so earnest, she pulled his face down so she could kiss him. "Who said I had a problem with it, hero? I was surprised, not upset. How could I be upset at the thought of having you around more?"

He cocked his head to one side, his beautiful smile returning. "You like the idea?"

"I just told you. I love it!"

"Then will you come with me tomorrow?"

"Of course. I'll help you figure out how you can make it feel like a home of your own."

His smile faltered at that. Why, though? That was what he'd asked, wasn't it? That she help him make it into a home. He nodded, but said nothing.

"Want to sneak downstairs for a glass of wine?" She had a feeling she wasn't going to get much rest tonight. She wanted to take a break, to try to get her head around the forgotten condom, before he was ready to go again.

He pressed himself against her, he was already hard. "Want a glass after?" He nibbled her ear, sending shivers down her back. She jumped up from the bed. "Yes, but let's have one before too."

He looked puzzled, but got up from the bed and pulled his pants on.

~ ~ ~

Dan opened the wine while Missy got two glasses from the cabinet. This whole evening, since they'd left the restaurant, had him confused. He poured the wine and looked at her. She said she liked the idea of him moving up here, but she seemed ill at ease. Something was bothering her and he had no clue what it was. Normally she was so forthright about everything. He didn't like this. She'd even wanted to come down here and drink wine rather than stay in bed with him. Right now he was too confused. There were too many emotions and he didn't know what they were. For once she wasn't making it easy for him to understand. His head filled with white noise, like it got when he was overloaded with people; he'd never felt that way around her. He put his glass down.

"I just remembered something in the RV, I'll be back." He escaped to the coach and sat down in front of the computer, feeling like a shit as he thought of the stunned look on her face when he'd walked out of the kitchen. He was angry with himself. He tapped on his keyboard and let out a big sigh. She deserved more than this. He had to go back in.

She was sitting at the kitchen table, fiddling with her wine glass. He couldn't read the expression on her face when she looked up, but he knew it wasn't good.

"Please forgive me, Miss. When I don't understand people, I walk away. That's what I just did, but I don't want to walk away from you. I want to understand. What's wrong, Miss?"

She sipped her wine and looked away.

"Please tell me? I'm no good at working these things out. I don't usually need to with you. Did I do something wrong? I'm sorry if I did. I didn't mean to."

She took hold of his hand. "No, honey. I'm sorry." This couldn't be good. She called everyone honey. It didn't feel like when she called him hero.

"Why?"

"You didn't do something wrong, we both did. We forgot the condom and I'm a little worried."

Oh! That was all? He put an arm around her shoulders and drew her to him. "That's nothing to worry about, beautiful."

She pulled away and scowled at him. "It is for me! You might want a baby, but I damned well don't!"

That shocked him. "What the hell makes you think I would want a baby?" He couldn't think of anything worse.

"Sorry." She visibly relaxed a little. "I've just got it in my head that that's where you are in life. You're at the stage where you should be getting married, sharing your life with someone, and having babies. I can't give you that, I've already been there. I don't want it."

Wow! He would never have guessed that was what she was thinking. "I don't want that. Well, not the babies part anyway, and you don't need to worry about getting pregnant. I can't have kids."

She looked at him, shocked. "You can't? Why not?"

"I had mumps when I was a kid. It's a rare complication, but it happens in a tiny percentage of cases. I was one of what they call the unfortunate few. I consider myself fortunate though. Can you imagine me with a baby?" He grimaced at the thought and was glad when she laughed.

"You should see your face. They're not that bad. Scotty was a little sweetheart."

"I'm sure he was, but most of them aren't. They're scary, demanding little creatures, constantly wet and noisy at both ends!"

She laughed again. She looked so very relieved that a thought hit him. "Did you really think that I would want to start a family?"

She met his eyes and nodded.

"But you don't want to?"

She nodded again.

"So, Miss, where did you think this was going?"

She shrugged, but still didn't speak.

"Please tell me?"

"I thought you were just coming up here on the weekends— that we'd date for a while. That you'd eventually meet someone more like you in San Jose who you wanted to start a family with. That you'd go off and start your life and we'd be over."

He took hold of her hands and cocked his head to one side as he looked deep into her eyes. "I have met someone I want to have a family with." She looked shocked. "Miss, I don't want to *start* a family. I want to become part of yours. You and Scotty, and me."

She just stared at him. He didn't know what that meant, so he pushed on. "I don't want to *go off* to start a life. I want to come here and start one. With you. I know it's too soon to be talking like this, and you don't have to say anything. But it's how I feel, it's what I want, and it's not going to change. So I need you to know. We can take our time getting there, if you want. I didn't mean to lay it on you like this. But honestly, if it were up to me, I'd have you both move in that house with me as soon as I can close on it. That's what I meant when I asked you to help me make it home, I meant by living there, with me. Like I said, a home is made from the people and the love that live there." He pulled her closer. "And I love you, Missy." He hadn't actually meant to pour all that out. Had intended to wait a while, build up to it, but saying it too soon didn't make it any less true.

Her eyes sparkled with tears. One big fat drop escaped and rolled down her cheek. Was that a good thing? He didn't know. She squeezed his hands as she smiled through the tears that followed the first down her face.

"It is too soon, hero." He sucked his breath in sharply. Of course it was, but he couldn't take it back, wouldn't want to anyway. "It is too soon, but I love you too."

His heart leapt and a huge grin spread across his face. "You do?"

"I do! How could I not love you? On paper we're all wrong for each other, but something about us just works. You're perfect,

perfect for me and I do love you." Her hands tangled in his hair as she pulled him down to kiss her.

When he eventually lifted his head, he held her tight. "I love you, little Miss Missy. I don't know how love works, I might not be very good at it. It's not something I thought I was capable of, but then I met you."

She smiled up at him, her eyes such a light gray, they looked like liquid silver. "I didn't think I was capable of it either, hero. I'm so glad we've proved each other wrong."

~ ~ ~

Missy lay awake, staring at the ceiling. Dan slept on beside her. She'd never had a man spend the night in all the years she'd owned this house. It just hadn't seemed right. Whenever she'd dated a guy, she'd tried to keep them separate from her home, from Scot. No one had ever come close to being good enough for her to have them around her son. Dan was different. Completely different. He'd gotten close to Scot in his own right. Now she wondered if *she* was good enough. Dan shared a bond with Scotty that she didn't—they were both so damned smart. She'd always felt a little guilty that Scot didn't have a guy in his life. She believed a boy needed a male influence. Ben had always been so good with him, hanging with him and taking him fishing when he could. Pete too, spent time with him whenever he could, but it wasn't the same as Scotty having someone of his own. She hesitated to even think it out loud, but what he had needed was a father figure. Dan fit the bill perfectly. He was the only person she had ever known who could talk to Scot on his level, and not just about his computers. Not only did Dan understand the kid, he was even smarter than him and could teach him, challenge him, help him along. She turned to look at his sleeping face, long dark lashes rested on his cheeks. His full lips turned up at the corners, smiling as he slept. In some ways she couldn't have asked for a more perfect match. He was everything Scotty needed. Damn, he was everything *she* needed! He was gorgeous, thoughtful, fun, he cared about her. Last night he'd told her that he loved her! That had come as a surprise, but not as big a surprise as hearing herself tell him that she loved him too.

It was true though. Despite the fact that they were so different, they gelled perfectly. Their differences complemented each other and, as Ben had said, they brought out each other's hidden qualities. It was all so much to take in. This time yesterday, she'd been thinking that all she could do was make the most of dating him for a while. Now he was saying he wanted to move up here. Buy a house, which just happened to be her dream house, and he wanted her and Scotty to move in with him! It was a lot to take in, for sure. On the one hand it was perfect. Perfect for Scot, and for her. But was it all just a little too perfect? Would the differences between them become more apparent over time? Would she drive him nuts if they did move in together? Would he be able to stand having her and Scotty around *all* the time? He was a loner, he needed his solitude. She was no fool. She believed he did love her, she knew she'd fallen for him, in a big way. But she also knew that might not be enough. Not when cold, hard, everyday reality set in.

If it was just about her, she'd happily be swept along by the excitement she felt, jump in both feet first and see where they ended up. But it was about Scotty too. She'd been so grateful to see his friendship with Dan grow these last few months. So happy to see the way he was growing in confidence, coming out of his shell more every day. The last few weeks, she'd noticed the way he'd been growing emotionally attached too. She hadn't missed all the hugs, or the way Scot turned to Dan whenever he was unsure of himself. She loved the relationship the two of them were building, but she was afraid of damaging it. If she and Dan got together and it didn't work out between the two of them, what effect would it have on Scot? Was it a risk work taking? She pursed her lips. What was the alternative? Her and Dan not getting together? Not even trying? That really wasn't an option. She loved Dan. Scot loved Dan. And he loved them. Between the three of them they'd work it out. It was a risk, but so was life. You didn't get anywhere good by not taking risks, she knew that much. If they were all honest with each other they'd be okay, whether it worked out or not. She hated the idea of Scot getting hurt, but more than that, she hated the idea of not even trying for something that could be so good for all three of them. All they could do was talk about it. She didn't like to hide anything from Scot; she felt it was important to involve him in decisions that affected him. He was smart enough, and after all he was becoming a young man in his own right.

Dan reached across and drew her towards him, sleepy eyes tender as his smile spread. "Good morning, beautiful."

She found herself pressed against his warm body, looking into deep brown eyes. "Good morning."

His hand closed around the back of her neck and she felt herself go limp. "C'mere little kitten, I need you." His eyes may be sleepy, but his body was wide awake as he pulled her on top of him.

"I need you too, Dan," she murmured as he ran his hands down her back. And it was true. She needed him in so many ways. As he rocked her against his arousal, she knew he could satisfy this immediate need. She could only hope that he might be able to meet her other needs even half as well.

Chapter Fourteen

"So, Mr. Planner," Ben looked at Pete, "what's the plan for your bachelor party? I know you've got all the scheduling figured out for the big spring wedding, but I've not heard anything about the guys' night. Please tell me we get to go to Vegas this time?"

Pete laughed. "Don't look at me. That's Jack's department. I'll go along with whatever my partner decides." He grinned at Holly. "That way, my bride can't hold *me* responsible."

Holly laughed. "Do what you like, Bigshot. Just don't ask about our weekend!"

Pete's cocky grin faded a little. "*Weekend?* What's the plan? This is the first I've heard!"

Holly was still laughing. "Never you mind. You take care of your own party."

Dan liked Holly. She was fun and confident. Until Holly came along he'd never known anyone but Jack and Missy who could put Pete in his place.

"In that case," said Ben, "my vote is definitely for Vegas. What do you say, Jack?"

Jack looked at Dan. "We'll have to watch this one if we go there."

Dan smiled as the whole group turned towards him. With this bunch, he didn't feel uncomfortable, or self-conscious at being the center of attention. Missy looked up at him enquiringly. "We'd come home a bit richer." He smiled.

"Oh, my God!" cried Holly. "You play the tables?"

He nodded. "It's just a numbers game."

"Yeah," said Jack. "And you should see the numbers he pockets!"

Dan looked at Missy, hoping she wouldn't disapprove. Olivia had given him hell when she'd found out he and Steven had been spending their weekends at the Bellagio. They weren't exactly wild party guys—to them it had been an interesting exercise in math and probability. To Olivia it had been unacceptable—until she found out how much they'd won.

Missy wrinkled her nose at him, but said nothing. He needed to know that she wasn't cross with him. "Do you like Vegas?" She shrugged. "I've never been. I always thought it would be fun though. I don't know how to gamble, but one day I want to go see the shows. That would be cool."

She'd never been to Vegas? He'd have to fix that. She'd love it. He smiled at her, but the conversation had already moved on. Ben was trying to convince Jack that Vegas was the only option for Pete's bachelor party. She smiled back at him and leaned a little closer. He'd love to take her to Vegas, even take her to a show. Give her a chance to get all dressed up. He realized that this was one of their many differences. As much as he loved this place, the beautiful lake, the great group of friends, breakfasts out on the Boathouse deck like this, nights spent listening and dancing to the band, to him it was all new and novel. To her, it was her everyday life and she craved the chance to get away from it sometimes. He put an arm around her shoulders, determined to give her all the chances she wanted.

"Whatever you guys decide," Pete was saying, "I'm up for it, but for now, we need to get going." He and Holly were heading back to LA for a few days.

As they stood to leave, Dan rose too. He wanted to talk to Holly. He was relieved when Emma turned to Missy to ask her about some recipe. "I'll be back," he said, and followed Pete and Holly out into the square."

"S'up, Dan?" asked Pete.

Dan looked back over his shoulder to make sure they were out of earshot. "I wanted to ask Holly a favor."

"Of course," she said. "What can I do?"

Dan shifted from one foot to the other. He'd been so sure of this, but as Holly looked at him expectantly, he wasn't so convinced. Maybe it was a bad idea?

Pete saved him "Was it about the fundraiser?"

"Kind of."

Holly raised an eyebrow.

"If Missy and I come, she'll need something to wear and I'd like to buy it. I wondered if you might help?"

The last of his hesitation dissolved at Holly's response. "Damn, Dan! You surprised me, sweetie. You're not as clueless as I thought!"

Dan grinned. This was why he liked her. She was straightforward, just like Missy. She wasn't mocking him, she was genuinely surprised, and pleased.

"I'd love to help, and I know her taste and what suits her. In fact I can probably get her into the store between now and then to try stuff on."

"That'd be great," said, Dan, "But do you think you could find her something this week too?"

Holly looked puzzled.

"Something she could wear to do dinner and a show in Vegas?"

Holly grinned. "I'd love to. You're really not the clueless geek you make out to be, are you?"

"Holly!" Pete scowled at her.

Dan laughed. "I hope not, but I have a lot to learn, I'm hoping you guys will help me figure it all out."

"I'll do anything I can, anytime. But I'm not so sure Bigshot here can help, he's pretty clueless himself. It would never occur to him to get *me* a dress." Holly gave Pete a pointed look, before turning back to Dan. "We'll be back midweek and I have the perfect one in mind for a little trip to Vegas. I'll call you, okay?"

"Thanks, I appreciate it."

"No problem at all."

Pete smiled. "Though it may become a problem if you keep showing me up!"

Dan grinned, "Don't worry, big guy, I'll give you tips on how to treat your lady right."

Holly laughed, delighted at the look on Pete's face. "Oh, Dan, you are priceless! You can help me keep this one in line."

Dan shrugged at Pete with a smile. "Thanks guys."

"Yeah, thanks a lot," Pete said with a rueful grin as he went to get in his truck.

"I'll call you," said Holly.

Dan made his way back to the table where Missy still chatted with Emma. Jack stood by the railing over the lake, talking into his cell phone.

Ben came out from the restaurant. "Here's the key, bud. You can go over any time."

"Thanks, we're going to go straight from here."

"We?"

Dan nodded.

Ben smiled. "Okay. They told me to let you know that they'd be happy to rent it to you. They really want to see some return on it soon. So even if you want to buy it, they'd be happy to rent it to you 'til you close."

Dan thought about that. "And the sale includes all the furnishings?"

"Right down to linens and cutlery. It's all good quality too. I love it. You could move in today if you wanted to. All you'd need is your toothbrush."

Dan liked that idea. "We'd better go take a look then."

~ ~ ~

Dan opened the front gate and let Missy walk up the path ahead of him. He was glad she'd agreed to come see the place with him. He already knew he wanted it. He didn't care what it was like inside. It was her favorite house. He wanted it for her. If she didn't like the way it was inside, he'd change it to whatever she wanted. He only hoped she would agree to come and live here with him. She started up the front steps then turned back to look at him.

"I can't believe this, Dan! I loved this house as a kid. I love it now. To think you might live here is crazy."

He smiled and put his arms around her. "You know that what I want most is for *us* to live here. You, me, and Scotty. That's my hope."

She nodded, her eyes liquid silver, strengthening his hope.

"Come on, then." He led her up the last few steps and unlocked the front door. "After you."

She stepped inside and he followed, into a grand entrance hall with a sweeping staircase. Missy looked at him, her face unreadable. She walked past the staircase, through to a huge living area. A row of French doors gave a beautiful view of the lake. They opened up to a brick patio area, filled with hanging baskets and edged by trellises with climbing flowers. Beyond the patio, lawns led down to the water's edge. There was a little sandy beach and what looked like a boat shed; the large dock had a boat-lift and a little screened-in room. Dan took it all in, loving what he saw.

He turned to Missy. She looked sad. "What is it, Miss?"

She shook her head. "Nothing. It's beautiful, isn't it?"

"It is, but what's wrong?"

"It's just me. It makes me sad that its soul has gone. I used to love coming here when it was the DeWinters' place. It was such a friendly place, full of laughter and love. Right now, it feels like your apartment. It is beautiful, but it's so impersonal. It's not a home, it's a showpiece."

He came to stand before her. "But we can change that, Miss. We can make it *our* home. Fill it with our life and our laughter. Fill it with our love, the three of us. What do you say?"

"I don't know, Dan. I can't see me and Scotty here. Can you imagine how long that rug would stay cream-colored? I couldn't relax around all this expensive furniture. I'd be too worried about breaking something."

"But it'll be our furniture, if we want to keep it, it won't matter if we break it. Or we can get rid of it all, furnish it how we want it, make it comfortable and homey." She looked so uncertain. He didn't know what else to say. He'd hoped she would be happy and excited. He needed to walk away again, just for a minute. He walked through to the kitchen and, seeing it, his need to be alone evaporated. He called back to her. "You have to see this, Miss."

She appeared in the doorway and grinned. "This hasn't changed much. This was the heart of the place."

"I can see why." It was an old-style country kitchen, now given the best of modern finishes. There was one of those big ranges and a double fridge, sub-zero. Sturdy pine cabinets lined the walls and a large island stood in the middle with bar stools along one side. Double sinks stood under a window that looked out onto a side yard with apple trees and a little herb garden. A sturdy farmhouse table stood in front of a bay window, with more French doors leading out to a pool. Dan went and sat at the table. This felt like a homey space.

"Can't you just see Scot sitting here doing his homework?" He knew from the smile on her face that she could, and that she loved the idea. He pushed his advantage. "And I'll bet his homework would get done a lot quicker if he knew we couldn't go in the pool 'til it was finished."

She laughed at that.

"Life would be a lot different for him here, Miss. It would be different for all of us. Better for all of us, don't you think?"

Her eyes were troubled now, but still light gray, not dark. "I think it would be, Danny." She'd called him Danny! That felt like a good omen. He relaxed a little as she continued. "I just don't know though. I mean, it's all so fast. Maybe we should take it slow? See how well we work together over time. I don't want you to buy a place for a family if we're not going to become one. I don't want you to become an even bigger part of Scotty's life if it's not going to work out." She came and sat on his lap at the table. "I want you. I want this. I want us, more than I've ever wanted anything, but it's all so fast. What if it's not real?"

He closed his hand around the back of her neck and felt her relax against him. "It's not really that fast Miss. We've known each other for months. We got to know each other as friends. There was no putting on a front to impress each other. You know me. You've seen who I am. You know I'm quiet, I'm messy, I don't cook, or clean. You know that sometimes I don't talk for hours on end. You know I need more alone time than anyone you've ever met." He bit his lip, but needed to say it, "You also know that sometimes, when there's too much emotion or it all gets confusing, I need to walk away for a while to clear my head."

She nodded; he knew she understood.

"And as well as you know me, Miss, I know you too. I know that you have the biggest heart in the tiniest body. That you laugh a lot and you work too hard. I know that you're bossy and you talk too much." She wrinkled her nose at him, but she was smiling. "I understand who you are, and you understand me, we just work. It's faster than normal, yes. But when you know something is right, time doesn't matter. If you want to look for worst case scenario—and you know I have—the worst that can happen is that we discover we don't match each other in everyday life. That we get on each other's nerves and that our blend of perfect isn't so perfect when reality sets in. But we both care about each other too much as friends to let it deteriorate into anything horrible. And we both love Scot too much to put him through any misery. So worst case is we discover we don't work, and we go our separate ways. I'm moving up here anyway. I want this life, I want this house.

Most of all I want you. If you decide you don't want me, I'll survive, but I'm hoping you'll decide you do want me. My relationship with Scot will continue either way. The two of us have our own thing. I hope it will be as part of our family, but if not, nothing is going to break the bond we share." He could see tears shining in her eyes now, but he was hoping they were happy ones.

She wrapped her arms around his neck and kissed his lips. "You're right. I am bossy, I do talk too much, but I'm better when I'm around you. I don't need to make everything happen when you're with me. I can relax and just be. I don't know what it is about you, hero, but you make everything feel better. You make *me* feel better." She made him feel better too, and they both knew it.

"Is that a yes? Are we going to do this?"

She nodded. "We'll have to think about how it will work, talk to Scotty, but yes. I think we should try it."

He held her tight, feeling happier than he'd known it was possible to feel. "We'll make it work, Miss. It's going to be great. I know it." He buried his face in her hair, breathing in the beachy scent of her, knowing this was one of the most important moments of his life.

~ ~ ~

Missy snuggled in Dan's lap. For something that sounded so crazy, this couldn't feel more right. They needed to talk to Scot—though she doubted he'd be able to see anything beyond the fact that he'd get to spend more time with Dan. Well, that and living on the lake *and* having a pool. She reached up to touch Dan's cheek. Looking into his eyes, she really couldn't believe how lucky she was. "I love you, Danny."

His smile was so soft and sweet. "Now I know you do. Only the people who love me call me that. And I love you, my little Missy."

She drew his head down to her and playfully nipped at his lips. He closed his hand around the back of her neck and rubbed his nose against hers. She lifted her lips to him as his mouth covered hers in a long, sweet kiss.

"Come on, then," he said when that kiss finally ended. "Let's go explore our house, shall we?"

She slid off his knee, hoping their exploring might lead them upstairs soon. When he kissed her like that, she found it hard to think of anything else.

His eyes twinkled as he took her hand. "Let's finish off downstairs first, shall we? I've got a feeling the bedroom may take a while."

He led her back through the living room and into a formal dining room where a beautiful oak table was set for ten with china and crystal. Dan rolled his eyes. "I don't see that getting much use, do you?"

Missy smiled. "It'd be nice to have the gang over for dinner." She'd love to cook for them all sometimes, but she couldn't even fit everyone in her house, let alone seat them.

"Oh." Dan grinned. "That would be quite cool. I can help—if we want to feed them pizza? Or you train me as your sous chef?"

She laughed. "Don't worry, hero. I'm not going to try to domesticate you. I love you just the way you are."

She especially loved the way his eyes shone when he smiled like that.

"I'd like to get the hang of some of the domestic stuff, though. I don't want you to be landed with all of it."

She smiled to herself. She appreciated the thought, but she could no more see Dan making dinner than she could see herself writing computer programs. It may not be 'politically correct', but she knew herself and she knew Dan. She loved to play house, he didn't. It was fine by her. "We'll work it out," she said. "Now let's see...Oh!" She'd opened the door to what used to be Mr. DeWinter's library. It certainly reflected the changing times. Where once there had stood beautiful bookshelves, filled with leather-bound books, there was now a full media room. A giant TV screen covered one wall and theater seating for twelve was set up in front of it.

"Wow! She exclaimed. "This will give a whole new meaning to movie night."

Dan grinned at her. "We can sit in the back row after Scot's gone to bed."

She laughed. "Can you see him ever going to bed when he's got this place?"

"Hm, maybe not. Especially once we rig up his game systems to play on it."

"Oh, no! I'll never see either of you again!"

He waggled his eyebrows. "Oh, you will. From what I saw online.... Come on." He took her hand and led her back to the entrance hall and up the grand staircase.

Missy looked around. "How many bedrooms are there? I never knew, it seemed like there were dozens of them."

"Six."

"Six bedrooms? That's a lot of space we're going to waste, Dan. Are you sure you need a place this big? You could just move in with us and save a fortune."

Dan stopped and turned to her. "I'd love that too. We don't need to do this, if you don't want to. I love your house, you know that. I thought you'd like this better, though. It's your favorite house. Everything it's got for Scotty. But if you don't want it, we don't have to live here. Can I show you something first though?"

She nodded and followed him up the rest of the stairs and into the master bedroom where she stopped dead. The whole room shimmered with light reflected from the lake. A balcony ran the entire length of the room, beyond sliding glass doors. Dan slid them back and it was like having an indoor/outdoor bedroom. She followed him onto the balcony, the view was spectacular.

"Look." He pointed at a hot tub.

"Oh, wow! I love those things."

"Me too. Skinny dipping and star gazing. Come back inside, though." He led her to the king sized bed that stood on a raised platform.

She laughed. "I hope I don't fall out. It's a long way down."

"You won't, I won't let you. Come on up." He climbed onto the bed and lay down. She lay down beside him and he rolled over to kiss her. Wonderful as this house was, she forgot all about it when his lips met hers. She was lost in his kiss, in everything he awoke in her. When he lifted his head she sighed. She wanted him, so badly.

It seemed he felt the same way. "I should probably sign on the dotted line before we christen the place, beautiful." He touched her cheek, "Don't look so disappointed, I can have the paperwork done within the hour."

She laughed, relieved. "Yes, please!"

"Okay then, but for now, close your eyes." She closed them and he lay back down beside her. "Now, when you open them, imagine that you're waking up in the morning and this is what you're seeing."

Missy opened her eyes and gasped. The way the bed was set up at this height made it seem as though it were floating on the lake. All she could see was sparkling water. She turned to Dan. "It's amazing! But you know the best part? What I'm looking forward to most?"

He shook his head. "What?"

"Waking up next to you."

His beautiful smile spread across his face. She felt her heart swell in her chest. Yes, this house was wonderful, but it was Dan she wanted. She'd happily stay in her own house, or go live in a tent if it meant she got to wake up with him every morning. The love shining in the big brown eyes smiling back at her told her he felt the same way.

"That's how I feel too, Miss. I just want to be with you. This house is awesome. I think we can make it a real home, the three of us. But what matters most is that we're together, not where we are."

She nodded happily.

"*But,*" he continued with a smile, "since we're lucky enough to be together *and* be in a great house, there are a couple more things I want you to see." He got up from the bed and beckoned for her to follow. He opened a door off to the left. There was an enormous walk-in closet and dressing area. Beyond that was a bathroom with a double steam shower and a huge corner Jacuzzi tub, surrounded by picture windows.

Missy wandered around the bathroom and wrinkled her nose. "It's gorgeous, but considering this bathroom and closet space is bigger than the entire upstairs of my house, you would have thought they'd have put in his and hers sinks."

Dan grinned. "They did."

She looked around. "Where? There's only one sink."

"In here there is, yes. What they put in are his and hers bathrooms. Come see."

She followed him back out through the dressing area, then the bedroom. He opened a door off to the right to reveal another closet, dressing area and bathroom that mirrored the first.

"Oh, my God!" She laughed. "I guess this is the *his* side?" she asked, looking at the silver toned tile.

"Yeah," agreed Dan. "If you don't mind, I'm not going to fight you for that peachy colored one. It's yours."

Missy wandered back out into the bedroom, a little overwhelmed at the thought that that would be *her* bathroom. She sat down in one of two armchairs beside the fireplace, caught up in a storm of emotions. She wanted him. She was in love with him, no question. She was so happy and excited at the thought of moving in here with him. She was thrilled that Scot's life would change so much. He'd have a guy in his life who loved him and could guide him. He'd have a pool and live on the lake. She didn't quite believe it was all real.

Dan came and sat on the floor at her feet. He picked up a remote and pressed a button. The fire sprang to life.

He grinned at her. "I love a real fire, but these imitation logs are so realistic."

She nodded, they were. And made for a lot less cleaning.

"And," he looked up at her through lowered lashes. "I thought maybe we could get a big sheepskin rug for in front of the fire...and after the hot tub."

The thought of writhing naked with him on a rug in front of the fire set her body alight. He ran his hand up her leg. "You know, I guess we don't *really* need to wait 'til the papers are signed." He tugged at her hands and she slid down from the chair to join him on the floor. They didn't need to wait 'til they had a rug either.

Chapter Fifteen

"Have you told Mom?" asked Jack.

Dan shook his head. "I haven't had chance to turn around yet. After we left you guys at the restaurant, Missy and I came to see the place. Then she went to get Scotty from Michael's. We thought it best if she talked to him first. I went back to see Ben, signed a rental contract for two weeks so we can move in right away while the sale goes through. Then I went to get the RV, brought it over here. Then you showed up."

"It's all happening fast, Danny. Are you sure about this?"

Dan nodded. "I remember asking you the same question when you first met Emma. My answer is the same as yours was then—Never been more sure of anything in my life."

Jack grinned. "That's what I was hoping to hear, little bro. I'm thrilled for you. I'm thrilled for me too. It's going to be awesome having you living up here. I know Mom will be over the moon, too. Call her when you get chance. She loved it here when she came for the wedding. Maybe with you here and bringing Lexi out here when I get the offices set up, we could persuade her to move here."

Dan cocked his head. He hadn't considered that.

"I guess the possibility of grand-babies would seal the deal too," grinned Jack.

Dan frowned. "Well, the grand-babies will be down to you. What do you think she'll make of a ready-made fourteen year old grandson?"

"Scot? You know she'll love him. He couldn't be more like you if he *was* your son!"

That made Dan smile. "He couldn't, could he? You know I've never wanted kids. When you brought me up here to meet him, I wanted to be like a mentor." He looked at Jack, "Hell, I'll say it, I thought if I could be half the big brother you are, then I'd be doing something great. But now, Jack, I want to be his dad. I know he's got a real dad somewhere, but I want to be a dad to him. Is that crazy?"

"It's not crazy, Danny. It's awesome! You're the best dad Scot could hope to find. And don't kid yourself that he already has one. He doesn't. There's a guy out there somewhere who is his biological father. Anyone can be a father." Jack stopped and looked at him. "Sorry bro. Any asshole can be a father, we know that better than most, but it takes someone special to be a dad. In Scot's case it would take someone very special indeed. You really are the best dad that kid could ever hope to find; you're perfect for him."

Dan smiled. He felt that it was true. "I'm going to work hard at it, Jack. I really want to be."

"You already are. There's no need to try. But tell me how you're managing to swing this. What's going on with Prometheus, are you really selling out? What are you going to do up here?"

Dan filled him in on the developments with the merger.

"You know I dislike Olivia, but I'm grateful to her. I think she's done you a huge favor in a roundabout way."

"I do too. It's like all her manipulating finally pushed me over the edge and I woke up to the fact that I've been sleep-walking through a life I don't want with a woman I don't even like. Now I get to come up here and a live the kind of life I really want, with the woman I love."

Jack grinned. "It's a great feeling, isn't it?"

Dan nodded. "And I even get to do new and challenging work that I'm looking forward to."

"What's that then?"

"Do you remember Ryan from Berkeley?"

Jack nodded, "Yeah, he's a good guy. Where is he these days?"

Dan told him about Ryan's visit and job offer.

"Wow, that's pretty cool. When do you start?"

Dan frowned. He was still waiting to hear back from Ryan. "Whenever they get done with the whole security vetting process. Ryan said it should only take a couple of weeks."

"So, soon you'll have a new job, a new house, and a new son. I have to ask, is Missy going to be your new wife?"

"I hope so. It's just that the whole getting married thing had never occurred to me before." He looked at Jack. "Should I have asked her to marry me first? I didn't think. I just want to be with her. Have us all move in here."

Jack smiled. "I don't think it makes any difference which way 'round you do it. You're made for each other. When I think of the two of you as individuals, you don't make any sense as a couple. When I see you together it's so obvious, you're perfect for each other."

Dan grinned. "That's something I've had to learn since I met Missy. Logic and reason don't take intangibles into account.

Just because things don't make sense, it doesn't mean they don't make sense."

Jack laughed. "That is so true. But I never thought I'd hear you admit it."

"Me neither. But that little lady is making me realize a lot of things I would never have believed before."

"I'm glad. Missy is good people."

"The best," agreed Dan. "And I want to give her the best, of everything."

"Well, you're making a good start with the best damned house in town!"

"You like it then?"

"I love it! Em's place is special. It's growing on me, and I do love being up at North Cove, but this place is something else. And for you, it couldn't be better, being right here in town and on the lake as well."

"I know. Miss has lived in town all her life. And can you believe this has been her favorite house since she was a kid? She knew the family and used to come to play with their niece."

"Wow! That makes it even more perfect.... And here she comes."

Dan looked up the driveway to where Missy was parking her minivan behind the RV.

"I'm going to get out of here, leave you guys to it," said Jack.

Dan nodded. It had been great to spend this time with Jack, but they'd be able to do that whenever they wanted and right now he wanted to show Scot their new home. Get a feel for what he thought about the whole idea.

"Thanks Jack. I'll call you."

"Sure bro. You can have us over for dinner when you're all settled in."

Dan smiled. Just like Missy had said, and he liked the idea.

"Hey Uncle Jack!" called Scot as he ran past Jack and flung himself at Dan.

Dan wrapped his arms around the kid. "Hey, champ."

"Dan, Dan, Dan! Mom says we can come stay with you here for a while!"

Stay here? For a while? Dan was thinking of it as live here. For good. He looked up at Missy who had been saying goodbye to Jack. She smiled as she came to join them.

"So you two are going to stay here for a while?" he asked pointedly. He relaxed when he saw her smile.

"Yeah. I told Scotty it's like when you and me were testing out hugs before we decided to go out with each other."

Dan understood. She needed to be cautious for Scotty's sake. Scot grinned up at him, still hugging his waist. "And we know how well the hugging turned out, huh, Dan? So, you gonna show me around our new house?"

Dan laughed as he led them through the front door. He had the feeling this was going to turn out really well.

Missy slid the tray of sweet potatoes into the oven with a smile. It still tickled her that Jack had told her his secret to making the best sweet potato fries she'd ever tasted. Emma had tried and tried to wheedle it out of her, but Jack had sworn her to secrecy. Emma prided herself on being the best cook of all of them, but she couldn't match Jack's fries. He claimed he kept his secret because she wouldn't need him anymore once she knew it. Missy knew how ridiculous that was. Despite a rocky start in learning to trust him, Emma was completely besotted with Jack and seemed to become more so with every week that passed since they'd gotten married.

Missy took a seat at the huge island in the kitchen. Was this really her life now? Would she and Dan get married, like Emma predicted? She hugged herself as she sat on the stool— she sure hoped so! She loved seeing how happy and in love Emma and Jack were. She was starting to believe that she and Dan could have that too. Right now, while she was making dinner, Dan and Scot were upstairs, supposedly coding, but from the occasional bang and yell, she guessed they were probably playing a video game instead. She'd always battled with Scotty about homework being done before games. Dan had explained to her that when he was a kid, he'd needed to give his mind a break from boring school stuff and play or code for a while before going back to it for homework. She hadn't been sure at first, but the two of them had played a video game while she'd made dinner on Monday night. After they'd eaten, Scotty had brought his books to the table and buckled down without being asked. It seemed that was becoming their routine. She liked it.

Her cell phone rang and she scooped it up, thrilled to see Chance's name on the display.

"Hey, big bruv!" She answered. "What's going on?"

"That's what I was going to ask you!"

Missy's heart sank. She'd told her dad she and Scot were going to stay with Dan for a couple of weeks. He'd met Dan a few times now, and seemed to like him. Her dad never gave much away, but he'd teased Dan about being so smart. He'd never tease someone if he didn't like them. She'd known she'd have to tell Chance too, but she'd wanted him to meet Dan first, so he'd understand.

"What do you mean?"

"Don't give me that shit, Miss!"

She gulped, he sounded mad!

"Who is he?"

"Chance, he's the guy I've been telling you about for months. The one who's been helping Scotty." She couldn't believe Chance would be too hard on a man who was helping Scot out.

"I thought that was some geek who was working with my nephew—not working on my little sister!"

She laughed. "Your little sister is a grown woman, Chance. A grown woman who is capable of choosing a good man."

"Hmph!"

"Oh, stop playing the badass! This is me you're talking to, remember." She was glad to hear him laugh. He rarely did these days. "I know it's all happening a bit fast, but he's a good man. He's good to Scot and he's good to me."

"We'll see."

"Yes, you will. I want you to meet him. Can you still come for my birthday?"

"I said I'd come, didn't I?"

"You did, but I know things can change." She loved her brother dearly, but she'd learned better than to expect him to come back to Summer Lake. It was too painful for him. She understood that.

"Well, they have changed."

Missy bit back the disappointment. She'd so wanted him to be there for her birthday, to meet Dan, spend time with Scot. She let out a sigh. "Maybe you can come sometime soon then?"

"I can. This change means I want to come this weekend...and stay for your birthday...and maybe a while longer."

"Really?" she squealed.

His deep laugh rumbled down the phone. "Really. I've got some stuff of my own going on, Miss. Before I can move forward in life, I think it's time I come back. Make peace with the past."

Missy didn't know what to say, Chance rarely mentioned the past. "Are you okay?"

"I'm fine, honey. And I think I'm starting to get better too."

"Oh, Chancey, I hope so. You can come stay here if you want?" She couldn't imagine him staying with their dad. He'd have to be a long way over the past before that happened.

"Thanks, but no thanks. How about you let me rent your place from you since you're staying with the geek-boy?"

"He's a man, not a boy!"

Chance laughed. "We'll see. And you're not arguing about the geek part?"

She pursed her lips. "Do you really think this is the best way to ask me a favor?"

It was good to hear him laugh so much. "I'm trying to do you a favor. Pay you some rent on your house."

"Yeah, right Chance. Whatever you say. Of course you can stay at my place and no you cannot pay me rent. How long do you think you might be here?"

There was a long silence before he answered. "We'll see."

That was his standard answer. He wasn't big on committing to anything. "At least tell me when you're coming?"

"This weekend. I'll be there when I get there. I've still got a key."

"Good, but Chancey, please let me know when you're arriving? I can't wait to see you. I can't wait for you to meet Dan. Promise me you'll go easy on him?"

"You know I don't do promises, Miss."

Damn! That had been a stupid thing to say. "Sorry. I'm just excited. Are you really going to stay 'til my birthday?"

"Sure am, honey."

"Thanks. You have no idea...."

"I've gotta go. Tell Shorty I'll see him next week, and tell geek-boy he'd better be good to you both. Love ya."

"I love you, Chancey, bye."

He'd already hung up. She couldn't imagine what was going on with him, that he was coming a week early for her birthday. She'd known he'd want to meet Dan—and scare him off if he could. But it sounded like it was about so much more than that. She slid down from the stool and went to check on the grill.

The house was so well laid out. A door from the kitchen opened out to a little deck where the grill stood. From there a path led down to an herb garden, then on to the vegetable garden. She could happily get used to living like this. Once the grill was hot enough, she went back to the kitchen to fetch the burgers. She looked at her phone sitting on the counter. She sure hoped, for Chance's sake, that he was ready to make peace with his past. She also hoped, for her own sake, that he would like Dan, the man who was starting to look like her and Scot's future.

~ ~ ~

Dan pushed his plate away. "That was wonderful. Thanks, Miss. I'm not going to tell Jack, but you make those fries better than he does."

Missy smiled, pleased that so far Dan had loved everything she'd cooked.

"Yeah, Mom. That was awesome, thanks." Scot wiped the ketchup off his face with his sleeve. She didn't have the heart to pull him up over it. He looked so happy.

Dan gave her a little smile that said he knew that her instinct had been to do just that and he was proud of her for holding back. To think she'd been a mom for almost half of her life, and he'd never had or wanted kids, yet Dan was teaching her a lot about what worked best with Scotty. Probably because he remembered all too well what it felt like to be in Scot's shoes.

"Come on, champ. Help me with the dishes so your mom can put her feet up?"

"Okay. Then who's up for a movie?"

"What about homework?"

"All done!" They both said at the same time. Dan held his hand up and Scot high-fived him with a grin.

"So. Movie?"

"Actually," said Dan. "I was wondering if you'd come for a walk into town with me?"

Scot looked at him. "Walk? Why?"

Dan laughed. "Because you've got to walk before you can run and I'm going to have you out running with me before Christmas."

Missy smiled to herself. She'd been surprised that Dan had managed to fit in his run every morning. He'd been walking with Scot to the bus stop, then running for an hour. She'd been leaving for work by the time he came back. She wasn't sure he'd ever be able to get Scotty to join him though.

"And I can't ask your mom to come with me because it's about a surprise for her." Dan's eyes twinkled and she wondered what he might have in store now. Yesterday morning he'd returned from his run with chocolate croissants from the bakery. Apparently when he'd learned that she loved them, he'd talked to Ben, who had added them to the menu. The twinkle faded though, as he said, "And besides, it doesn't seem fair to ask your mom to walk anywhere since she works so hard all day."

She frowned. He'd been trying to persuade her to at least cut back on her cleaning schedule. He may be right that she worked too hard, but she didn't know how to do anything else. "I'm not too tired. I'll come for a walk with you."

"Sorry, but I do have a surprise in store for you, so you can't." He looked so pleased with himself, she couldn't even feel upset. And she was still tired, though nowhere near as bad as last week. "Okay. Maybe I can figure out how to set up the movie for when you get back."

Dan and Scot exchanged a look.

"Don't worry about it, Mom," said Scot with a laugh.

"Err, yeah." Dan smiled. "Maybe you should have a go at the computer in your office instead?"

He'd tried to convince her that they did need six bedrooms, by setting them each up with an office. His own was the biggest, and looked to her like something out of a SciFi movie with huge monitors and server racks sitting around. Scot's was almost as bad, and apparently was going to get even more so over the weekend when they got rid of all the bedroom furniture and brought in more desks and equipment. Her own 'office' was beautiful. It looked out over the lake and had its own fireplace and little balcony. The computer in there was a big, scary thing though. She had yet to get the hang of it. Dan wanted her to cut back on the cleaning, not just to get some rest, but also so that she could start taking classes online and working towards her degree. It'd take a while though, before she trusted that all this was real, that it would last, before she would loosen her grip on her only source of income.

"Maybe I will take a shot at it." She could go and sit and stare out at the lake while the computer went through its drawn out boot up. Hopefully they'd be back before she needed to attempt to log on to it.

"Go on," said Dan. He seemed to know what she was thinking. "Enjoy the sunset up there. We'll see to the dishes and set up the movie."

She got up from the table. He curled an arm around her waist and pulled her to him for a kiss.

"Hey, where's mine?" asked Scot when Dan let her go. He hugged her waist and pecked her cheek. "Love you, Mom."

Missy grinned. "Love you, son." Not only was he hugging on Dan every chance he got, he was showing her much more affection too. "Give me a shout when you get back," she said and headed upstairs.

~ ~ ~

"What's the big surprise?" asked Scot as they set out on the short walk to the resort.

Dan smiled at him. "We're taking your mom to Vegas, to see a show!"

Scot pulled a face. "*We?* As in, including *me?*"

"Yeah. Is that a problem?"

Scot's face was a picture of disgust. "Have you ever been to the kind of shows she likes? I have. They're dumb. People singing and dancing and they go on forever. It's soooo boring!"

Dan had to laugh. He understood how Scot felt and his face was so expressive it was quite comical. "I know what you mean, champ, but this one is awesome. It's more like the circus, with people flying around and doing acrobatics and such. You'll love it."

Scot did not look convinced.

"We get to fly up there too."

That sparked a tiny flicker of interest, though it faded quickly. "When is it?"

"Tomorrow night. We'll pick you up from school and head out."

"Oh. Do I *have* to go?"

Dan thought about it. He'd wanted the three of them to go together, but he didn't want to force the kid if he hated the idea. "Why, what are you thinking?"

Scot grinned. "I'm teaching Ethan how to use Linux. I'll bet his dad would let me stay there again."

"Maybe. We probably need to ask your mom first though."

"But that'll ruin your surprise!" Scot looked crestfallen. "I don't want to do that."

"It won't. All she needs to know is that you're staying at Ethan's. Not that it's so you don't have to go to Vegas."

Scot brightened. "Oh, yeah. Cool."

Dan took out his phone. "I'll text Michael and check with him."

~ ~ ~

When they got back to the house, Scot grinned at Dan. "I'll set up the movie while you go hide the dress."

"Thanks, champ."

"No problem. You got me out of seeing one of Mom's shows *and* got me a night at Ethan's. I owe you one."

Dan laughed to himself as he ran up the stairs to hang the dress Holly had given him in his closet. It was a beautiful blue color. He knew Missy would look stunning in it. Holly had told him that Missy had loved it when she'd seen it in the store. He'd been stunned when she'd told him how much it cost. Pete had grinned at him, "I did warn you that expensive dresses are Holly's specialty."

Holly had seemed worried. "Is that okay?" she'd asked.

Dan had smiled and nodded while Pete had reassured her. "Don't worry about it, sweetheart. Dan's not only a tech genius, he's a financial one too. He could buy and sell the rest of us without ever touching his savings."

That had felt uncomfortable—because it was true. Yet even with all his money that was supposed to make such a big difference, the woman he loved was still going out scrubbing other people's toilets every day. He needed to find a way to make her see sense.

He knocked on the door to her office before he went in. She smiled at him, looking a little guilty from her spot in the armchair looking out at the lake. Her computer blinked at the login screen, just as he'd expected.

"You don't need to knock."

"I like to."

He pulled her up from her chair and slid in underneath her. She nestled in his lap and he closed his hand around the back of her neck and kissed her deeply. She did go limp when he did that.

When his lips left hers she smiled. "You know you can do whatever you want with me any time you get me by the scruff of the neck like that."

He laughed. "Not this time, I can't. Scot's waiting for us to go watch the movie. What I want to do with you will have to wait 'til he's gone to bed."

She put her hands on his shoulders and rubbed her nose against his. "I hope it's a short movie."

Dan did too.

Chapter Sixteen

Missy looked at Scot across the breakfast table. She was still amazed at the way he'd gotten up every morning this week without her having to call him. She looked at Dan sitting next to him, the two of them working their way through the bacon and eggs she'd made. She'd been concerned at first that she might be spending her nights sleeping alone in that big bed, while Dan worked on his computer. So far though they'd gone to bed together every night. She smiled at the memories. They'd woken up together too. Though she thought of Dan as a night owl, one part of him was definitely a morning person! She hoped that this was the pattern they were setting, not just a honeymoon period that would slip away.

"Scot, honey. I'm thinking maybe you should come home after school and get your homework done. Uncle Chance is coming this weekend and we both know you won't get anything done while he's here. We can take you over to Ethan's once you're done."

Instead of the argument she'd feared, Scot grinned at her, then looked at Dan. She saw Dan wink at him.

"Okay, what's going on?" she asked.

"What do you think, champ? Should we tell her now?"

Scot nodded eagerly. "Go on, tell her. I want to see her face."

Missy laughed. "Hello? I'm sitting right here! Will someone tell me something?"

Dan smiled his beautiful smile and she knew that, like Scot, she would have no argument to offer.

"Scotty can't come home after school, because we won't be here."

"Why? Where will we be?"

"Vegas!" said Scot. "He's taking you to see one of your shows and I don't have to go!"

Missy looked from Scot to Dan. "Vegas? How can we do that?"

Dan reached across the table and took her hand. "We're flying up this afternoon." There was concern in his eyes as he squeezed her hand. "If you want to? I got us tickets for Cirque du Soleil."

"Really? I've always wanted to see that!"

He looked relieved. "So you want to?"

Her heart sank. "Only if you got us the cheap seats, I don't have anything I could wear otherwise."

Scot jumped up, grinning at Dan. "Can I go get it?"

Dan grinned back at him. "Please, champ."

As Scot shot upstairs, Missy looked at Dan. She was a little concerned. "We could have taken him you know. I've taken him to see shows before."

Dan smiled. "Don't think I'd leave him out. That was my original plan, but apparently he'd rather have a tooth pulled than see another one. He asked me to help him get out of it. Do you mind? We don't have to go if you don't want to, but he was so keen to get another night at Ethan's that I thought this might be okay."

He looked so uncertain. The poor man was trying to do something nice, both for her and for Scotty. She squeezed his hand back. "Oh, Danny. I do want to. I'm just surprised. And Scotty will be fine. It's a treat for him not to have to go, I'm sure."

"It is. A real treat," said Scot as he reappeared carrying a dress. "I wish I'd get to see you in this though, Mom. You're gonna look so good. You haven't worn a pretty dress since Auntie Em's wedding."

He held up a beautiful midnight blue colored evening dress. Missy caught her breath. It was the one she'd seen in Holly's store last weekend. It was gorgeous. And she knew it cost more than she made in a month! She looked at Dan.

"I hope it's alright?" he asked.

"Alright? It's fabulous! But Dan, it...."

He held up a hand with a stern look. "I know what you're going to say, but please, Miss, leave it?"

He spoke with such finality that she said nothing.

He looked at her, eyebrows raised. "Please? How about you go try it on so Scotty can see you in it?"

"Yeah," said Scot. "Go put it on, Mom."

She took the dress into the guest bathroom. It fit perfectly. It was absolutely beautiful. She hurried back to the kitchen and saw two jaws drop open.

Dan's face as he said, "Damn!" was a picture she'd never forget. It sent the tingles racing through her to know she could have that effect on him.

"Wow, Mom! Just, wow." Scot grinned. "You should wear pretty dresses all the time."

Dan nodded. "We'll have to work on that, huh, champ?"

Missy smiled at them, delighted. Delighted with the dress and with both of their reactions. "Thank you, Danny. It's beautiful."

"No, Miss. *You* are beautiful. The dress just shows you off, right Scotty?"

"Right."

"Well, thank you both." She checked the clock. "But for now I need to get out of this, and we need to get moving if you're going to make the bus. Have you got everything you need for tonight?"

"Oh, no! I need to...." Scot ran off back up the stairs.

Dan came and put his arms around her. "So beautiful," he murmured. "Are you sure you want to go? If you're worried about him, we could stay here?" He ran his fingertip along her collarbone. "I'm sure we could find something to do?" He touched his lips to hers. "Maybe dance in the bedroom? Or you can let me take you to the Bellagio, see your show, and dance in a different bedroom?"

She pressed herself against him. "Take me to Vegas, Dan."

He grinned and kissed her again. "I was hoping you'd say that."

"Dan, Dan, Dan! The bus just left!" Scot came bounding down the stairs."

"No worries. It was my fault." He looked at Missy. "Can I borrow the van?"

She nodded. He'd just bought her a dress that was worth more than her old minivan. She looked at Scot. "Are you sure you've got everything now?"

He nodded. "Yep. Don't worry, Mom. You have a great time." He gave her a hug. "Love you. See you tomorrow."

Missy swallowed around the lump that had formed in her throat. "Love you, sunbeam. You make sure *you* have a great time, okay?"

He grinned back at her as he headed for the door. "I will. See ya!"

~ ~ ~

Missy stepped out of the limo in front of the Bellagio. She felt like Cinderella. Her Prince Charming came to take her arm. She looked around, thinking he'd forgotten their bags, but of course the bell-boy was taking care of them.

She smiled up at Dan. "Looks like you've done this before, hero?"

"Yeah. We used to come up here most weekends last winter."

Missy's heart sank. She shouldn't be jealous of his past, she knew that, but she was.

He stopped to look at her, head cocked, that serious expression on his face. "Miss, when I say 'we', I mean me and Steven. Corey sometimes. I never brought Olivia to Vegas. Or any other woman for that matter."

It was silly of her, but she was pleased to hear it. "It's none of my business, Danny, but I'm glad."

His eyes twinkled. "Me too. This feels like coming for the first time."

"Oh look!" Missy had caught sight of the fountains springing to life. "They're so beautiful!"

Dan smiled. "Wait 'til you see them after dark. We can come out after the show. You'll love it."

Missy couldn't wait.

"Mr. Benson. Welcome."

The man behind the desk greeted Dan warmly and nodded at Missy.

"Good to see you, George. How've you been?"

"I'm just fine thanks, and you?"

Dan put an arm around Missy's shoulders. "Better than ever, thanks, George. I'd like you to meet my girlfriend, Missy." George came out from behind the desk to shake Dan's hand, then Missy's. He held on to her hand as he said, "I'm so pleased to meet you, Missy. Dan here is one of the kindest, most decent men I've ever met."

Missy smiled. "It's nice to meet you too, George. And I have to say, I feel the same way." She looked up at Dan. "He is a very special guy."

"He is that, and you must be a special lady yourself. I've only ever known him head straight for the tables." He grinned at Dan, "But tonight I've got you down for a table at Picasso and VIPs at Cirque? I thought it must be another Dan Benson when I saw that, but requesting your suite, it had to be you. Are you waiting on your other guest, or will they be joining you later?"

Missy looked at Dan, wondering what other guest.

"No, it's just us in the end. Scot couldn't come."

"Should I make that a table for two at Picasso then?"

"Yes, please. And, George, would you see if there's any chance we can get a table outside, after the show, too, for dessert?"

"I'll make sure you get one, Dan."

Missy was surprised, and at the same time not surprised, to see how the concierge treated Dan. Just like Herb, at Dan's apartment, this guy obviously liked and respected him. That didn't surprise her at all. What did was Dan's confidence and relaxed manner. He seemed more at home here than he did even at the Boathouse with the gang. This side of him she was getting to see more of could never be described as shy, definitely not clueless as he sometimes described himself. No, he was very much the wealthy young man-about-town. She smiled to herself—and he was all hers!

"Here's your key card," said George. "Your bags are on the way up. Your butler will take care of anything you need, but please give me a call if I can be of service."

Dan shook his hand again. "Thanks, George. We'll be sure and stop by before we leave."

"Enjoy yourselves. It was a real pleasure to meet you, Missy."

"Thank you. You too."

Dan led her to the elevator where he swiped his card in the slot.

"Private floor?" she asked.

He nodded.

"Poor dumb country boy, my ass!" She laughed as the elevator doors closed behind them.

Dan grinned. "I told you. I never claimed to be dumb."

"Well, you can't claim poor or country either, can you?"

"I guess I can't anymore, but it's where I come from. It's what I am, Miss. I learned all this stuff because it's what you do when you're living the life I was trying to live. I never really got the point of it before, but I do now."

"Yeah? What's the point of it now?"

He put his arms around her. "I want to share it all with you. It's fun with you. Seeing you enjoy it makes me enjoy it."

The elevator stopped and the doors opened. She looked around as he took her hand and led her over a bridge across a reflecting pool. "I think you're going to enjoy our suite." His smile was so sexy and so sweet as he added, "In many ways."

~ ~ ~

Dan closed the door behind the butler and turned back into the suite to find Missy. She was out in the atrium. She turned to him, eyes wide.

"It's sooo beautiful, and we've got our own fountain out here, Dan! Come see."

He grinned as he took her hand and she led him to the fountain. He didn't remember ever coming out here in all the times he and Steven had stayed in this suite. Beautiful hadn't meant much to him until he'd met Missy. Before he'd only noticed the upload speeds he could get inside, and the video and audio quality on the huge TV and sound system. Now he noticed that the fountain really was beautiful, as were the flowers out here, but he only noticed them because of how happy they made Missy. And she was truly beautiful.

"We have a great view of the main fountains too, see."

As she stood looking out at the famous fountains shooting up into the air, Dan stood behind her and slid his arms around her waist. As they watched, a wedding party came into view and posed for photographs with the water dancing behind them.

Dan lowered his lips to her ear. "Would you like to get married here, Miss?"

He felt her tense; a few moments passed before she replied. "I've never really thought about it. It's not something I thought I'd ever do."

Hmm. Apparently he hadn't phrased that right. He tried it again. "Would you like for *us* to get married here?"

She spun around to face him. "Danny, what are you saying?"

Her eyes widened. Why did she look so shocked? Then it dawned on him. He was supposed to ask her *if* she wanted to marry him first. Damn! He didn't want to mess it up. He hugged her to him. "Nothing, I just wondered, that's all." She rested her head against his chest and hugged him tight. That was good, right? He'd figure out a way to ask her properly before he brought it up again.

~ ~ ~

Missy felt as though she was living in a dream, sitting on the patio overlooking the fountains. They'd had a wonderful dinner here earlier. The show had been spectacular, she'd never seen anything like it. She felt like a million dollars in the dress Dan had given her. She smiled across the table at him, he *looked* like a million dollars. Gorgeous! She felt all the tingly excitement bubble up, remembering his question about if she'd like to get married here. At first she'd thought he must have been asking a general question, like you'd ask a friend—would you rather get married in church or in Vegas? But then he'd said, for *us* to get married here! Part of her wanted to ask him what he'd meant, if he was asking her to marry him—if he was, that part of her would say yes in a heartbeat. But another part of her was more cautious. She knew she loved him and believed he loved her, but marriage wasn't about the hearts, and flowers, and great sex type being *in love*. Marriage was about the long-haul, getting through the tough times together type *love*. She knew they could do the hearts and flowers—and the great sex, but would their differences tear them apart instead of drawing them together when they hit life's storms? You could never really know 'til it happened, but she had Scotty to think about, so she needed to be sure. Besides, who was she kidding? He hadn't actually asked her. It had probably just come out wrong and that wasn't what he meant at all.

She looked up to find him smiling at her. "Thanks so much, Danny. I don't think I've ever enjoyed a night as much as this."

His smile widened. "I know I haven't, Miss. And this is just the beginning, we can do this whenever we want."

Wouldn't that be wonderful? To be able to do this, with Dan? To think that her life could be like this, and that she could share it with the amazing man sitting across from her? She was at a loss for words. She gasped as the fountains shot up into the air, seeming to dance to the music, sparkling in the light-show that accompanied them. This night could not be more perfect.

Dan's eyes twinkled at her. "I know it's a bit early, but Happy Birthday, beautiful." He held out a jewelry box.

She caught her breath as she took it. "Thank you!"

He grinned. "Open it. See if you like it before you say that."

She opened the box and tears filled her eyes when she saw the necklace inside. It was a delicate silver chain, with a pendant made up of two linked hearts side by side. A smaller heart threaded through the bottom of the other two, so that the pendant looked like one big heart made up of three smaller ones. She felt a tear spill over as she smiled at him.

"I think you know what I mean?" he asked, his head cocked to one side.

She nodded. "It's you, me and Scot, isn't it?"

He nodded.

"Danny, it's gorgeous. *You* are gorgeous. Thank you so much."

He smiled and took her hand. "Happy Birthday, Miss."

"It's not for another week, but it's already the best birthday I've ever had!"

~ ~ ~

Missy clung to his hand as the plane took off from McCarran. He was getting used to having his fingers crushed whenever they flew. He kind of liked it. It reminded him how strong she was, in so many ways. Last night had been awesome. He'd even enjoyed the show, and not just because Missy had enjoyed it so much, either. His original plan had been for them to stay the whole weekend. But they had to get back for Scot. That was okay. They'd come again soon, he was sure. He liked the idea of getting married here. Missy seemed to love the place so much. He'd talked to George this morning and he'd said the Bellagio did packages where they took care of every little detail. He liked that idea too, so that Missy wouldn't be able to overwork herself setting it all up. He bit his lip; he had to figure out how to ask her first though.

Another reason they needed to get back today was that Missy's brother was coming at some point this weekend. He was feeling a little wary about Chance. He knew he'd be under some scrutiny and he hoped it would work out okay. It sounded like Chance was a man to be reckoned with. He was understandably protective of his sister and nephew, but Dan felt the same protectiveness towards them, at least that was something he and Chance had in common. It didn't sound like there would be much else.

Smoke's voice filled the cabin. "You can unbuckle now, if you want, but we may be in for a bumpy ride this morning. I'll let you know if you need to strap back in."

Missy finally released her grip on his fingers. "Sorry, hero" She looked apologetic as he shook his hand trying to get some sensation back. "You'd think I'd be getting used to it by now."

"I don't mind. I like it, you know that. And you'll have plenty of chances to get used to it. How about coming to San Jose with me this week? I want to get some more gear and clothes from my apartment and I need to talk to Leanne, hopefully see Ryan."

Her smile disappeared. "I'd love to, but I can't."

He thought he knew what she was going to say, but he had to ask. "Why not?"

"Scot's in school."

He bit his bottom lip. She was avoiding it. "I know. We could leave after he takes the bus and if we go on Wednesday, he won't be finished at chess club 'til six. We'll easily be back by then. So, what do you say?" He felt bad pushing the issue, but it had to be done.

Her eyes were dark gray now. "I have to work."

There was the real problem. "You don't though, do you, Miss?" he asked gently.

"Yes, I do!" she shot back.

"Miss, we need to talk about it."

She let out a big sigh. "I don't know what to say though, Danny. Or what to do."

He knew she'd arranged for one of the girls from the resort to cover for her so they could leave early yesterday. There had been so many little things he'd wanted to do last week, but hadn't brought them up because he knew she wouldn't take the time off. "We need to figure out what we're going to do though, don't we?" He put an arm around her. "You work too hard. You're still worn out and I don't like to see you doing all that when you don't need to."

"I do need to, though! I have bills to pay, a son to take care of."

"But I can take care of you both, if you'll let me."

She shook her head. "I know you want to be my hero and part of me wants to let you, but I've always made my own way in life. Who would I be if I gave up my job and let you pay for everything? I wouldn't know what to do, or who I was. It would change things between us, too, and I don't want that."

She did have a point. He did want her to give up her job, not worry about money, let him take care of it, of her and Scot. But Missy wasn't exactly the stay-at-home housewife type. She was a doer, strong and independent, that was part of what he loved about her so much. "As I said, we need to talk about it. I know you don't want to be a kept woman." He hoped for a laugh, but didn't get one. "There's got to be some compromise between that and you killing yourself every day cleaning up after other people."

She pursed her lips, but at least she nodded; it was a start.

"How about we both think about it. See what ideas we can come up with and we'll talk about it tomorrow night, after Scot's gone to bed?"

He was liking the ritual they'd started of going up to their room when Scot went to bed. A couple of nights they'd sat in the hot tub, talked and watched the stars. A couple of nights they'd sat in the armchairs by the fire and talked. He'd found and ordered online a big sheepskin rug, so that soon they'd be able to do more than just talk in front of the fire.

"Okay," she said. "Let's do that, but please, Dan, don't expect me to come with you this week. I have a lot of work already lined up and I won't let people down."

Dan nodded. He respected that.

The intercom crackled, then Smoke said, "Sorry, guys. I'm going to have to ask you to strap in."

Dan grinned and let his seat-belt all the way out. He attached it to Missy's buckle. "There," he said, putting his arms around her. "All strapped in."

She smiled up at him. "Thanks. I feel safer now."

As she snuggled against him, he knew she meant it. If only she'd let him make her feel safe in all the other ways he wanted to, too.

"Have you talked to Laura lately?" she asked.

"No. We've been playing phone tag. Have you? Is she coming for your party?"

"I hope so, but we've been playing phone tag too. Her last message said she wants to, but she's not sure if she can get up. It's quite a drive from the Bay area isn't it?"

Dan put a hand to his face, annoyed with himself. He'd been using Papa Charlie and Smoke's services a lot lately, but he forgot, he was the exception, not the norm. Laura couldn't do that. She'd never ask Jack if she could use the plane, there was no way she could afford the fuel.

"What's wrong?" asked Missy.

He smiled as an idea came to him. "I don't know if you've noticed, but I think Laura and Smoke like each other."

Missy laughed. "It's kind of hard not to notice."

"And I'm guessing Smoke's coming to your party?"

Missy nodded.

"So, how about when I go to San Jose, I drive back so I've got the Jeep. That way Smoke can stay over there and they'll get some time together, then he can fly her up for the party?"

"That's a great idea. Do you want to talk to her, or shall I?"

"How about you talk to Laura and I'll talk to Smoke?"

Dan did intend to talk to Laura himself, but that wasn't anything he wanted Missy to know about yet.

Chapter Seventeen

Dan circled his arms as he ran. He'd thought about skipping his run today, but since Missy had said she was going to her dad's after she collected Scot from Michael's place, he'd decided he may as well fit it in. He needed to figure out how to get his gym equipment up here. He missed it, but in the meantime, his run had become an important part of his day. The days were getting cooler now and the breeze off the lake made him feel alive in a way sitting in front of a keyboard and monitor never had. He'd discovered a few routes that gave him a good hour's run. The one he'd chosen this morning was less challenging. He'd followed the cycle path along the lakeshore and out of the resort before looping down to the old road by the river that would lead him back into town and home. He'd already come to think of their house as home. He hoped that Missy and Scot would too.

He picked up his pace as the old road climbed a little. There were hardly ever any cars out here, but he kept to the edge anyway. At the top of the rise he could see a big black pick-up truck parked in the shade under the trees. As he approached a man stepped out, leaving the door open and standing in Dan's path, arms folded across his chest. His eyes were shadowed by his black cowboy hat. Dan slowed to a jog, not sure what to make of this. The guy was taller than him by a good few inches. He was probably thirty pounds heavier too—thirty pounds of solid muscle. From his intimidating stance, it didn't look like he was after a friendly chat either. Dan slowed to a walk as he got closer, trying to make out the face under the brim of that hat.

"Afternoon," he said, deciding that an attempt at conversation was preferable to a silent staring match.

"Are you the kid that's been seeing Missy?"

That caught him off guard—and riled him. He wasn't a kid and he wasn't just *seeing* her. They were living together, hopefully she was going to marry him—when he figured out how to ask her. He stilled himself and balled his fists, every instinct telling him he was going to need to fight. "I am. What's it to you?"

"What if I told you to leave her alone?"

"I'd tell you to go fuck yourself, because that's not going to happen!" Dan surprised himself with his words and his tone, which came out sounding like a threat. He was even more surprised that the guy started to laugh.

He tipped back his hat and Dan saw light silvery-blue eyes, crinkling as he laughed. He stepped forward holding out his hand. "Nice to meet you Dan, I'm Chance."

Dan pursed his lips, but smiled in spite of himself as the adrenaline receded. He shook Chance's hand. "Yeah. Nice to meet you too. Sorry about that. I didn't know who you were, or what to make of you."

Chance laughed again, the sound raspy, as though he were out of practice. "No, I'm sorry, Dan. I didn't know what to make of you either. I thought you were some little geek-boy, sniffing around my sister. Wanted to see how easy you might scare off."

Dan met his gaze. "I'll admit I was scared of you, but not you, or anyone, or anything is going to scare me away from Missy."

Chance nodded. "I can see that. I'm glad to be wrong about you, kid."

Dan frowned. He didn't want to push his luck, but he didn't want Chance to think of him as, or call him, kid. "I'm glad you weren't what I thought either, but do me a favor?"

"What's that?"

"Don't call me kid."

Chance narrowed his eyes and gave him an appraising look. "Why not, kid?"

Dan wasn't going to back down now. "Because you don't know me. In your sister's eyes, I'm her man. In Scot's eyes, I'm becoming a kind of father figure. Can you respect how they see me, what I am to them?"

Chance pushed his hat back off his head and ran his hand through unruly black hair. He nodded slowly. "In my book, respect has to be earned, not just given."

"I'm with you. I'm asking you not to disrespect their faith in me. As for you respecting me, I'll earn it over time, or I won't." He smiled. "If I don't then you can call me kid and I won't argue."

Chance smiled. "Fair enough. So what do I call you?"

"Dan, nerd, geek." Dan smiled. "See, it's not about ego, I'll accept being called what I am."

Chance grasped his shoulder. "I think we'll do just fine, you and me, Dan. Now, do you want a ride back into town?"

"Sure. Missy and Scot have gone to your dad's. You could drop me on the way if you want to go there?"

Chance's face changed so fast it took Dan by surprise. His smile was replaced by thinned lips, his eyes narrowed and hard. He got back into his truck. Dan went around and climbed in the passenger side and waited, not wanting to question the sudden change. Chance turned the key in the ignition, then looked across at him. The anger was gone, but he looked pained. "I'd sooner come hang with you 'til they get back. You can show me this house she's been raving about."

"Sure."

"Do we need to pick up some beer?" asked Chance as he put the truck in gear.

"No." Dan smiled. "We've got plenty, and they're stinging cold."

"I'm liking you more by the minute, kid." Chance shot him a quick grin. "Dan, I mean Dan!"

~ ~ ~

Missy was thrilled to see Chance's truck parked in the driveway when they got back to the house. She looked across at Scot. "Looks like Dan's met Uncle Chance already, huh?"

Scot nodded, his face solemn. "Do you think they'll be okay?" he asked.

"We'd better go find out. Come on." She'd been looking forward to seeing Chance, looking forward to him meeting Dan, seeing the house, but now he was here, she was a little afraid of how he might react. What he might do if he took a dislike to Dan. She hurried up the steps and into the house, Scot following her closely. From the look on his face, he shared her concerns. "Hey! We're back," she called. The house was silent. Scot looked at her; she shrugged. They checked the media room—no one there. She went out to the patio and, to her relief, heard the sound of laughter. She beckoned to Scot to follow and they made their way down to the workshop down by the dock. She couldn't believe her eyes when she saw both doors standing wide open and inside they weren't working on a boat or even a motorcycle as she might have expected. Oh, no. There was a pool table in there! The two of them were playing pool and drinking beer!

Dan was the first to spot her. He grinned and came over to her while Chance took his shot. "Hey, Miss! Can you believe this? I'd never bothered looking in here, thought it was just a boat shed. We got a pool room instead!"

She smiled and pecked his lips. "Wonderful. I see you found my brother too."

"Oh. Yeah." Dan grinned.

"In fact," said Chance, once he'd taken his shot. "I found him." He came around the table and Missy threw herself into his arms. Chance lifted her up so her eyes were level with his own. "Good to see you, Miss." He set her down and turned to Scot. "Hey, Shorty!"

"Hey, Uncle Chance." Scot looked a little unsure of himself until Chance held an arm out.

"Got a hug for me?"

Scot grinned and gave him a quick hug. When he let go, he went and wrapped his arms around Dan's waist. "So how did it go? Did you enjoy Vegas?"

Chance caught Missy's eye and nodded. Seemingly he approved of Dan. Although it should be none of his business, Missy was relieved—and pleased.

"It was great, champ. You would have enjoyed it."

Scot pulled a face at him.

"Don't look at me like that. You would. You can't knock it 'til you've tried it. But how did it go at Ethan's? Did you two have fun?"

"We did. Is it okay if he comes here tonight, so we can keep working on it?"

"We'd best check with your mom."

Dan looked at her and Missy smiled. "I said we'd need to ask you."

Dan looked puzzled. "Why?"

She could feel Chance's eyes boring into her. "Because it's your house."

Dan frowned, hurt brown eyes fixed on her. "It's *our* house, Miss. You don't have to ask who can come over."

Scot grinned. "See, Mom! That's what I said."

Missy stared at them, not knowing what to say, until Chance laughed. "Take it easy on her, guys. She might need a little time to get used to this." He turned to her. "Don't take too long though, Miss. You've found yourself a good 'un here. Now, are we playing, or not? It's your shot, Dan, and you're not going to beat me this time." As Dan went to take his shot, Chance looked at Missy. "You could have warned me he was hustler!"

She laughed. She would have if she'd known. It was just another of his many hidden talents she was learning about.

~ ~ ~

Miss still looked tired. It was starting to really get to him. They'd had a great weekend, first Vegas, then hanging out with Chance. He'd stayed the night and Dan had gone to get them all breakfast and the papers this morning. Missy had wanted to take Chance to see the gang for breakfast at the restaurant, but he wasn't keen to be around people. Dan could relate to that.

Tonight, Chance had gone to stay at Missy's. He'd said he didn't want to interrupt the Sunday night, back to school routine. Dan suspected he just needed to be alone.

They'd seen Scotty off to bed and now they sat in their bedroom, by the fire. It was time to see if he could persuade her not to work so hard all the time. He reached out to touch her cheek. The dark smudges under her eyes were still visible, even though she thought she covered them with her makeup. It made Dan feel sad. Sad that she worked so hard and wouldn't let him help. Sad because it reminded him of his mom and the black eyes she used to try to hide in the same way. When Missy smiled at him, like she was doing now, he felt like he could conquer the world for her. The only trouble was, she was too stubborn to let him. To be fair though, it had only been a couple of weeks. Like Chance had said, she needed time to adjust. He hoped that tonight he'd be able to persuade her to see things his way.

"You look tired, beautiful."

"I am." She smiled and placed her hand over his. "Can we save the talk for another time, and just go to bed?"

He frowned, not knowing if she was too tired, or trying to get out of the conversation they needed to have.

She moved her hand from his cheek to his chest and slipped it inside his shirt. "I know we need to talk Danny, but I am tired. I don't think I've got the energy to talk and...." She slid her hand down to the waist of his jeans and tugged on his belt.

All his hesitation disappeared when she slid down to the floor and pulled her top off over her head.

"We don't have the rug yet, but this carpet is nice and soft." She wriggled out of her jeans and smiled at him.

All thoughts of conversation left him as he unbuttoned his shirt and shrugged it off. He knelt on the floor facing her, caging her against the chair with his arms. She fumbled with his zipper and got him out of his jeans. Seeing her breasts overflowing her bra, he ached to be inside her. He freed them and buried his face in them, teasing her nipples with his lips and fingers until she moaned. He turned her around to lean on the armchair and pulled her panties down. Kneeling behind her, he spread her legs. She leaned into the seat of the chair, her hands grasping the arms when he reached around to touch her. She moaned and pressed her ass against him. He had no choice but to hang onto her hips as her heat yielded to him. He saw her knuckles turn white against the chair as he settled into her. He'd have to take this slow. He was already on the very edge, and the sight and sound of her panting shoulders threatened to take him over at any moment. He leaned forward and filled his hands with her breasts as he withdrew slightly. She moaned as he fingered her nipples and slid back home. He moaned with her as she closed around him, she was so wet and tight. He set a slow, steady rhythm, feeling the pressure build each time he thrust deeper. She clutched the cushions, moaning as she moved with him. He slipped a hand down between her legs to touch her. The way she moaned his name and pressed back against him touched the fuse that had him thrusting deep and hard, the pressure building, and building until he could no longer contain it. He let go, seeing stars as he clung to her, throbbing inside her as she writhed beneath him, gasping her own pleasure. She really was a perfect fit for him.

Dan lay on his back, staring out at the water. It still sparkled in the darkness, even though there was no moon and only a few stars to reflect. He was getting used to this bed, this view of the lake. He curled his arm tighter around Missy. He was getting used to sleeping like this too. He lay on his back, she lay on her side, head on his shoulder. His arm was around her waist, her leg wrapped around his. It felt so comfortable, so right. He didn't know how he'd slept without her 'til now. Didn't think he'd ever be able to again.

"G'night, Danny," she murmured.

He dropped a kiss into her hair. "G'night, beautiful. Tomorrow we talk. Don't think I've forgotten."

She nodded and snuggled closer, but said nothing. He wrapped both arms around her and held her tight.

~ ~ ~

Missy pulled the minivan into the driveway. She was happy to see that Chance's truck was already there. Even happier at the way he and Dan had hit it off. Dan had seen more of her brother this week than she had. It seemed the two loners enjoyed each other's company. She was glad of it, even though it didn't make much sense to her. She smiled as she got out of the van; being together with Dan didn't make much sense either, but they were getting closer every day. He'd insisted that he'd be in charge of dinner tonight, since she'd worked late.

She let herself in, wishing she could just go take a shower and lie down. She was still so tired. She was starting to think there must be a way to do as Dan said, and find a compromise that would mean she didn't have to work so damned hard all the time. She found them in the kitchen. Scot sat close to Dan, as he seemed to whenever he could these days.

"Hey, Mom!"

"Hey, sunbeam. How was your day?"

"It was good."

"Hey, beautiful," Dan's face was full of concern. "You look beat. Come and sit down. Do you want a drink?"

"I'd love a glass of wine, thanks. I am beat today."

Chance turned to her. "So why not give it up, Miss? You shouldn't be working your ass off when your man here wants to take care of you. You're being stupid."

Missy stared at Dan, shocked. Dan, who had gotten up to get her wine, stopped dead and shifted from one foot to the other, looking very uncomfortable. She'd managed to avoid having the conversation with him since Sunday night, but she was shocked, and a little hurt, that he would have talked to Chance about it. "What have you said?"

Chance cut in. "He hasn't said a word. He doesn't need to. Any fool can see what's going on here, Miss. He's trying to give the two of you a life, and you're clinging to your independence."

She looked at Chance. "I am not stupid! We only just moved in together. We're still figuring out how things are going to work. And *you* need to butt out, thank you very much!"

Chance continued as if she hadn't spoken. "I'm not going to watch you work yourself into the ground when you don't have to. I'm not going to watch you mess things up with Dan here. He's the best thing that's ever happened to you, and to Scot. You've never known someone to be there for you, take care of you. I'm partly to blame for that, but Dan's different. He's here for you. He's not going anywhere and he wants to take care of you. Let him, Miss. We all know you can do it all by yourself, but you don't have to anymore."

Missy looked from Chance to Dan. He smiled at her, nodding his head.

"Yeah," Scot piped up. "It would be nice if you weren't always working."

That stung! "But, Scotty! I always try to be home for you."

He smiled at her. "I know, and you are, but you're always too tired to have any fun."

She sagged in her chair. She couldn't deny that. Just now she'd been wishing she could rest instead of looking forward to the evening ahead. She put her head in her hands. Dan was at her side in an instant. He put his arm around her shoulders.

"Leave it guys. We'll work it out with time." He tipped her chin until she looked up into big brown eyes. "We care about you, Miss, that's all. We want you to be happy, not exhausted." He winked at Scot. "We're being selfish, too. We want more of you for us."

She nodded; she wanted more of them too.

Chance stood up. "Come on, Shorty. Come see if you can beat me at pool while these two talk about it."

Scot patted her shoulder as he followed Chance out the French doors.

She looked at Dan. "What do you want me to do?"

"Selfishly? I want you to quit cleaning. Quit working. Get yourself some rest, have time to hang with Scot, time to hang with me. I'd like to see you taking classes online, working towards your degree so that eventually you'll be able to work as a guidance counselor, do something you love that won't exhaust you. But that's me being selfish. What matters is what you want to do, Miss. Do you know what you want?"

She nodded slowly. "I want to rest. I want to have the energy to have fun with Scot." She touched his cheek. "And with you.

But Chance was right. I've never known what it's like to have someone there for me. I only know how to do it all myself." She shrugged sadly. "Even though I don't do it very well." He closed his arms around her. "Miss, you do brilliantly. You've raised a wonderful young man, kept your head above water. I could never have done what you have." She let out a little laugh. "And you know damned well, I could never have done what you have." "Exactly. We're so different, we fill each other's gaps. You and Scotty are giving me a life I would never have imagined possible without you. Can you see that?" She nodded; she could see the truth of it. "I'm asking you to let me do the same for you. I think we'll work best when we learn to lean on each other, Miss. I'm already taking the risk. I'm leaning on you for a family, a home. For the things I've never had that come naturally to you. Can you trust me? Lean on me for the things that you've never had that come naturally to me?" She rested her forehead against his. "I want to, but it's scary, you know?" "I do know. It's scary for me too, but I trust you. Can you try to trust me?" "I am trying." "I know, beautiful. Listen, would you be angry if I told Ben you need to take a few weeks off? We can do what we did last time. I'll pay him to find someone to cover for you. You can get some rest. I'll talk to him when I go pick up dinner." Missy thought about it. She didn't want to leave Ben in the lurch again, but taking a couple of weeks off did sound good. "How about I talk to him myself? I'll finish out this week, give him chance to find someone to cover for next week?"

Dan shook his head. "Please, Miss, let me sort it tonight?" He closed his hand around the back of her neck, making her close her eyes and relax. She was close to giving in.

He smiled. "I can do whatever I want with you now, right little kitten?" He gently squeezed her neck. "Wouldn't you rather spend the next couple of days hanging out by the pool, playing in your herb garden, and getting ready for your party, than scrubbing floors and toilets?"

She smiled. "Well, when you put it like that...."

They both knew he'd won.

"Good. I'll go get dinner and talk to Ben. You put your feet up, I'll be back."

She watched him walk down to the boat-shed. She did trust him, and Chance was right, she would be stupid to refuse his help. It was his way of loving her.

Chapter Eighteen

Dan looked out of the window while he listened to Smoke talking to ATC. He'd seen Scot to the bus stop this morning and left Missy sitting in her robe at the kitchen table, ready for her first day relaxing at home. His chat with Ben had worked out better than he'd hoped last night. Tourist season was winding down and Ben was happy to have more work to divide among the cleaning crew. There was never enough to go around over the quiet season. Dan knew that would help in him trying to convince Missy to give up the cleaning completely. If she kept at it, she'd be taking work away from people who genuinely did need the money, when she didn't, not any more.

Smoke looked across at him. "Thanks for this, Dan."

"No problem at all. It works out great for everyone."

In a few minutes they'd be landing in San Jose. Dan had a busy day ahead, he was meeting with Leanne later. Hopefully he'd get to talk to Ryan, too. He was going to load the Jeep with more of his clothes and gear, and drive back to Summer Lake. He hated to spend the night away from Missy and Scot, but this way, Smoke would get some time with Laura, Missy would get some time with her son and her brother, and Dan would get some time alone. It surprised him that he hadn't missed the solitude he used to crave. He was curious how it would feel to sleep alone. There had only been a handful of times in the last few weeks when there had been too many emotions floating around for him to process. He'd been able to walk away for a while, get straight with himself. Missy had understood.

This weekend would be a long and busy one, with Missy's birthday, and the party. As much as he looked forward to everyone coming to their house, as they no doubt would, he figured that getting some alone time in advance would help see him through a people-filled and important weekend.

"Would you ask Laura to call me, when she gets chance?"

Smoke grinned at him. "Are you doing what I think you are?"

Dan bit his lip, and nodded. "Did she tell you?"

"God, no! I just remember her talking about making Emma's ring for Jack. I figured when you got around to asking Missy, you'd do the same."

Dan nodded. "I still haven't figured out how I'm going to do the asking part, but at least with Laura's help, I know the ring will be perfect."

Smoke nodded as ATC came over the radio and handed them over to the tower for their approach into San Jose.

~ ~ ~

Missy sat out by the pool, enjoying the morning sunshine. It wasn't warm enough to swim, but she didn't have the energy anyway. She was simply making the most of the peace and quiet, of not having to do anything—anything at all. It was a strange feeling, but it wasn't as bad as she'd expected. She heard a car door slam. Chance appeared around the side of the house. He came out to the pool and sat beside her. He was still handsome, but he did look older. Touches of gray flecked his dark unruly hair. His face was rugged. He looked weather-worn, but then who wouldn't, spending all their time outdoors in Montana? He didn't speak, just sat staring out at the lake. She waited, knowing he'd talk if he wanted to. He'd been here almost a week now. He hadn't talked about himself at all. He had gone to see their dad, but hadn't spoken about it. Eventually he turned to look at her. His smile reminded her of the old Chance, of the kid he'd been, always laughing and joking. He'd been captain of the football team, the most popular guy in school. That was before, though.

"I like him, Miss."

She smiled back. She already knew it, but was relieved to hear him say it out loud. "I like him too, Chance."

"He's good for you, and for Scot. I'm happy for you."

"Thanks. And thanks for telling me I was being stupid!"

"Anytime." He grinned.

"You are going to come to my party on Saturday?" She hoped he would. He'd lain low all week, but all her friends, and many of his knew he was here, and hoped to see him.

He nodded. "I'll be there. I gave Dan my word."

She looked at him, surprised.

"That's different from a promise, Miss."

"If you say so."

His face had shut down.

"Are you going to tell me what's going on with you?" she asked.

He stared back out at the lake, seeming to think it over. "I'm doing better."

"I can see that."

"Nah, let's not go there today, huh?"

She nodded. He'd talk when he was ready, there was no point pushing. He really did seem to be doing better though.

"Maybe Dan could bring the two of you up to see me some time?"

Wow! "Really?"

"Yeah, it's about time you saw the place, and now you've got Dan, I won't need to worry about keeping all the guys away from you."

"Chance, I'd love to!" She knew he managed a big cattle ranch somewhere near Yellowstone, but she'd never visited him up there. Whenever she'd asked, he'd made excuses about why she couldn't come. "When?"

"We'll see."

A *we'll see* from Chance usually meant never.

Seeing her face, he shook his head. "We will see. We'll talk to Dan, huh?"

That bothered her. "I know you like him, but don't you dare start treating me like the little lady, while you men folk go making all the decisions!"

He laughed. "I'm not. I just want to include him, and you'd better get used to it. If you two are going to become a team, you need to stop defending your independence so hard and think about including him in your decisions, too."

"Oh!"

Chance laughed again. "Yeah, you might well say, oh. Let him in, Miss. Don't push him out."

"And when did you get into couples counseling?"

"When I saw my little sister in danger of screwing up the best thing that's ever happened to her. And don't tell me to butt out again, because I'm not going to. Not 'til you relax and accept what he's offering you, okay?"

She sighed. "I am trying! Look, I'm here, at home, not at work. Is that not enough?"

"It's a start. I'll give you that."

"That's big of you! Thanks!"

"Look, Miss, you pride yourself on being able to handle anything life throws at you, right?"

She nodded. She did.

"Well, remember life can throw good stuff at you as well as the tough shit. You need to learn how to handle the good stuff. You haven't had much practice at that, you've been too busy dealing with tough shit."

"Thanks, Chance." He was right.

"What did you ever see in that woman?" Leanne pushed her long blonde hair out of her eyes and shook her head at Dan. "She's such a bitch!"

Dan laughed. "Calm down, Lee. You've been telling me that for years. I finally get it. Just tell me how to get out of it all. That's all I care about now."

They sat in a restaurant around the corner from his apartment. As usual, Leanne drew the attention of every man in the place. Round glasses framed her big blue eyes. Her pale gray suit fit her figure perfectly, emphasizing large breasts and a tiny waist. The split in her skirt showed off shapely legs underneath. Dan had always been aware that she was beautiful, but for some reason she just didn't appeal to him in that way. He admired her mind. They'd been friends since the first lecture they'd shared at Berkeley, but he'd never been attracted to her. She felt the same way about him. They'd often laughed at the way they left a trail of men and women drooling in their wake, while neither of them got what it was all about.

"It's getting interesting," she said. "Steven's been stalling me. I told him if he doesn't get back to me by tomorrow, I'll advise you to sell direct to Systech. That should get him off his ass."

"I don't think it's him sitting on his ass that's the problem, it's his being under Olivia's thumb."

"Maybe so, but in the meantime, Corey called me, and he's interested in buying your shares himself."

"Really?" That puzzled Dan. "Did he say why?"

"No, but think about it. If you sell to him, then he'd win either way. He could go into Systech in a very strong position, or he could even decide to put a stop to the merger completely, since he'd be the majority shareholder."

"Jesus! That would really piss Olivia off."

"So, what do you want to do?"

Dan cocked his head. "I don't know. I just want out. I want the best price I can get, obviously. But I don't want to screw Steven over."

Leanne tutted. "He didn't give a shit about screwing you over!"

"It's not his fault, Lee. Olivia and their parents push him around, they always have."

"Well, if he refuses to grow a pair, that's his problem—not yours."

Dan laughed. For all Leanne looked so soft and pretty, she was a real tough cookie. "What do you recommend?"

"As your attorney, I'd suggest you create a bidding war, pit Corey against Olivia, and then bring in Systech."

Dan frowned.

"As your friend, I know you're not going to do that. So, I'd say we wait and talk to Steven. If he can't or won't make a fair offer himself, then we get you the best price we can from

Corey and leave them to battle it out. You can't do anything for Steven while he's under Olivia's control."

Dan thought about it. "I'm going to call Steven one last time. I'd like to sell to him and let him decide. We started Prometheus together, I hate to see it torn away from him."

"You're too soft, Dan. It's not being torn away. He held his hands up and surrendered when his sister came in to take it. So did you, for that matter."

Dan nodded. He couldn't deny that. "Yeah, I did, but I don't want it anymore. She set me free to go live the life I do want, Lee."

Leanne's smile transformed her face. "I know! That's why I can't hate Olivia as much as I want to. Her plan to snare you *and* Prometheus has backfired in her face. She lost you, and I have to say, I hope she loses out on the company, too. That you end up selling to Corey. But, Dan, I've never seen you like this. Never thought I would. You, my friend, are a man in love. It's written all over your face!"

"It is?"

"Oh, yeah, buddy! I need to meet the lady who can do this to you. When are you going to bring her to town?"

"I don't know. You'll like her though, Lee. She's amazing."

"She must be."

"Oh. I know. If nothing else, I'm going to bring her to the Phoenix fundraiser this year."

"She must be truly amazing! You just said you're going to come to the fundraiser *and* you said it with a smile on your face! Normally you run for cover at the mention of it." She sighed. "I guess that means the days of my representing your ass are over."

"No, way. That's what I'm saying, you'll definitely meet her then, if we don't manage anything before."

"But I'm guessing I have to buy my own ticket, right?"

Dan shook his head. "Nope. I'll still get it for you. In fact, I'll even snag you an escort, as well as a ticket."

"An escort?!" she laughed.

Dan joined her laughter. "Not a paid one, idiot. I mean a date."

"And why would I want one of those?"

"Because he's a great guy. He's a friend of Jack and Pete's from Summer Lake. Sounds like he usually goes with them, but since their table is turning into a couples table, he was going to give it a miss this year. I said I'd ask if you wanted an escort."

Leanne's eyebrows knit together. "He usually sits with Jack and Pete?"

"Yup."

"What's he look like?"

"A bit taller than me. Dark blond hair."

"Ooh!" Leanne's face lit up. "His hair's a bit long, green eyes, big shoulders, big hands?"

Dan laughed. "I can verify longish hair and big shoulders. Can't say I've noticed his eyes or his hands."

"I guess I shouldn't have admitted that either, but if he's the one I think he is, then yes, please! I'd like him as an escort." She gave him a raunchy grin. "In any sense of the word!"

"Jesus, Lee! Down, girl!"

"Whatever," she laughed.

Dan hoped he was doing the right thing with Leanne and Ben. He had to check. He studied her face closely as he asked. "Did you know Ryan is in town?"

She covered it well, but he saw her pupils dilate and a tiny crease appear in her forehead in the second before she smiled. "I didn't. How's he doing these days?" Her hand trembled slightly, making the ice-cubes tinkle as she sipped her water.

"He's great. I'm going to be working with him, by the looks of it."

"Oh. So, are you all set to close on the house?"

Dan cocked his head. "You're not even going to try for a *subtle* change of subject?"

Leanne shook her head vigorously. "I spent years putting that man behind me, Dan. I can't go there. Don't make me?" Her big blue eyes pleaded with him.

"Okay, but don't you think it would help to talk about it?"

"There's nothing left to talk about. He's the past. Now tell me about this house of yours. Is everything set to close?"

"Yep." Dan let it go. "The appraisal was fine. It's all straightforward. A clean, easy deal."

"Good. I hope you're going to invite me up there soon? Not only do I want to meet Missy, but I also want to see the place. I can't believe you got so much house for so little money!"

Dan smiled. "It's a different world up there, Lee. We'll have to figure out when we can get you up."

Leanne's phone rang. "What is it, Karen?.... Okay...tell them I'll be there in twenty." She hung up and stood up. "I've got to go. Are you going to talk to Steven, or am I?"

Dan thought about it. "I'll call him and let you know what he says. Either way, I'm going to turn it all over to you after that."

Leanne smiled. "Wise move. I'll see you soon." She bent down to peck his cheek.

Dan laughed. "Weren't *you* supposed to be taking *me* out to lunch?"

She rolled her eyes. "I'll get it next time."

"You always say that."

She laughed as she walked away. "Yeah, and you always fall for it!"

Dan shook his head at her as she turned back to blow him a kiss from the door.

Missy went to open the front door. She couldn't get used to the ridiculous chime that played when someone pressed the doorbell. She'd have to go to the hardware store to see if she could pick up a straightforward bell. She smiled to herself, or maybe she'd ask Dan if he would.

She was thrilled to see Ben standing there. "Hey, you! Come on in."

"Hey, Miss. I hope it's okay to invite myself over, but it's quiet at the restaurant and I wanted to check in with you about the party."

"Of course it's okay. I've been wanting to talk to you too. It's just that...." She looked over her shoulder. It was that Chance was there and he still didn't seem to want to see anyone.

Ben seemed to understand. He'd no doubt seen Chance's truck in the driveway. "I know. I don't have to stay."

Chance poked his head out of the kitchen. "Ben Walton! How you doing?"

Ben grinned. "I'm good, Chance. How about you?"

Chance nodded. "Happy to see our Miss doing so well. Don't leave because of me, will you? I don't bite."

"I just needed to talk to Miss a minute."

Missy decided to risk it. "Come on through. Have you got time for a beer?" Chance could make himself scarce if he wanted to, but she hoped he would stick around. He'd always liked Ben.

"Yeah, come on in. Be good to catch up."

Missy grinned and led Ben through to the kitchen. She opened the fridge and smiled at the way Dan had the beers arranged. They were lined up neatly, ordered by brand, all the labels turned to the front. It was just another of his quirks that she loved. He left clothes wherever he stepped out of them—or threw them! She'd ventured into his bathroom once, and had no intention of returning any time soon. But the beers were neatly ordered and displayed. To her surprise and amusement, he'd done the same thing with her jewelry box one evening while they'd sat talking. She didn't have much in there, but he'd organized it systematically and logically—and beautifully!

She handed beers to Ben and Chance, and took one herself. It was Friday night after all, why not?

"I wanted to check if you want anything special for tomorrow night."

"I'm fine with whatever you want to do, Ben. I really appreciate it."

"It's your birthday, Miss. And you deserve a party. I've moved the band upstairs and we're doing the food up there too."

"Oh, hon. You don't need to do all that!"

"I want to. It's your birthday present." He grinned. "And besides, I'm looking forward to it, too. It'll be like old times." He looked at Chance. "Are you going to come over?"

Chance nodded. "Yeah, I can't miss her birthday, can I?"

"I hoped not, but I wasn't sure," said Ben. "I didn't know how much of a low profile you were keeping. I've had people in the bar asking after you all week."

Missy hoped Ben would shut up. She didn't want Chance to change his mind, and his face was hard now, eyes narrowed.

"And what have you been telling them?"

Ben shrugged. "You know me. I never know anyone's business. Too busy working. I'd heard you were here. Hadn't seen you though."

Chance's face relaxed. "Thanks, Ben. I'll be there." He looked at Missy. "That's not saying I'll stay for the duration though."

Missy nodded, she didn't expect him to.

"What time's Dan back?" asked Chance.

"He should be here soon," said Scot who had just come downstairs. "I talked to him earlier."

Missy smiled. Dan had only left yesterday morning, but Scot had spoken to him several times. She missed him. That big bed wasn't the same without him. She'd realized how right he was about what made a home. This house had started to feel like home, but she needed him to come back now, to keep it that way.

~ ~ ~

Dan turned the Jeep onto Route Twenty. It had been a long time since he'd driven up here. He'd gotten used to flying. He had enjoyed his time alone on the road though. He'd needed it after his conversation with Ryan. He still wasn't sure what he should do, whether he should talk to Missy first.

Ryan had told him that the vetting process was complete and that they could get together next week to go through everything else and get Dan read in so he'd be able to start work. Ryan had also told him there had been two red flags raised in the vetting process, and they both had to do with Missy. The first one hadn't surprised him at all. He'd already known that Chance's past might be an issue—because Chance had told him all about it. Dan had decided immediately that he would back out of the job rather than have the past raked up. When he'd told Ryan that, his friend had reassured him that it

wouldn't cause any problems; Ryan had simply been looking
out for Dan. When he realized that Dan already knew, he was
cool with it—in fact he said he'd be interested to meet Chance
someday. It was the second issue that had him confused over what to
do. He'd known that Scot did have some contact with his
father. Scot had told him that he received birthday and
Christmas cards every year, and sometimes there was money in
them. What he hadn't known, and didn't believe Missy did
either, was that the guy had spent the last ten years in and out
of prison and that now he was living only half an hour away
from them, just down Route Twenty. Again, it didn't affect his
security clearance, but Ryan had wanted him to know. Now
that he did know, he didn't know whether Missy would want
to, or whether Scot should. He was approaching the
conclusion that he would talk to Chance about it and ask his
advice. Chance was family. Dan almost wished he didn't have
the information himself, but he had asked Ryan to tell him if
anything came up about Scot's father. Dan had decided that he
wanted to talk to the man.

Following the road as it twisted and turned its way through the
mountains, he looked forward to his first view of the lake.
Rounding the corner, the water sparkled before him in the late
afternoon sunshine. Home. For the first time in his life, he felt
like he was coming home. To his family. He was hoping that
before the weekend was out, Missy would say that she would
marry him, become his wife. He was also hoping that Chance
would help him to figure out what to do about Scot's father, so
they could become a real family, and he'd have a son, and a
brother-in-law, too.

Chapter Nineteen

"Dan, Dan, Dan, can you come to Ethan's with me while Mom's getting her hair done?"

Dan ruffled Scot's hair. "Sorry, champ. Uncle Chance and I have got a couple of things to take care of. I could get there a bit earlier when I come to pick you up this afternoon though?"

Dan felt bad seeing Scot's face fall.

"Okay."

"I'll get back as early as I can, Scotty. Sorry."

Scot smiled at him. "It's okay."

Dan didn't like that he was spending less time with the kid than he had been doing, but today's little outing with Chance was important. He wanted to have everything in place by tonight. Laura was bringing the ring with her. He still didn't know *how* he was going to ask, but he wanted to ask Missy to marry him tonight, on her birthday. He wanted Missy to be his wife and Scot to be his son.

Missy came into the kitchen. "We need to get going, sunbeam."

Scot scampered upstairs to get the textbooks that Dan had bought. As he'd expected, Scot had claimed them as his own when he'd found them in the RV, and now he was using them to teach Ethan too. Missy came to Dan and stood on her tiptoes to plant a sweet kiss on his lips. He closed his arms around her and breathed her in.

"I love you, Danny."

It took his breath away whenever she said it. He still couldn't believe how lucky he was. "I love you more, beautiful. Happy Birthday."

"It is. The happiest birthday I've ever had." She smiled and touched the earrings he'd given her this morning. They matched the necklace he'd given her last week. Three little hearts sat at each ear.

He framed her face between his hands and rubbed his nose against hers. "It's not over yet. Hopefully you'll be even happier by the time we go to bed tonight." He hoped she'd be wearing another new piece of jewelry by then.

She rubbed her hips against him, making him hard. "I'll definitely be happier once we're *in* bed, hero."

As Dan held her against him, Scot came skidding back into the kitchen and Chance let himself in through the French doors. He let go of her reluctantly.

"Come on, Mom. Ethan just texted. He's waiting. See you later guys."

Dan smiled as he watched them go, loving this new life they were building.

~ ~ ~

"You want me to come in with you?" asked Chance when they pulled in to the trailer park.

Dan shook his head. "No thanks. I've got this."

Chance looked around as they drove. "You don't know what you're going into."

Dan had a fair idea. Judging from the sofa he'd seen in one yard, the various old cars, sitting on blocks, or just rusting away, the gang of kids smoking on the corner they'd just passed, and the pit-bull roaming loose, he wasn't expecting to be invited in for tea! He bit his lip and looked at Chance.

"I appreciate it, but I need to do this myself." He shrugged. "Though I won't pretend I'm not glad that you're going to be outside waiting."

"I've got your back, bro."

Just hearing that buoyed him up. "Thanks. Look, that's it." He pointed at one of the trailers. The number 1511 hung lopsided next to the door. Clothes hung on a line in the front yard. Dan rubbed a hand over his face as Chance pulled the truck over. "Wish me luck," he said as he climbed down.

The man who opened the door wasn't what Dan had expected. His disheveled hair was light brown, his eyes blue. Dan had expected him to look like Scot. He didn't. At all. Maybe this wasn't him?

"Are you Travis Gibbs?"

The guy nodded, looking wary. "That's me. What do you want?"

"I want to talk to you about your son."

The guy rolled his eyes. "Which one? What have they done now?"

That caught Dan off guard. "How many have you got?"

"The two of them...." Travis stopped short. "Do you mean Scot?"

Dan nodded and was shocked to see Travis' face turn pale. "Is he okay? Tell me he's alright? Is Missy okay?"

"They're fine," Dan reassured him. "They're both fine."

Travis looked over his shoulder and came outside, closing the door behind him. "Then what do you want? Why are you here? What's going on with Scot?" He walked down the side of the trailer and took a seat on a log in the yard.

Dan saw Chance move to get out of the truck, but shook his head and waved him back as he followed Travis and sat beside him.

"Scot's doing great," he said. "I want to marry Missy." He looked Travis in the eye, "And I want to adopt Scot."

Travis let out a big sigh. "I would have been there for him, you know. I didn't even know about him 'til he was two. It took 'em that long to find me."

Dan nodded. "She told me."

"I was married by then. Already had my daughter and another one on the way."

Dan nodded again. He didn't know what to say. The guy seemed to be apologizing.

"I had nothing to offer him." Travis put his head in his hands and said nothing for a long while. When he looked up again, he swept his arm out over the trailer park. "This is the nicest place we've ever lived. I've spent most of the last ten years inside anyway. Joy and the kids have been on their own. I figured Scot would do better without me in his life than with me."

Dan silently agreed.

"What's he like?"

"He's a great kid. Smart, really smart. Loves his mom. Loves his computers."

Travis pursed his lips. "He wouldn't even have one, if I'd been his dad. My lot pester me for one, but I can't afford that shit." He looked at Dan now. An appraising glance that took in his clothes, his boots, his watch. "Money's not a problem for you though, is it?"

"No."

Dan couldn't help but respect the guy when he said, "It's not just about money though. Being a dad is so much more than that. You need to love 'em. Show 'em right from wrong. Teach 'em to be good people. That must sound like so much horse-shit coming from me, but it's what I believe. I always hoped Scot might have a chance to find a real dad, if I stayed out of the picture."

"That's what I want to be," said Dan. "I love him. I think he loves me. I came here to ask if you'd have any objections to my adopting him, trying to be a dad to him."

Travis nodded. "I'll sign anything you want me to, but I do have one condition."

Chance had warned him that Travis might try to get money from him. Dan wouldn't mind giving him some, but he didn't believe that was what Travis wanted from him. He was right.

"Let me know how he's getting on? Send me photos sometimes?"

Dan smiled. "Of course." He took out his wallet and gave Travis a photo he'd been carrying for a while now. Scot was sitting on the back step of the RV, playing on his GameBoy. Missy had taken it when they were all up at Emma's. Scot was oblivious to the camera and everything else. The lake sparkled in the background.

Travis smiled. "He's gotten so big. Is that your rig?"

Dan nodded. It occurred to him that the RV that he and Scot used as a workshop and game-room was much bigger than the trailer Travis and his family lived in.

Travis rubbed his arm over his eyes and nodded sadly. "What was your name?"

"Dan. Dan Benson,"

"Well, take good care of him, Dan Benson." He stood up. "I'd better be getting on, but you send me the papers. I'll sign 'em." He held out the photo.

"You can keep it if you want?" Dan wanted him to have it. He'd send him more too. He understood that Travis believed he had done the best he could for Scot by staying out of his life. Dan respected that—and was glad of it.

"Thanks." Travis held out his hand and Dan shook it firmly. "I want you to know I'll do my best for him. Always."

Travis nodded and walked away.

~ ~ ~

They were almost back to Summer Lake when Dan's cell phone rang. When he saw Leanne's name on the display, he muttered a quick *sorry* to Chance and answered it. He'd seen a voicemail from her this morning, but hadn't had time to check it yet.

"Hey, Lee. Is everything okay?"

"I'll let you decide that. Have you heard from Olivia?"

"No."

"Well you can expect to. I've had her on, bitching me out."

"Why? What's going on?"

"Seems like she got some insider information from Systech."

"Insider information? Like what? And how?"

"Considering it's the weekend and considering Corey is disillusioned with her, my guess is that she's screwing one of them now and that's how she found out that what Systech wanted most out of Prometheus was *you*. She thinks the deal is going to fall through if you're not part of the package."

Dan tried to process this. He couldn't. "So?"

"So watch out, my friend. She'll be hunting you down now that she thinks she needs you again."

Dan gave an involuntary shudder. He'd been pleasantly surprised that Olivia had made no attempt to contact him after he'd told her he was done with her and the company. "So, what do I do?"

Leanne laughed. "Hide! Block her calls, and let me draw up a deal with Corey."

Dan thought about it. He didn't need to hide, he was up here at the lake. He could easily ignore Olivia's calls. He had no desire to talk to her. Especially not today. He'd talked to Steven, it seemed his old friend had given up, he'd even encouraged Dan to sell to Corey. "Okay then. Do it."

"Will do. Call you later."

Chance looked at him as he hung up. "Everything okay?"

Dan nodded. "I hope so." He explained the whole situation to Chance as they spent the last few miles crawling along in the weekend traffic heading in to the resort.

"Watch your back," said Chance. "You know what they say about a woman scorned."

Dan smiled. "I do, but there's nothing she can do to me now. She's part of my old life. Everything and everybody I really care about is up here now."

Chance looked at him, eyes narrowed, jaw set. "Watch. Your. Back."

~ ~ ~

Missy sat between Emma and Holly in the big pedicure chairs at the salon. Emma's birthday gift had been to bring Missy to get her hair done, ready for the party. Holly had decided that they should all get manicures and pedicures while they were there.

"So." Emma grinned at her. "Are you all ready for tonight, birthday girl?"

Missy nodded happily. "Yep. I'm having my best birthday ever. The party will be the icing on the cake."

Emma's grin grew bigger. "Speaking of cake, I made your fave. Though how we're going to fit all those candles on top, I don't know."

Missy slapped at her arm. "Give it a rest with the old lady thing, Em. I already feel ancient!"

Holly laughed. "Don't feel too bad, Miss. You're the one who has snagged yourself a young hottie. We landed ourselves with a couple of old men, compared to your Dan."

Missy smiled. "It doesn't feel like he's younger than me though. He's so smart, and he takes such good care of us, you know?"

Holly smiled back at her. "I do know. I wasn't so sure at first. I honestly thought he was a bit clueless, but he's not, is he? When he asked me to find you a dress, he knew what he was doing alright." She laughed. "He even showed Pete up, and you've got to love anyone who can do that!"

Missy nodded happily. She did love him, but she wasn't going to tell the girls that yet.

Emma watched her with that knowing smile, though. "Are you still going to argue about being my sister-in-law?"

Missy felt the heat in her cheeks. She could no longer trot out her arguments about being at different places in life. Since he'd mentioned it in Vegas, she kept hoping that he *might* ask her to marry him.

Holly laughed. "Your silence says it all, sweetie. Sorry, but it was obvious from the beginning that he wanted you more than he might want to go off and start a family."

Missy nodded. "I get that now. But honestly, I could never forgive myself if he wanted babies and he missed out on that because of me."

"Hopefully you believe that he doesn't, now?"

She nodded. She really did. Knowing that he couldn't have children made it so much easier too. She wasn't depriving him of having a family of his own. She was sharing something with him that he would never have known otherwise.

"Anyway," she said. "What time is Laura getting in? We've been playing phone tag for weeks, but I still haven't managed to talk to her."

"She's going to call before they take off," said Emma. "The poor thing was so excited that Smoke was going to get her, but then she had some diamond people show up, and she's spent the last couple of days with them. She won't even get to see Smoke 'til she gets to the airport."

"Aww, what a shame!" Missy had been looking forward to hearing how Dan's plan to get those two a couple of days together had worked out.

"At least they'll both be at the party tonight," said Holly.

"Hopefully," replied Emma. "Jack said he'll pick them up from the airport, whatever time they arrive. What time are you going over there, Miss?"

"I don't know, I'm waiting for my men to tell me what we're doing."

Emma laughed. "It must be love! I never thought I'd see the day you would wait for a man to tell you what your plans were."

Missy nodded. "I know. It's weird isn't it? I like it when it's Dan though."

"I definitely hear more wedding bells on the horizon," said Holly. "Just do me a favor and coordinate with Pete before you decide on a date? You know what he's like for planning and he has to make sure nothing clashes!"

Missy looked up as a glass crashed to the floor. A woman, sitting in the waiting area a few feet away, had knocked it over, along with a pile of magazines. She stood up and looked around. Missy offered her a friendly smile, knowing how embarrassed she would feel if it were her. The expression on the woman's face as she looked back at Missy wasn't one of embarrassment, or even humor. It was a look of pure venom that took Missy's breath away. She tucked a strand of her angular cut bob behind her ear before turning and stalking out of the salon.

"Wow!" said Holly as the door slammed shut. "Who the hell was that, and what did you ever do to her, Miss? It's a good thing looks can't really kill, or this would be your last birthday!"

"I have no idea!" Missy was stunned.

Jackie, the owner of the salon, came over to clean up the broken glass and soggy magazines.

"Who was that?" asked Emma.

"A tourist, I guess," said Jackie. "She came in saying she just wanted a blow dry. I told her it'd be at least an hour before we could fit her in, but she wanted to wait. I guess she changed her mind, huh?"

"I wouldn't worry about it," said Holly. "She might have turned us all to stone, giving out looks like that!"

~ ~ ~

Missy sat in front of the mirror in her dressing room. This really was the best birthday ever. She'd had a great time with the girls, getting pampered. It had been far too long since she'd done that. Now she was getting ready for her party. Dan had gone out to collect Scotty a while ago. How could she ever have hoped to find a man who would be so close to her son that he apologized about leaving her to go and help him and his friend before they came home? She didn't mind one bit. It had given her time to take a long soak in her tub. She'd even had a glass of bubbly in there as she'd sat and stared out at the lake. Life was good. So very good.

She was applying her mascara when she heard Scot come bounding up the stairs, followed by Dan. Scot came into the dressing room and started to laugh when he saw what she was doing.

He looked at Dan. "She always sticks her tongue out when she does that."

Dan smiled at her. "I know, and I don't even know why she does it. She doesn't need makeup, she's beautiful."

"You should see some of the other stuff she does to look beautiful," said Scot, laughing again.

Missy wondered what he was about to give away.

Dan's eyes were twinkling now. "Really? Like what?"

"She pulls her eyebrows out!"

Missy laughed, remembering Scot's face when he'd seen her plucking her eyebrows. As a male, and a very logical one at that, she had not been able to make him understand it.

"Isn't *that* weird?" he asked Dan.

"No." Dan smiled at her. "It's not necessary, but it's not weird."

"Not necessary?" She laughed. "If I were to leave them to grow wild for a couple of months, you'd understand how necessary it is. I'd look like something from Planet of the Apes!"

Scot laughed, but Dan ran a hand over his face. "Do I look like something off Planet of the Apes? I'll shave it off before we go out."

Missy was horrified. She loved his scruff. He was gorgeous clean-shaven, but there was something even sexier about him stubbly. "Please don't! You look like *you* with your stubble. You look like you're trying to be someone else when you shave it off."

There went his beautiful smile again. "I'm so glad you get it. That's how it feels to me, too."

She smiled back at him, looking into those big brown eyes.

"Enough sappiness guys!" said Scot. "Are you going to put your angel costume on so we can see it?"

"No. You're going to go take a shower and put your cowboy clothes on. I'll see you downstairs."

She really wanted to walk down that grand staircase in her costume and see their faces.

"Come on, champ," said Dan. "She's not going to show us 'til we're ready. Let's go get you that hat, and get showers."

Scot grinned. "I'm going to be cool as a cowboy, Mom. Dan's letting me wear one of his hats to go with that shirt you got me."

"I know. I can't wait to see. You go get a move on, while I finish up here."

Scot went off to take his shower and Dan came to stand behind her chair. He bent to drop a kiss on her shoulder, then met her gaze in the mirror. "It's going to be a great night, Miss."

It would be a great night, even if she never moved from this spot. She could lose herself in those eyes for hours! "It is. I'm so looking forward to it."

"Not as much as I am," he said with a mysterious smile. He dropped another kiss on her neck, leaving her with hot shivers racing down her spine as he turned and left.

~ ~ ~

Dan stood in the hallway with Scot, waiting for Missy to appear. He felt more comfortable than he would have ever believed he could be going to a party. Everything about this felt right. It was all for Missy. He was going with her and Scot. They would spend the evening hanging out with people whose company he enjoyed. No one would give him a hard time if he didn't say much, yet with them, he found he usually did have something to say. He was comfortable in his own skin these days. He was definitely comfortable in these clothes. He'd brought them with him when he'd driven back from San Jose. He was wearing black jeans and a black denim shirt, and these black boots were the comfiest he'd ever owned. He'd dug out an old silver belt buckle too and had brought another one for Scot. He'd been a little surprised by the shirt Missy had bought for the kid to wear—a plaid thing that had made him look more like a hillbilly than a cowboy. He'd bought one himself at a big outfitters outlet store on his drive back to the lake. He smiled at Scot now, the shirt was almost the same as his own, and Scot loved it. He'd gotten him some boots too, so now the two of them were dressed almost identically. The kid was thrilled.

"Are you nearly ready yet, Mom?"

"Nearly," Missy shouted down the stairs. "My halo's all wonky!"

Dan smiled to himself. "I'd leave it," he shouted. "A straight one wouldn't suit you anyway."

He heard her laugh. She sounded so happy. He looked up and his breath caught in his chest as she appeared at the top of the stairs. She looked more beautiful than he'd ever seen her.

"Wow, Mom!" he heard Scot say.

He couldn't find any words of his own as he watched her come down the stairs. Her outfit was shorter than anything he'd seen her wear before. She might be small, but she had the longest legs. The outfit was a shimmery gold color. It clung to her, showing off her plump breasts. Little wings peeked over her shoulders and when she turned, he saw a barely covered, shimmery gold backside. He shifted his hands in his pockets. The feelings she was arousing were far from angelic.

As she reached the bottom of the stairs, she smiled at them. "Now that's what I call a pair of good-looking cowboys!"

Dan grinned. He couldn't drag his eyes away from her breasts. "Now that's what *I* call a pair of...."

She slapped his arm and pointed at her eyes with a laugh. "I warned you, cowboy! Up here!"

He met her gaze with a smile. "Sorry, beautiful."

"Hey, Mom! Do you like my shirt? It's the same as Dan's. He got it for me."

Dan had been concerned that she might be cross with him about it.

"I love it, son. It's miles better than the one I found. You look great."

Dan felt his heart expand in his chest as she looked back at him. "So do you, Danny. Just great!"

From the look in her eyes and the way she looked in that outfit, he would gladly have forgotten all about the party. The way her halo tipped over to one side, it seemed to be teasing him to find out how naughty a beautiful little angel could be.

"Can we go now?" asked Scot, pulling Dan and Missy back into the moment.

He gave her a regretful smile. "I think we better, while we still can."

Scot threw a puzzled look back over his shoulder as he headed for the door. Missy took Dan's hand and squeezed it. She knew what he'd meant.

Chapter Twenty

Dan sat out on the upper deck of the Boathouse. The party was off to a good start. Missy was inside catching up with some of her old school friends. He'd stayed by her side and she'd introduced him to them, but she'd sensed his discomfort. She'd made it easy for him, like she always did. Instead of making him stay, which he would have done for her, she'd asked him if he'd mind leaving them alone for some girl-talk. He'd gratefully obliged.

Chance appeared out of the shadows at the top of the back steps up to the deck. Dan grinned. He'd wondered whether Chance would really come.

"Hey, Dan." He came and sat down at the picnic bench. "How's it going?"

"It's going great. She's happy."

Chance nodded. "She is. It's not just the party that's making her happy though. It's you."

Dan was relieved that Chance was articulating his approval. "Your dad gave me his permission to ask her. I'd like yours too."

Chance looked him in the eye. "That's not how it works. You don't need my permission."

Dan shrugged. "Technically no, I don't need it. I'm asking because I *want* it. What do you say?"

Chance smiled, the tension completely gone from his face for once. "I say you've got it. My permission if you want it, but you've also got something more than that."

Dan was puzzled. "What's that?"

"My respect. I told you, in my book respect is earned, not just given. Watching you this last week, seeing you with Miss, and with Scot, you've earned my respect, Dan. I'll be proud to call you brother, not just bro."

Dan nodded. He had no words that could come anywhere near expressing how much that meant to him.

Ben came to the table with a bucket of beer. "Thought you might be needing these." He looked at Chance. "And I thought you might want a heads up that the gang are on their way. Pete and Holly just arrived with Michael. I saw Jack's truck pulling in, so that's him, Emma, Smoke, and Laura. And a few of your old buddies are downstairs, talking about coming up when it fills up a bit."

Dan saw Chance glance back towards the dark stairway from where he'd appeared. Dan of all people understood the desire to escape from too much company.

Chance caught his eye. "Are you going to do it tonight?"

He nodded.

"In that case." Chance plucked a bottle from the bucket. "Thanks for the warning, Ben, but I'm not going anywhere."

Ben grinned. "Glad to hear it. I'll catch up with you in a little while."

Once Ben had gone, Dan said, "I might not ask her 'til we get home. I don't know what to do yet. I don't want you to stick around for that, and then me not have the nerve to ask her here."

Chance shook his head. "Doesn't matter to me when you ask her. It's not that I need to see it. I just know tonight is going to be one of the happiest nights of her life. I want to be a part of it. Have her remember that, for once in her life, I was part of something good. I was there."

Dan nodded. He could understand that.

~ ~ ~

"Damn, Miss! Look at you," exclaimed Jack as he leaned down to hug her. "Happy Birthday! You look great. Though I have to say, angels looking like you could get devils in trouble!"

Missy laughed as Emma pushed him away so she could get a hug herself. "Hey, hon. You look great."

Emma rolled her eyes. "Thanks, but I look good. *You* look great. As the size of my husband's eyes proves!"

Jack hung his head and gave Emma a sad puppy dog look. "Am I in trouble, baby?"

Emma laughed. "Not at all. In fact, why don't you stay here and admire Missy's costume a while longer?" She was looking over Jack's shoulder as she spoke. "I've just seen your brother and I need to go say hello."

"To Dan?" asked Jack, looking behind him.

"I think she means *my* brother," said Missy with a laugh as Emma disappeared into the crowds who had started to arrive.

Jack's face was a picture as Emma caught Laura by the arm and led her out to the deck. Once there she pecked Dan's cheek and then threw herself into Chance's arms.

Jack turned back to Missy. "I think I preferred it when she was running scared!"

Missy laughed. "We both know you don't mean that. You love that she's got her confidence back, and you're the one that gave it to her."

He grinned. "I know. It is great." He glanced back to where Emma was clinging to Chance's arm as she gazed at him adoringly. "But it does ding the old ego a bit to see that. I mean, we're all dressed up as cowboys, and some of us can pull it off, but your brother there is the real deal."

Missy shook her head at him. "It'd take more than that to dent your ego, Jack. And look, Dan isn't daunted by him. In fact, the two of them have really hit it off."

Jack nodded. "Isn't that cool?"

Missy nodded happily. "You have no idea how cool that is for me, and looking at the two of them together, you'd think they'd both come straight off the ranch. You Benson boys must have some cowboy in your blood somewhere, because you can both pull it off. Unlike *you!*" She turned to Pete who had just joined them with Holly at his side, and Michael and Smoke in their wake.

Pete's eyebrows came down. "Unlike me what? What have I done now?"

"It's what you've not done, Hemming," said Missy with a laugh. "I'm just saying you're not cowboy enough."

Holly put a hand on Pete's shoulder and waggled her eyebrows. "Oh, he's cowboy enough, Miss. Why do you think we're late?"

Pete wrapped an arm around Holly. "Yeah, my fiancée is thinking about starting a 'Save a Horse' campaign!"

Missy put her hands over her ears and started to hum loudly.

Jack laughed. "Enough already! We don't need to know!"

Holly laughed and tugged at Pete's hand. "Come on. Let's go meet Missy's brother. See if we can get you any tips from a *real* cowboy. Catch up with you later, Miss."

After making the rounds a couple of times, Missy needed to sit down for a while. She was loving the party, loving the attention. She really did feel like the birthday girl in her costume, she'd had so many compliments about how good she looked. What she loved most was finding Dan watching her whenever she'd looked outside to where the gang was sitting. The way he'd catch her eye and give her an encouraging smile. They'd had to pull two of the picnic tables together out there to make room for everyone. As usual, Dan was sitting on the end and she headed straight for him. Chance, who was sitting next to him, shifted up to make room for her to sit between them. She happily slid in between her two favorite men. She was very pleasantly surprised when Dan turned to sit sideways and folded both his arms around her.

"Are you having fun, beautiful?"

She nodded and leaned against him. "How about you, are you doing okay?" She knew this wasn't exactly his comfort zone, but he did seem to be enjoying himself.

"Couldn't be happier," he murmured into her hair.

She turned to look up at him inquiringly. "Honestly?"

He smiled. "Well, honestly, I'm hoping I will be even happier later." He rubbed his nose against hers. "But that will depend on you."

The tingly excitement rippled through her as she thought of ways she could make him even happier later.

"What do you say, Miss?" asked Ben. "Do we need to reinstate this as an annual tradition?"

Missy nodded. "I'd love to. What do you all think?"

"Definitely!" said Emma.

"You can put my name down for next year," said Smoke.

Missy smiled at him. He seemed like a good guy, and was certainly easy on the eye. She hoped he and Laura might hit it off, if they ever got the opportunity to spend some time alone together.

"If you're coming, then maybe we should make it pilots and flight attendants," said Holly.

"Can we stick with cowboys and angels?" asked Chance. "That way I can enjoy the views *and* feel at home."

Dan laughed and held Missy a little tighter. "That one gets my vote too. In fact...." He cocked his head to listen as the band played the first few chords of a new song. "They're playing it now. Come dance with me?"

Missy took hold of his hand and followed him out onto the dance floor. She looped her arms around his neck and smiled up at him. He rested his hands at her waist. As she pulled him closer, his hands slipped down and closed around her ass cheeks. She looked up at him, shocked.

His eyes twinkled. "It's the only place to put them, Miss. I don't want to damage your wings."

She couldn't help but smile back at him. He looked so pleased with himself. Her eyes widened as he held her closer, pulling her against his arousal. "Dan! Everyone can see!"

He brought his lips to her ear. The feel of his words against her skin had her clinging to him, just to stay upright. "I keep telling you, beautiful. You've gotta dance like nobody's watching."

She looked deep into his big brown eyes. She was starting to think he was trying to tell her something whenever he said that. "What does that mean to you, Danny? To most people it just means don't be afraid to act like a goofball if you're having fun. That doesn't sit right with you though."

His gaze was so soft. "You're right. It does mean something different to me. It's more about being brave enough to do what you really want to do. Even if it doesn't fit what everyone expects of you. Even if it doesn't fit what you would expect of yourself. When I was a junior in high school, we had a formal dance. I really wanted to go. No one expected me to go, or to be able to dance. I was making myself miserable, because I wanted to go, but I thought I'd mess up and make a fool of myself if I did. I made myself so miserable that Jack was worried about me. When he found out what was wrong, he told me I needed to figure out a way to do what I really wanted to. He helped me. He went to all kinds of dance classes, because I was too shy to go. He would come home and teach me what he'd learned in this big old barn near the house."

Missy smiled at the thought of Dan and Jack as boys, dancing together. "Did you go to the dance?"

"Yeah, and a lot of the girls wanted to dance with me. I was that good by then. The point is, I wanted something that it didn't seem logical for me to want. Dancing didn't seem to fit with who I was, but I wanted it anyway. Once I stopped trying to only do the things a guy like me is supposed to do and started doing what I wanted to, I got good at it. It changed my life. I learned about confidence and I learned about trusting myself. I believe I became a better person, because I became a stronger person.

She smiled as he closed his hands tighter around her ass.

"Being with you is the same thing, Miss. I wanted you so badly, even though on paper we don't make any sense. I wanted you anyway. I didn't think I was the kind of guy who could fall in love with a woman and start hoping and dreaming about forever. Once I stopped focusing on who I thought I was supposed to be and started going after what I really wanted, that's exactly what happened."

She drew his head down 'til his lips were an inch away.

"I love you, Missy. Please be my forever," he murmured before his mouth came down on hers.

There was nothing clueless about his kiss. He explored her mouth, tongues tangling. They clung to each other as they kissed. And danced. Like no one was watching.

~ ~ ~

When they returned to the table, Emma gave Missy a big hug.

"It's so good to see you enjoying yourself! You don't have nearly enough fun anymore."

"It's true," said Ben. "I remember the days you girls used to dance on the bar. Not seen you do anything like that in years, Miss."

Missy took Emma's arm and looked around the table. "Well, there's another tradition that needs to be reinstated. Holly, Laura, care to join us?"

Holly leapt to her feet. Laura wasn't far behind. This would be fun. When Ben had redone the upstairs as a function room, he'd left the old bar that ran along one wall in place. On their way over to it, Missy stopped where the band was taking a break and had a word with Chase. He grinned and nodded and talked to the others.

Missy kicked her shoes off before climbing up on the bar and turning to help Emma. Once Holly and Laura had joined them up there, she gave Chase the thumbs up. Since most of the partygoers were looking at the band, no one but the guys noticed them at first. Missy was glad of it as she struggled to find her balance and her rhythm as the first song started. Soon though she was dancing and laughing happily with her friends. As the band launched into the next song, Chase spoke into his microphone. "It's great to play a party where the birthday girl knows how to have fun." He pointed over at them. Heads turned and people started laughing and applauding. Soon quite a crowd had gathered around them, with the guys at the front. Pete pawed at Holly's legs as she danced, making a big show of looking up her skirt. Missy laughed, those two just could not keep their hands off each other. She found Dan, leaning against one of the pillars, arms and legs crossed as he watched her. She could honestly say, she'd never seen a man look so much in love. And he was in love with *her*! As the song came to an end, she held out her arms to him. He came and reached up to close his hands around her waist, effortlessly lifting her down. When she touched the floor his arms closed around her, but before he could kiss her, Jack's hand came down his shoulder.

"Wanna show 'em how we do it in Texas, bro?"

She saw Dan's face light up. He pecked her lips then vaulted up onto the bar. Jack followed him, laughing.

Ben came pushing through the crowd. "What you waiting for, Hemming? Get your ass up there!" he called to Pete as he joined Dan and Jack. Smoke and Michael joined them and soon Missy's sides were aching from laughing at them clowning around up there.

"It's okay fellas." Chase shouted mid-song, when Pete made like he was about to start stripping. "You can leave your hats on, we don't need a full Monty!"

When the band started to play Wagon Wheel, Missy saw Dan and Jack exchange a look and Dan tipped his hat further down over his eyes. The two of them tucked their thumbs into their pockets and started to mark out steps in perfect time with each other.

"Oh, my goodness!" cried Emma. "They can line dance!"

Missy couldn't believe her eyes as Chance pushed through the crowd and vaulted on to the bar to join Dan and Jack. He'd been lurking most of the night, avoiding attention, and now here he was dancing on the bar, with everyone in the place watching. The three of them were all tall, dark, and handsome, looking like a girl's cowboy fantasy come true! The others had climbed down and left them to it. Dan's gaze held hers as he peeked out from under the brim of his hat. *Damn*! She'd be making him dance like this for her again. Hopefully shirtless! As the song came to an end, the crowd around them cheered and wolf-whistled. Chance tipped his hat, jumped down and seemed to melt into the crowd.

Missy started toward Dan, but a dark haired woman got there before her. Hands on her hips, she looked up at him on the bar.

"Daniel! What do you think you're doing?"

Missy was stunned. Who the hell was she? She looked familiar for some reason. Oh. She was the woman from the salon this morning. Dan's face was still, giving away no clues as to what he was thinking.

"This is a private party. You need to leave."

"I'm not going anywhere until you come with me. We need to talk."

"We have nothing to talk about, Olivia."

Missy looked around. The whole gang was watching and listening to the exchange.

"Actually we do. Now get down and stop making a fool of yourself."

Missy wasn't going to let this bitch talk to him like that! She stepped forward. "Like he said, this is private party. *You* are the one making a fool of yourself, and you need to leave!"

Olivia gave her another one of those venomous looks. This morning it had stunned her, now it just made her good and mad.

"Actually *you* are about to make a fool of *yourself*. You see, he's not going to walk away from his company, or from me when he hears what I have to say."

Dan sat down on the edge of the bar. "Olivia, I already have. Weeks ago."

"Danny, we really need to talk. I know you needed a little break, but just wait 'til you hear the deal I've managed to get you with Systech. You need to come home, with me. Back to your life. You're not being fair to her." She looked at Missy as though she were something she'd scraped off her shoe. "The poor thing actually believes her friends." She sneered at Emma and Holly. "That you want to marry her. If she can believe that, she really doesn't know you at all, does she? You'll never marry her. She can't give you anything, certainly not what I can." Missy was stunned by the self-satisfied look Olivia gave her.

Dan seemed to explode. He jumped down from the bar and stood toe to toe with Olivia, his fists balled at his sides. "No! See that's where you're wrong. *You* don't know me. You never even wanted to know me. All you were interested in was what

I could do for you. How much I could make that you could take. It's *you* that can't give me what *she* can."

"Don't be ridiculous, Daniel! What could *she* ever give you?"

"Something you wouldn't understand, Olivia. Love. See, Missy does know me, she understands me and she cares about me. And I know her."

Missy felt her insides melting as his gaze found hers and held it as he spoke.

"I understand her, and I love her."

Olivia's harsh, brittle laugh sliced through the magic. "Don't be ridiculous, Daniel! You don't know what love is!"

Missy wanted to throttle her, but Dan silenced her much more effectively. His beautiful smile spread across his face as he came and put an arm around Missy.

"I'll grant you, Olivia, that when I knew you, I didn't know what love was. It took meeting Missy and Scot for me to find out. And to discover that I'm capable of loving deeply. I owe you my thanks. If you hadn't tried to screw me over the way you did, I might have spent my whole life believing that love was some strange emotion that other people felt, but not me. Your scheming set me free and allowed me to explore what I feel for Missy, to discover that I love her with all my heart and soul."

"Oh, how touching!" Olivia sneered at Missy. "Believe me, he doesn't know what love is. You might be keeping him happy in bed, for now, but you could never make him happy long term. He'll come back to me when he realizes what it will cost him not to. Sex and infatuation can't compare to the life he could have with me."

Dan's voice was low and firm when he spoke again. "You're talking as if I'm like you, someone with superficial values who cares more about how much things cost than how they feel. Someone who values money more than love."

"Stop talking as if you know what love is. It doesn't suit you!"

"Oh, but I do know what love is, and it does suit me. I'm new to it, yes, but I learn fast. What I've learned is that when you love someone, making them happy is all you can think about. You can't wait to see them, to be with them, to make them smile. But it's so much more than that, too. When you love someone, you see them and accept them for who they are. And you see yourself for who you are. You want to become a better person, so you can be what they need." His arm tightened around Missy's shoulders. "You want to share everything you are, and everything you have, with them. You want them to share everything they are with you. You want to be perfect, but you know you're not. Then you look in their eyes, and you know that they see you as perfect. Perfect for them. Just as they are perfect for you. Missy loves me the way I am, with all my flaws. She loves me because she sees inside and likes what she sees. And I love her, she is my perfect. I see inside, to the heart of gold that would do anything for anyone. It makes me want to be the one who does everything for her. She's as beautiful on the inside as she is on the outside. I don't expect you to understand, Olivia."

Missy's heart overflowed as he looked down at her, his face as earnest as she'd ever seen it. "I need *you* to know, that's how I feel. That's what you mean to me."

"Pathetic!" Missy was barely aware of Olivia turning and stalking away. She was too busy drowning in big brown eyes full of love.

Chapter Twenty-One

Dan looked around at everyone staring at him. Everyone was staring, but no one spoke. He was a little shocked at having poured out his feelings like that, for everyone to hear. Shocked but kind of proud of himself, too. He looked back down at Missy. At least he hadn't been wrong. Her eyes were liquid silver, her face glowing with what even he knew was love.

Chance stepped forward, his arm around Scot's shoulders. The two of them grinning at him.

He winked. "Now would be a great time, brother."

Chance was right. Dan took a deep breath. He'd just claimed to know what love was. Claimed that he loved Missy, and that he wanted to become a better man for her. What better way to show it than right here, right now, with all their friends looking on? He smiled as he turned to face her. He took hold of her hand and slid his other inside his pocket to get the little box Laura had given him earlier.

Missy's eyes grew big as he got down on one knee in front of her.

"I just told you, and everyone else, how much I love you and what I think love is. I need you to know how much I want to spend my whole life loving you. And Scotty." He glanced over to where Scot was grinning and nodding at him. "The two of you are my home and my family. You already are my perfect, Miss. Say you'll be my forever? Will you marry me?"

He held his breath as she stared down at him. She didn't say a word for what felt like minutes. His head started to fill with white noise. He could feel the blood pounding in his temples. Was she going to say no?

"Oh, Danny." She wrinkled her nose.

Oh, shit! She was going to say no!

"*Yes!* Yes, yes, yes, yes, yes! I love you, hero! I don't quite believe this, but yes!"

It felt like his heart was exploding in his chest. Jesus, she'd scared him! He could feel his face wanting to split in two as he smiled. Then he remembered he hadn't even shown her the ring. He opened the box and held it up for her to see before he slid it onto her finger.

"I'm going to spend the rest of my life making a believer out of you, beautiful."

She pulled him up to his feet. "It's beautiful, Dan."

He grinned. "*You* are beautiful. But we've had this conversation before. You know what it symbolizes."

She nodded happily, as she looked at the three diamonds sitting on her finger.

He drew her to him. He was aware of the applause and slaps on his back, but they seemed to be happening at a great distance as he held her to him and kissed her deeply.

~ ~ ~

Missy stared out at the lake. She loved the way it sparkled in the afternoon sunshine. She looked down at her ring. She loved the way it sparkled even more. She loved everything it meant, but most of all, she loved the man who had given it to her. He came back out to the patio with a fresh beer for each of them and sat across the table from her.

"Thanks."

"Miss, I want to give you an engagement present."

She wrinkled her nose. "You already gave me this beautiful ring, and the best present I could ever have, hero. The promise of a future with you in it."

She loved the way he cocked his head to one side, loved knowing that she'd get to see his beautiful smile every day for the rest of her life.

"I feel like you got that backwards. They are your gifts to *me*. That you're wearing my ring and *you*'ve promised me a future with *you* in it,"

He truly meant it too. What had she ever done to deserve this man?

"So will you accept an engagement gift? Say you'll accept it in the spirit that I give it?"

She frowned. "Want to tell me what it what it is before I answer that?"

Big brown eyes twinkled at her. "No. I don't. I want you to trust me."

She nodded. "Okay then. I do. I trust you, Danny."

"Good. Then enjoy college. My gift is your tuition. I signed you up. Get your degree done, Miss. You don't have to wait any longer."

Missy's mouth fell open. She was at a loss for words. "Oh, Danny!" was all she could manage.

The poor man looked so worried. "Is it okay? Did I do wrong? Should I have asked you first?"

She couldn't help but laugh as she came around the table to sit in his lap. "You did wonderfully. Thank you. We both know that if you'd asked I would have said no. But we both also know that it's what I want, and need. I love you Danny, so much!"

Before she could get lost in his kiss, she heard car doors slam out on the driveway. Dan lifted his head, hearing it too.

"Sounds like our boy is back."

Scot came running around the side of the house, with Chance not far behind.

"Dan, Dan, DAD!"

Missy's heart stopped in her chest. She felt Dan go completely still, his arms stiffen around her. Even Chance stopped in his tracks and fixed his gaze on Dan.

Scot stopped when he reached the table and looked at Dan with a big grin, apparently oblivious to the tension in the air.

"So can I call you Dad now then? I don't have to wait 'til you actually get married, do I?"

Missy looked up at Dan, she had no idea what to expect. He looked nervous. She hoped he wasn't scared by this development, but how could he not be? When they had talked about not letting their relationship affect his friendship with Scot, she had never dreamed that it might mean demanding more of Dan than he knew how to give.

Dan looked at her; there was no question he was nervous. Oh, how she hoped this would turn out okay.

He smiled at Scot. "I wanted to talk to you about that, champ."

Oh, no. She knew she couldn't expect Dan to suddenly step into the role of father. How she wished they'd talked about this first. Decided how they could handle it, without pressuring Dan or disappointing Scot.

"Okay?" Scot was still grinning.

Dan looked down at her. "And to talk to you about it too, Miss."

Missy, let out the breath she'd been holding. Wishing he'd just spit it out now, so they could start to deal with whatever it was he had to say. "I think we better."

He looked back at Scot, "If you want to call me Dad, I would love that. And if you want me to *be* your Dad, I would love that even more. We already are a family. But, if you want to, I'd like to make it official, become your Dad, adopt you."

"*Yes!*" Scot punched the air, before wrapping his arms around the two of them. "Thanks, Dad! Isn't that awesome, Mom?"

Missy didn't know what to say. She was stunned that was what Dan wanted, and a little apprehensive as to whether it was possible. Scot did have a father. Somewhere.

"It'd be great." She smiled, not wanting to dampen Scot's excitement.

Dan's hand closed around the back of her neck. "Please don't be mad at me, Miss."

"Mad? I think it's great. I just don't know if it's possible. Legally."

Scot stood back, looking concerned. "Say it is, Dad?"

Dan looked so sure of himself now. His nervousness gone. "It is, son. I already got it all set up in the hope that you would both want me. All I need is for the two of you to say yes, and we can get the papers."

"*Yes!*" Scot punched the air and ran back to Chance. "Dan's my Dad! Dan's my Dad, Uncle Chance! Isn't that awesome?"

Chance grinned at the kid. "It is awesome, Shorty. And I get him as a brother too!"

Missy put her hands on Dan's shoulders and rubbed her nose against his. "I hope you really are prepared to work at making a believer out of me, hero. It's going to take an awful lot to convince me that I got this lucky!"

His beautiful smile melted her heart. "I'll do everything in my power, beautiful. Every single day. Forever;"

A Note from SJ

I hope you enjoyed visiting Summer Lake and catching up with the gang. Please let your friends know about the books if you feel they would enjoy them as well. It would be wonderful if you would leave me a review, I'd very much appreciate it.

To come back to the lake and get to know more couples as they each find their happiness, you can check out the rest of the series on my website.

www.SJMcCoy.com

Smoke and Laura are up next in Fly Like You've Never Been Grounded

Additionally, you can take a trip to Montana and meet a whole new group of friends. Take a look at my Remington Ranch series. It focuses on four brothers and the sometimes rocky roads they take on the way to their Happily Ever Afters.

There are a few options to keep up with me and my imaginary friends:

The best way is to Sign up on the website for my Newsletter. Don't worry I won't bombard you! I'll let you know about upcoming releases, share a sneak peek or two and keep you in the loop for a couple of fun giveaways I have coming up :0)

You can join my readers group to chat about the books on Facebook or just browse and like my Facebook Page.

I occasionally attempt to say something in 140 characters or less(!) on Twitter

And I'm always in the process of updating my website at www.SJMcCoy.com with new book updates and even some videos. Plus, you'll find the latest news on new releases and giveaways in my blog.

I love to hear from readers, so feel free to email me at AuthorSJMcCoy@gmail.com.. I'm better at that! :0)

I hope our paths will cross again soon. Until then, take care, and thanks for your support—you are the reason I write!
Love
SJ

PS Project Semicolon

You may have noticed that the final sentence of the story closed with a semi-colon. It isn't a typo. Project Semi Colon is a non-profit movement dedicated to presenting hope and love to those who are struggling with depression, suicide, addiction and self-injury. Project Semicolon exists to encourage, love and inspire. It's a movement I support with all my heart.

"A semicolon represents a sentence the author could have ended, but chose not to. The sentence is your life and the author is you."

- Project Semicolon

This author started writing after her son was killed in a car crash. At the time I wanted my own story to be over, instead I chose to honour a promise to my son to write my 'silly stories' someday. I chose to escape into my fictional world. I know for many who struggle with depression, suicide can appear to be the only escape. The semicolon has become a symbol of support, and hopefully a reminder – Your story isn't over yet

Also by SJ McCoy

Summer Lake Series

Love Like You've Never Been Hurt (FREE in ebook form)
Work Like You Don't Need the Money
Dance Like Nobody's Watching
Fly Like You've Never Been Grounded
Laugh Like You've Never Cried
Sing Like Nobody's Listening
Smile Like You Mean It
The Wedding Dance
Chasing Tomorrow
Dream Like Nothing's Impossible

Coming next
Ride Like You've Never Fallen

Remington Ranch Series

Mason (FREE in ebook form)
Shane
Carter
Beau
Four Weddings and a Vendetta

Coming next
Chance

About the Author

I'm SJ, a coffee addict, lover of chocolate and drinker of good red wines. I'm a lost soul and a hopeless romantic. Reading and writing are necessary parts of who I am. Though perhaps not as necessary as coffee! I can drink coffee without writing, but I can't write without coffee.

I grew up loving romance novels, my first boyfriends were book boyfriends, but life intervened, as it tends to do, and I wandered down the paths of non-fiction for many years. My life changed completely a few years ago and I returned to Romance to find my escape.

I write 'Sweet n Steamy' stories because to me there is enough angst and darkness in real life. My favorite romances are happy escapes with a focus on fun, friendships and happily-ever-afters, just like the ones I write.

These days I live in beautiful Montana, the last best place. If I'm not reading or writing, you'll find me just down the road in the park - Yellowstone. I have deer, eagles and the occasional bear for company, and I like it that way :0)

JUL   2019

$ 19.95

Made in the USA
Middletown, DE
23 June 2019